TOMBS
OF
TERROR

T. Lynn Adams

Bonneville Books
Springville, Utah

The views expressed within this work are the sole responsibility of the author and do not necessarily reflect the position of Cedar Fort, Inc., or any other entity.

ISBN 13: 978-1-59955-326-9

Published by Bonneville Books, an imprint of Cedar Fort, Inc., 2373 W. 700 S., Springville, UT 84663
Distributed by Cedar Fort, Inc., www.cedarfort.com

LIBRARY OF CONGRESS CATALOGING-IN-PUBLICATION DATA

Adams, T. Lynn (Terri Lynn), 1962-
  Tombs of terror / T. Lynn Adams.
     p. cm.
  Summary: A young man accompanying his archaeologist father to Machu Picchu falls through a rotted plank, landing in an Inca tunnel deep inside the Andes mountains.
  ISBN 978-1-59955-326-9
  1. Adventure stories, American. 2. Young adult fiction, American 3. Archaeologists--Fiction. 4. Machu Picchu Site (Peru)--Fiction. 5. Mormons--Fiction. I. Title.
   PS3601.D397T66 2010
   813'.6--dc22

2009042951

Cover design by Angela D. Olsen
Cover design © 2010 by Lyle Mortimer
Edited and typeset by Megan E. Welton

Printed in the United States of America

10 9 8 7 6 5 4 3 2 1

Printed on acid-free paper

TOMBS
OF
TERROR

DEDICATION

This book is dedicated to all my Peruvian friends, old and new. I love them like my family and Peru like my home.

To my American family, *muchísimas gracias!*

CONTENTS

AUTHOR'S NOTE

WHILE living in Peru, I was fascinated by the legends of underground tunnels crisscrossing the country. Those legends and the warm, loving people of Peru were the foundation for my adventure novel, *Tombs of Terror*. The book is based on fact. The tunnels do exist. The Shining Path Terrorists are a current and deadly threat to the mountain people of Peru. Even the tomb traps used in the story are real. Lastly, I will admit to personally pouring oil into an Inca Kola bottle.

As I worked to create speed and adventure on each page, I wanted to take you into situations you would never want to encounter and let you realize you could manage them if you did. I believe most teens are as resilient and resourceful as Jonathon.

¡Disfruta! I hope you enjoy every rapid step of your journey through Peru.

ONE

LIMA, PERU. The creature stared through the glass, its thin brown lips drawn back in a mocking smile or muted scream—Jonathon couldn't tell which. He slid the headphones off his head and let them wrap around his neck. Silence enveloped the giant room. Sending a nervous glance around him to make sure he was alone, Jonathon stepped closer to the protective case.

The eerie thing inside peered through the glass. Stained teeth snarled at him from within a dry and pinched face. Black hair framed the skeletal head in a dusty mane, and bony, brown limbs were grotesquely twisted forever in silence. Jonathon stared in horror at the unwrapped mummy.

"The mummy is *fea, sí?*"

Jonathon jumped. He thought he'd been alone in the vast exhibition hall. The unexpected voice behind him rattled his nerves. With his heart pounding against his chest, the youth clipped the iPod to his belt and gave a casual nod. "Yeah," he answered in English, his voice flat. "The mummy is very ugly."

Jonathon stepped away from the case, pretending to be interested in some woven baskets, but his light brown eyes shifted to the mummy's corpse. He wanted to stare at the thing some more. It fascinated him.

It scared him.

He could still feel the prickling of goose bumps on his arms and spine.

The man peered into the display case of ancient baskets next to the young American. "*Canastas antiguas,*" he offered.

Wanting to avoid speaking Spanish, Jonathon reached for his headphones. "Whatever." The teen realized the man probably thought he was a Peruvian; Jonathon's brown hair and light brown skin confused most Peruvians. The man's presence bothered him. He didn't care what the stranger had to say about mummies or ancient baskets. He just wanted to be left alone.

Jonathon moved to a display of pottery. The man followed, staring into the same case of clay vessels. Irritation grew inside Jonathon. The stranger had an entire museum to browse. *Why is he following me?*

The Peruvian spoke again. "*Tu padre me dice que hablas español.*"

Jonathon groaned inwardly. He should have known that his own father would tell a complete stranger that Jonathon could speak Spanish. His father didn't understand that Jonathon used English as a defense mechanism. He could act oblivious when the locals approached him, answer their questions in English, and watch them wander off. It worked great, and people left him alone.

This system prevented annoying situations like the one he was currently in.

He only wished he'd found something that could have prevented him from being in Lima, a coastal city of ten million people. He wanted to be home in his bedroom in the United States. He wanted to drink the water without boiling it first and eat food without wondering what it was. Jonathon wanted to listen to his music, play his video games, and enjoy his solitude. He definitely did not want to spend the day speaking Spanish to some stranger about ancient pots.

Jonathon glared at the man. "Sorry, I speak English." Hooking the headphones over his ears, he cranked up the volume on his iPod and moved away. Music would drown out the man and Jonathon's feelings.

The stranger didn't seem disturbed. He moved after the boy, continuing to speak in Spanish. Jonathon rolled his eyes in frustration. *This guy obviously can't take a hint,* Jonathon thought, shaking his head.

Just then an image of Jonathon's mother came into his mind. He could see her, hands on her hips, chocolate-colored hair pulled off her face, her mouth turned down in a frown. If she knew he was standing in Peru and refusing to speak Spanish, she would give him a lecture in *two* languages. And she could do it, too.

The image brought a smile to Jonathon's face. A native Guatemalan, Jonathon's mother was fluent in both Spanish and English. She met Jonathon's father while grading Spanish papers for a professor at Cornell University in New York. Jonathon's father was pursuing a degree in archeology. Because his emphasis was in Central and South American archeology, he enrolled in Spanish classes to augment his studies. She liked to tease him about his Spanish. He tried to tease her back—in Spanish—but mixed up his words and proposed marriage instead.

At least, that was the story Jonathon's mother liked to tell.

His father never refuted the story. Instead, he always smiled and said his Spanish had improved since their marriage, and he wouldn't make the same mistake twice. His mother would laugh and say he would do it all over again because he'd mixed up his Spanish on purpose.

"*Puede be*—could be," his father always responded, and they both laughed together.

They married a week after Jonathon's father earned his degree and Jonathon was born a year after that. With hair and skin darker than his father's and lighter than his mother's, Jonathon's appearance was a perfect blending of two worlds. His language was, too.

His mother told Jonathon she spoke Spanish to him before he was even born, wanting him to learn the beautiful language of her heritage. His father said she really just wanted to make sure he learned it properly.

So Jonathon grew up in a world of English and Spanish—"Spanglish" some people called it. He could ask for a glass of *agua* or a drink from a *copa*. Because of his parents, he could flip between two languages as quickly as some kids flipped through television channels.

But now, because of his parents, he was stuck in Peru.

The thought jarred him back to reality, and Jonathon's smile faded.

He really didn't want to be here.

The man leaned close to Jonathon and tapped on one of his earphones. "I like their *Living With the Dead* album better." The words, spoken in perfect English, shocked Jonathon, and he turned to stare.

A playful smile greeted him. "Yes, I speak English. I studied at Cornell with your father and we both listened to a lot of music while we were there." The man continued in English. "Your dad sent me to find you. He is concerned for you. He knows it will be a while before he finishes reviewing the recent findings from Cusco. Working vacations are often like that."

The mention of his father's work disgusted Jonathon, and he moved away. "Yeah, more work than vacation."

"At least you get to come and see a part of the world you have never seen before. You should enjoy this opportunity."

The youth scowled at the sterile museum. "Some opportunity. I get to see another museum."

"You didn't have to come."

"Yeah, right."

"Did your father drag you onto the plane?"

Jonathon exhaled, his annoyance growing. "No."

"So why are you here?"

Deciding his short answers weren't working to deter the man's obnoxious interrogation, Jonathon opted for the "too much information" route: "Because my dad purchased a ticket four months ago when he didn't think the museum would pay for one then found out they had, so when he couldn't get a refund for his own ticket, I got stuck with it."

It didn't work. "Someone else could have been stuck with it instead."

"No," Jonathon frowned, defeated by the man's persistence and his own situation. "You may know my father but you don't know my mother. She made me come." Jonathon's mind went back to two weeks ago. He remembered standing in the kitchen with his mother, furious because she made the decision—while doing the breakfast dishes—that Jonathon needed to spend more time with his father. That morning, between washing the glasses and the silverware, she had announced that she would not be going to Peru with the other ticket—Jonathon would go instead.

"But I don't want to go!" he had shouted despite the fact she stood only a few inches away.

But she had merely continued doing the dishes, her voice quiet. "I know, but you are going anyway." She gazed out the window for a moment, and her voice softened even more. "*Es tiempo*. It is time, Jonathon, for you to develop a relationship with your father. You need to appreciate him more."

Still standing in the kitchen, filled with anger, Jonathon knew she was right, though he would not say it. He couldn't think of the last time he'd been grateful for something his father did . . . not even this trip; but he had come to appease her, not to please his father.

Now, standing in a dimly lit museum thousands of miles from home, feelings of anger washed away beneath feelings of defeat. A single trip to Peru wouldn't help the relationship. The only place Jonathon ever found his dad was at work or in a museum somewhere. Since Jonathon didn't like either place very much, he wasn't sure how two weeks of standing in Peruvian museums while his father continued to work would change that.

But he loved his mother, so he was stuck here while his dad played researcher in a back room and some strange man followed him through the exhibits. *So much for building relationships*, he thought.

The man introduced himself. "My name is Juan."

Stopping in front of another glass case, Jonathon scowled. "You and five million other Peruvians. Can't you guys think of another name?"

"Not really, *Juan*-athon."

Juan's response coaxed a smile over Jonathon's frown. "Okay, good one. You got me there."

Extending a hand in greeting, Juan smiled. "Well, Juan-athon, just so you don't confuse me with the five million other Juans living in Peru, my full name is Juan Victor Chanteco Espinoza Mayari. And what is your full name?"

Taking Juan's hand, Jonathon took a deep breath then announced his full name, speaking each syllable with intentional clearness. "Jon-a-thon Brad-ford."

Juan's dark eyes danced. "Good. When I come to the States I will have no problem finding you with such a unique name, *sí*? I mean, how many Jon-a-thon Brad-fords can there be?"

"You're welcome to try and find me there anytime. Someone will know me."

He turned back to the case, but his smile disappeared. Once again Jonathon found himself standing in front of the mummy's display. His stomach tightened at the sight, and his nerves tingled. This time he let himself absorb the full impact of the apparition before him. The mummy was more grotesque than any Hollywood creation, and he knew the reason: this mummy was real.

Juan leaned close, his voice a whisper. "I dated a girl at Cornell who looked just like that."

Jonathon's view did not shift from the mummy. "Remind me to go to Penn."

"She did not say a word the entire night. I did all the talking."

Jonathon glanced at Juan. "Somehow that doesn't surprise me." When the Peruvian chuckled at his comment, the teenager softened. Maybe Juan wasn't so bad.

The man nodded at the case. "You know, the ancient Incas used to think this was beautiful."

Turning back to examine the hideous figure, Jonathon blew out a dismayed breath and shook his head. "They would have loved the girls at my school."

"Then I feel sorry for you."

"Me, too. It's my school."

Nodding toward the mummy, Juan approached the case. "Did you know the Incas never buried their dead?"

"I think my dad mentioned it once or twice." Following, Jonathon also stepped closer to the glass partition. "But he's an archaeologist. He knows more about rocks and tools than mummies."

"It is said archaeologists have rocks for brains."

The comment caused Jonathon to laugh out loud. "Ah, you *do* know my dad." He disconnected his headphones. "I like that one. I'll have to remember it." Inspecting the man standing next to him, Jonathon nodded his acceptance. "So, if you've met my dad, you must be an archaeologist too."

Juan smiled and straightened. "Oh, no. I do not have rocks in my brain. I am an anthropologist."

"So you study dead people." Jonathon's thought quickly. "That must mean I'm talking to a 'dead head.'"

This time Juan laughed. "*Me gusta.* I like that one. I will remember it. Actually, I started my degree in archaeology with your father but discovered I preferred the study of ancient cultures and their beliefs— not their rocks." Juan turned to the mummy. "I finished my doctorate in anthropology but, because I have a background in archaeology and know your father personally, the museum is sending me to Cusco with you tomorrow. They want me to show your dad some of the ancient Inca sites that are still off-limits to tourists."

"Oh, great. You're coming to show us more rocks?"

"I can show you a mummy or two if you'd like . . . and they will not be in glass cases."

Jonathon's gaze returned to the silent, shrieking mummy. Her open, sunken eyes stared out through the glass, and a chill iced down Jonathon's spine. The thought of being close to a mummy without the protection of a thick glass case bothered him. He would hate to get any closer. "I don't know. I think I'd almost rather see the rocks."

"Most would agree with you. They do not like mummies."

"But you do. I mean, it's your job to find these things, right?"

"I try, but I've never found one. I have only studied the ones already in our collection."

"Either way, yuck." Jonathon moved closer to the atrophied corpse. The placard said she was about sixteen years old at the time of her death—the same age as Jonathon. He let his gaze skim over the dried skin and contorted face. He could see her arms, her clothing, her feet—even each hardened and twisted finger and toenail. "Did someone have to unwrap her and dress her in these clothes?"

"No. She was found that way. Inca mummies are not wrapped like Egyptian ones. They are quite different."

The youth glanced at Juan. "How so?"

"In ancient Egypt, they removed the insides and filled the bodies with embalming fluid. Then they wrapped their mummies in strips of herbal-soaked linen to protect the skin, placed them in stone coffins and left them alone. The Incas did not do that. They wanted their loved ones preserved the way they were when they died, so they didn't remove anything."

"How did they turn them into mummies without embalming them?"

"Some were dehydrated using herbs. Others were smoked over low fires. This particular mummy was left exposed to the cold altitudes until she freeze-dried."

Jonathon shook his head. "Smoked or freeze-dried? Sounds to me like they were preparing dinner, not mummies."

Juan gave him a teasing smile. "They *were* preparing to invite them to dinner. The Incas brought their mummies home to live with them."

Jonathon stared in horror at the Peruvian. "Oh, that's sick."

"They just wanted to keep their loved ones close to them."

"Looking like this, all decayed?"

"Not decayed, preserved. There is a difference. Everything is still there—her eyelashes, hair, skin, even her intestines, lungs, and heart. In fact, she is so well preserved that we can tell what she had for her last several meals."

"Okay, now you're really starting to gross me out." Jonathon moved back a step. "I don't even want to know who researches what she had to eat or how. I'm sorry, but I think I'll stick with my father on this one. Rocks are better than mummies." He continued to stare in horror at the contorted figure, his own thoughts twisting around each other.

Juan spoke, his voice respectful. "Jonathon, to the Incas this was not gross. Mummifying their dead was an act of love. They believed as long as the body existed, the spirit remained near by. Keeping mummies in their homes was a way to keep the *spirits* of their loved ones close by."

Completely stunned, Jonathon turned and stared at Juan. "They actually wanted ghosts in their house? What for?"

"You are using the term *ghosts*. The Incas called them *ayaq*, or "spirits," and they believed the spirits of their loved ones would help them make important decisions and guide them. They also believed that as long as the body remained intact, the spirit could re-enter the body and come back to life, so they took great care to preserve the body so it could resurrect."

"Looking like that?" Quick refusal came from Jonathon. "I'm sorry, but if I saw something like her coming back to life, it'd scare me to . . . well, to death! If this is what we're going to look like if we come back to life, leave me buried . . . and leave her buried, too. How could they believe something like that? That's just creepy."

"Jonathon, creepy or not, there are many people who believe the dead resurrect. Look at all the stories and movies about zombies and mummies."

Jonathon grimaced as he checked out the body in front of him. "Yeah, but that's just it—they're stories and movies. They're not true."

"You don't know that. All legends have some truth in them somewhere."

Jonathon didn't like the implication. "Are you saying there may be some truth to mummies coming back to life?"

Gazing beyond Jonathon into the darkness of the museum, an odd expression settled on Juan's face. "Maybe, maybe not. I know there are museum workers who believe the walking dead exist, right here in this building. They say they've seen the mummies move in their cases at night—"

A muffled sound passed through the museum behind them then disappeared. His heart hammering, Jonathon turned to look, but his gaze met only eerie blackness. Had the museum been so dark earlier?

Juan's voice continued. "They say the mummies scratch on the cases, moaning for their release. Some even claim to have heard the sound of dried feet scraping across the marble floors as they search for human flesh. Mummies can smell human flesh. That's what they do. They go out at night and hunt for living flesh, to make it their own." He stared at Jonathon. "Oh, they don't move fast, but nothing will stop them once they decide they want you—your skin, your blood. They will track you, coming closer and closer until you smell smoke and rotted corpses. Then you will hear dry limbs shuffling in the dark and their eerie moans."

Another sound passed through the museum expanse, disappearing before Jonathon could find it's source.

Juan saw the teen looking into the darkness and shook his head. "Oh, you won't see them until it is too late. Once you see a mummy walking it is too late. You *will* die."

Jonathon didn't know Juan well enough to know if he was still teasing. Uncomfortable, he eased away from the man, wanting to go someplace with some actual light—like the back room, with his father.

Juan stepped closer to the teenager, his expression unreadable. "When an army of mummies finds you, they surround you, and there is no escape. They fall on top of you and, while you are still alive, each one of them claims a piece of your body—your skin, your eyes, your tongue. Then you become one of them . . . one of the *undead*."

Contorted hands from behind closed on Jonathon's shoulders, gripping his flesh. Startled, Jonathon yelped and twisted away, spinning to face his captor from the dark.

A new man burst into laughter. "Look at you jump! If I didn't know better, I'd say Juan had you going there."

Disgusted, Jonathon knocked the hands away. "Cut it out, Dad."

Still laughing, David Bradford stepped beside his son. "I'm sorry, but when I heard Juan's story, I just couldn't resist." Nodding a greeting to his friend, David spoke to his son with a laugh. "I see you've met Juan."

Jonathon scowled. "I didn't have much of a choice."

"So, what did you think of his mummy story?"

"It's just a story."

Juan shrugged. "Not to some of the workers. They really do claim the museum is full of strange noises and occurrences at night. We have a hard time keeping night guards here. Many become so frightened they leave in the middle of their shift and never return, not even to collect their pay."

David smiled at his friend. "That's because you probably frightened them with your stories, Juan!"

Despite his father's laughter, Jonathon didn't find much humor in the conversation. The whole topic made him feel uncomfortable. He felt grateful he didn't have to spend time in a dark museum at night, guarding distorted human remains. He might start hearing things too.

David draped an arm around his son's shoulders. "You don't believe that stuff, do you?"

Though he didn't move away from his father, Jonathon distracted himself by untangling his headphones. "Believe what, that Juan scares away the workers? Yeah, I believe it."

"No," David refuted. "I mean about mummies coming to life."

"It's just a bunch of stupid legends, Dad." Jonathon adjusted his iPod, but his stomach still felt tight. He knew Juan was right. Every legend held some truth. Glancing at the hideous corpse trapped in glass, Jonathon didn't like the thought that maybe mummies did come to life in some bizarre, creepy, or evil way.

As the mummy's twisted face stared back at him, Jonathon didn't know what truth the legends held. He just knew he didn't want to find out.

TWO

YUNKA WA-YUNA, PERU. In the corner of a *restaurante*, a stranger was trying to buy companionship with cheap alcohol and easy talk. Lifting his brown bottle of booze, he waved a drunken invitation to those who looked his way. Most of the locals ignored him. They didn't know where he came from and they didn't need another troubled drunk in their mountain village. They had enough concerns of their own.

Seeing a teenager walk through the restaurant door, the stranger swayed in his seat and motioned to the boy. "Do you want a drink?"

Severino placed a bundle a bundle of recently purchased goods on the floor and glanced at the man. Drunks were just a part of Peru's impoverished mountain life, but Severino had learned to stay away from them. Like a stray dog, *borrachos* either turned aggressive or followed you home. Neither was desirable. Walking past the drunk, Severino moved to the back of the restaurant.

If being ignored bothered the man he dealt with it by taking a rapid swallow from his bottle. Alcohol spilled down the sides of his mouth, and he wiped the sour liquid away with the back of his hand. He pointed the container's narrow neck, like a warning finger, at Severino. "If you don't drink now, boy, you will after hearing my story."

Severino had not come to the restaurant to smell alcohol or listen to stories. He'd come to town early that morning to buy supplies. With the task accomplished, he now came to the restaurant to await the last bus home.

Finding the familiar face of the restaurant owner, Severino smiled. "Carlos, *¿qué tal?* How are you?"

The owner's dark eyes shifted to the drunk in the corner but he waited until the teenager reached the counter before leaning over to give an answer only Severino could hear. "I will be better once the *borracho* leaves." He'd heard the drunken story and did not want the man around.

Severino glanced at the drunk, shrugged his shoulders, and took a seat. "He does seem to be drinking too much."

"He is also talking too much."

Noting the expression on his friend's face, Severino frowned with curiosity. "You've heard too much talk before. Why does his bother you?"

Paused with polishing rag in hand, Carlos glanced around the empty restaurant before replying with a whisper. "I don't like stories about mummies."

All his life, Severino had heard rumors about the mummies, yet something in Carlos's expression caused the words to knot in his stomach and his skin to prickle. "He talks of mummies?"

"And gold."

"What has he said?"

Carlos' scowl deepened. "He says he has seen both in the mountains near here . . . that he has seen the mummies' hideous faces, stared into their lifeless eyes, and lived to tell about it."

Concern crossed Severino's face. His voice became quiet and strained. "Do you think he speaks the truth?"

Carlos glared at the drunk. "If he does, he had better shut his mouth, or he will die."

The stranger in the corner did not see Carlos. Hunched over his bottle, he watched the street, searching for someone to listen to his story and keep him supplied with fermented brew.

Carlos opened a tiny refrigerator, withdrew two sandwiches and passed them to the youth. "You had better go. The last bus will be here in a few minutes. Give a sandwich to Delia when you get home." Severino withdrew money from his pocket, but Carlos waved it away. "Save the money for a taxi ride. It will be dark when you get off the bus. I do not want you walking home."

"I will be fine."

Carlos shook his head. "You will be dead . . . just like your father. You do not know the evil that waits here, in these mountains."

"I do not fear it."

"You should. Every man who has faced it fears it. Now go. I see the bus."

Severino glanced out the open door. An orange and red bus came up the dirt road, dust swirling behind it like brown ghosts. Feeling apprehensive, Severino glanced at the drunk in the corner then turned to his friend, uncertain. "What if he really has seen the mummies?"

"He is full of drunken stories. Nobody sees the mummies and lives to tell about it. You know that." Carlos nodded at the road. "The bus is here. Go home, my friend. Keep your wits about you and be safe. I feel *they* may be out tonight."

Severino grabbed the sandwiches then moved between the tables to retrieve his bundle of goods. As he stepped out to catch the ancient transport home, worry caused him to peer back through the open door of the restaurant at his friend. Carlos wore the same expression. Hesitating one final moment before swinging on board, Severino passed his gaze to the drunken stranger. He almost wished he had stopped at the drunk's table and heard the tale for himself.

◆   ◆   ◆

As night fell around the restaurant, the stranger's talk of mummies bought him another cheap bottle of booze and more men to hear his tale. They poured him liquor and listened to his drunken stories, but now the drink and the men were gone, the restaurant closed. Now only fear accompanied the drunk.

Eerie blackness claimed the earth. Staggering down the deserted streets, he reeled with a misstep and fell forward. Only inebriated luck kept him from landing in the dirt. Righting his body, the drunk swayed on his feet, reclaiming his balance.

Nearby, a cat hissed, its amber eyes staring—not at the man, but at something hidden in the night. The animal then darted away, fleeing into the shadows.

Worried, the drunk looked behind him, squinting at the darkness. He did not like cats. He'd been told they could see the undead, and the man truly feared the undead might be following him. He had seen too much and he knew it, even if no one else believed him.

Coldness moved across the valley. Its icy fingers found the drunk and pierced his ragged clothes, penetrating his flesh. He shivered at its grip, wanting a warm, safe place to sleep. Maybe someone on the street would realize his need and take him home. It was a desperate, unfounded hope. He was a ragged stranger with only a mummy's story for his recent past. People didn't want to hear about mummies with the moon announcing midnight.

He didn't want to remember them.

No one was on the streets, and he shouldn't be either. It wasn't safe. Fear filled him. He needed to keep moving. Continuing his wobbling progress along the dirt road, he searched for a place to sleep that would be both warm and safe. The drunk saw a tall concrete wall. He knew it would take great strength for evil to break through the concrete, yet concrete held the cold, and he didn't want to be cold. He stumbled on.

Some distance later, the man's red, swollen eyes tried to focus. He saw a car parked near the end of a deserted street. Rubber tires were warmer than cement walls, and a car's metal underbelly would provide a safe shelter. Anxious, he staggered toward it. He would crawl beneath the car and go to sleep. He'd be safe there.

A mummy wouldn't search for him under a car.

Arriving at the vehicle, the man gazed one final time into the night to make sure no evil followed to the end of the street. Finding only emptiness behind him, he lowered himself to the dirt beside the car and wiggled forward on his belly. He managed to only drag his upper body beneath the shelter before the alcohol gained its victory. The drunk passed out in the dirt, his open mouth dribbling sour saliva onto the earth, his legs exposed to the night, unaware that evil watched.

A cloud blindfolded the moon, and an icy breeze escaped a mountain canyon. It blew its way down the dirt road toward the car, stirring up dust and debris. In the distance, a dog barked a frightened warning. Close by, rats squealed their discontent. Nearer still, a mange-eaten cat arched its back, yowled in alarm, and fled as evil moved toward the car.

Only partially hidden, the drunk slept on unaware.

Something locked onto the man's legs, awakening him, dragging him from beneath the car in its deadly grip. Dirt and rocks pelted the drunk's eyes as his body slid with tremendous speed over the ground. Earth entered his nose and mouth, gagging him, preventing him from crying out. Desperate, he clawed for a handhold in the dirt and grabbed at the tires as they slid past. His efforts, though, did not stop the harrowing slide.

Pulled free of the car, the frightened drunk tried to scramble to freedom but could not break the hold on his legs. Twisting his body, he fell onto his back. His gaze, still blurred by booze, moved upward, and what he saw filled him with horror.

He only managed a partial cry of terror before the night became deadly quiet.

◆   ◆   ◆

The next morning, a woman found his body lying in the dirt, life-less eyes staring with horror into heaven. His lips were drawn back in a silent scream while a puddle of his own blood browned and thickened around him.

As she stared in shock, a tremor shook the earth. It pulsated across the ground and rippled the congealing blood. The woman turned and fled.

The tremor did not stop. It reached deep inside the mountain. Boulders groaned in complaint. Rocks and dirt shook free and rained down in subterranean passages. Moans echoed through the darkness.

Surrounded by stone, thirty-two Inca mummies quivered in the falling debris. For more than six centuries, they had been imprisoned in their mountain catacomb. As the rocks trembled, the mummies' twisted faces and silent mouths snarled through the darkness. Contorted limbs and gnarled fingers shuddered with the quaking of the earth.

Death had come to the mountain valley, and few knew how to stop it.

THREE

DAVID BRADFORD opened the hotel curtains, allowing morning light to stream through the glass. He looked over the ancient city. "It's going to be a perfect day for seeing Cusco."

Postured on the hotel bed like he often was at home, Jonathon's eyes followed the action on a game screen while his thumbs worked the buttons. He wasn't interested in watching the sun rise over an ancient city. His dad might enjoy Peru, but Jonathon preferred the United States, where life was electronic or attached to wheels. To emphasize his feelings, he attacked the game with renewed vigor. Beeps and squeals filled the hotel room.

Jonathon's father looked back at him and tried to gain his son's interest. "Did you feel the earthquake this morning?"

"No."

"They have a lot of them here. I remember that from my time here as a student."

"Good for them."

His father sighed. "Maybe you should put that game away and get ready."

"I am ready."

David hesitated. "Jon, you know this trip could be a real blessing."

Jonathon punched a few more buttons. "Oh, it has been a blessing. I got to level seven in my game last night."

David forced a smile. "That's not what I mean, Jon. I mean this could be an opportunity for some quality time." He zipped the camera bag closed, his voice remorseful. "I know I've had to do a lot of work, but I'll be finished with the museum's requests today. After that, we have four days until our flight home. Maybe we could relax here and see some local sights or fly back to Lima. We'll do whatever you want. I want you to enjoy at least part of this trip."

Fingering the strap of his camera bag, David's emotions brimmed. "I know you didn't want to come, but I'm glad you did. I've enjoyed being with you. I just want us to enjoy our time together—like we used to." David's voice quieted. "You're a good kid, Jonathon, and I'm proud of you. I want you to know that; and I also want you to know that I do love you."

Jonathon didn't respond. To his father, he appeared unaffected, but he had heard every word. On his game screen, he missed a simple move.

✦   ✦   ✦

Trying to ignore the tightness in his chest, Jonathon squinted at the pale blue sky. Standing almost two miles above sea level, his body felt the lack of oxygen, even when he fully filled his lungs. Exhaling through his mouth, Jonathon sucked in another deep breath, hoping the constricted feeling would go away.

It didn't.

Raising cupped hands to his mouth, he blew into the cavern made by his fingers, trying to warm them. His hands were numb from the cold and hard to move. Even with the sun sparkling in a clear sky, the air stayed cold. It chilled his face and ears and drew the warmth from his skin. Jonathon wondered how the people of Cusco survived so high in the mountains. How could they breathe or stay warm enough to do anything? Yet they'd built an entire city here, and even now the streets were filled with people working and living.

He watched the native people move through their daily routines around him. They looked different than the Peruvians in Lima. Here, in the tops of the Andes Mountains, their brown skin appeared darker, toughened, their cheeks constantly tinged red from the cold. Their black hair looked stiff and dry. Even their posture differed. After a lifetime of climbing steep mountain slopes, with backs often burdened by cargo, their legs were bowed and sinewy and their bodies bent.

Despite such physical hardships—or maybe because of them—many of the people in Cusco wore bright-colored clothing. To keep warm, the native women wore brilliant *mantas*, or blankets, pinned around their shoulders. The native men dressed in heavy ponchos decorated with Inca symbols of earth and heaven. All around him, the men and women wore hats. Juan told Jonathon you could tell where the people were from by the hat or blanket they wore. One style of hat was worn by natives living in the mountains between Peru and Ecuador. Those living around Lake Titicaca, the world's highest lake, wore another style. Even in Cusco, the natives claimed their own special hats and blanket designs.

The mountain people also had their own language.

Jonathon listened to the unfamiliar chatter as two older women shuffled by with blankets full of herbs strapped to their backs. The sound of their speech intrigued him.

Juan leaned toward the youth. "That is *Quechua* you are hearing," he explained. "It is the ancient language of the Incas."

"I thought everyone spoke Spanish in Peru." Shaking his frozen hands, Jonathon returned them to his PSP.

"Oh, no," Juan corrected. "In fact, over ten million people still speak or understand *Quechua*. Until just a few hundred years ago, *Quechua* was the most common language in Peru. It was only after Pizarro and his two hundred men destroyed the mighty Inca empire that the natives were forced to learn Spanish."

Jonathon frowned. "If two hundred men destroyed them, their empire wasn't that mighty."

"Mighty enough that they built the giant stone walls still here in Cusco. They also built the fortress of Sacsayhuaman, the city of Machu Picchu, and hundreds of other cities that still exist throughout South America. They even built Q'oricancha, the Temple of the Sun, which sat right here." Juan waved at the curving rock foundation beside them. David moved along the foundation, carefully taking pictures and documenting each photo in his notebook.

Observing the wall of dark stone still visible beneath the Catholic church of Santo Domingo, Jonathon teased Juan. "Their temple must not have been that great, either. Another church is sitting on top of it now." He turned and walked away.

Following him, Juan smiled at the opportunity to share his knowledge. "That church has been rebuilt many times, but the Inca foundation beneath it has never been damaged, not by centuries of earthquakes, rains, floods, mudslides, or wind."

The comment caused Jonathon to laugh and shake his head. "In case you haven't noticed, *something* did damage it, Juan. The Inca temple no longer exists."

"*Qué bien.* You do not miss much, do you?"

"Just my stereo and warm hands." Flexing the fingers in his right hand, Jonathon tried to get the blood circulating while gazing at the Catholic church. "Obviously the Incas couldn't have been that great, Juan. Their temple is gone, and Bizarro destroyed their entire empire with two hundred men."

"Pizarro," Juan corrected.

"Whatever."

Breathing in the thin mountain air, Juan studied the church. A cold breeze blew across the plaza, ruffling his dark hair. "Did you know the ancient Incas did not use cement?"

"Yeah, my dad told me. He said they were so good at notching and fitting stones together without cement you still can't slide a knife blade or piece of paper between them."

Juan sat on a public bench, and Jonathon joined him, his fingers continuing to work the buttons on his game. Juan nodded in agreement. "Your father is right. Somehow they cut, moved, and lifted giant stones into perfect position. Some weigh more than twelve tons. We still do not know how they did it, and we cannot replicate it today, even with all our computers and modern equipment. The Incas used stone for everything, including their building tools and weapons of war. The sharpness and strength of steel was completely unheard of by them."

"And Pizzaro and his men had steel swords."

Juan glanced at the boy. "You have heard this before?"

"No, but it doesn't take too much to figure it out. Kind of like this new game here." Jonathon dropped it into its lap. "It's stupid."

"Oh, the Incas were not stupid. They were prepared to fight Pizarro and his men. When the Spaniards rode into the valley of Cajamarca, they found eighty thousand warriors waiting for them."

"What did the Spaniards do?"

"The only thing they could do." Juan looked over at him. "They captured the Inca king."

Jonathon's face reflected his approval. "That would work. But how did they capture him? Did they just ride through eighty thousand warriors and take him?"

"No. The Inca king always led his people. He showed up at the front of his army, and that's why the Spaniards were able to take him hostage. The Inca warriors fought to free their king but they were only dressed in leather and decorative war feathers. They were no match for the steel swords and full body armor of the Spanish. Every time a Spaniard swung his sword or fired a cannon, he killed an unprotected Inca soldier. Over six thousand Inca warriors died in that battle, and not a single Spaniard lost his life or was seriously wounded."

Jonathon whistled. "That's a lot of killing for just two hundred men."

Leaning against the bench, Juan viewed the ruins of Q'oricancha. "A lot of husbands, fathers, and sons died that day. The Incas did not know how to fight against armor and horses, but the gunpowder frightened them most. It seemed to be a magical force."

Jonathon turned over his PSP and picked at the manufacturer's sticker on the back. "What happened next?"

"When the Incas saw they could not free their king, they tried to buy his freedom. They promised to fill his prison cell with gold as high up as the king could reach." Turning, Juan observed Jonathon's reaction. "That cell was seventeen feet wide and twenty-two feet long."

Shock sounded in Jonathon's voice. "That's bigger than my living room at home."

A small shoe-shine boy approached with a box of polish. Juan passed him some money but waved the child away and continued his story. "The Incas also promised to fill two large huts with silver. Of course, the Spaniards agreed to the trade, so the Incas brought gold and silver artifacts from all across the empire. For days it came into the city. The Incas even took down seven hundred golden walls from here to pay the ransom."

"This place had golden walls?"

"They were actually sheets of solid gold placed over the rock walls. When the sun came up each morning, it made the temple glow as if it were on fire. That is why they called it the Temple of the Sun. You could see it across the entire Sacred Valley."

"I bet."

"They even had a special golden sun disc outside the temple. It was positioned to catch the sun's light and reflect into the temple. It illuminated the mummies they kept inside, along the walls."

"Oh, now that's gross. Mummies in a temple?"

"They were the bodies of their greatest rulers. As I told you, the Incas loved and revered their dead ancestors and preserved their bodies so they would resurrect. The Temple of the Sun held the bodies of their royalty. But the Spaniards raided the temple, melted down the golden walls and all the rest of the gold the Incas brought to free their king. They weighed it at more than twelve thousand pounds. At today's prices, that's over a hundred million dollars worth of gold, and estimates are that the Incas also brought more than twenty-five thousand pounds of silver."

Engrossed in the story now, Jonathon watched the man. "So did all that gold work? Did the Spaniards free the king?"

"No. Pizarro heard a rumor that the Incas were planning a new attack as soon as their king was safe."

"Were they?"

"No. Many believe that some of Pizarro's own men started the rumor, hoping to scare off other Spaniards so they could get a larger share of the gold."

"That was greedy."

"Very, but Pizarro did not know it was a rumor. Fearful for their lives, he ordered the king burned at the stake. He hoped the empire would be thrown into chaos by the execution and that he and his men would have time to escape with their gold."

Jonathon frowned. "What happened then?"

"When the Incas learned they were planning to burn the king it *did* upset their nation. They did not want their king to be burned to death, and do you know why?"

Jonathon rolled his eyes at the question. "Because he would die?"

A chuckle came from Juan. "No. Think again."

He did and understanding flowed into Jonathon's mind. "The Incas turned all their dead into mummies. They couldn't turn the king into a mummy if he was burned to death."

"You are right. So the king made one last deal with Pizarro. He knew their religion only let them burn heathens and heretics, so he asked to be baptized a Christian if Pizarro promised to strangle him instead and return his body to his family. Here's another question for you: Why do you think the king and his people were so anxious to mummify him?"

This time puzzlement filled Jonathon's mind for a minute, but then a smile of knowledge began to grow on his face. "Because the Incas believed mummies could return to life." He looked at Juan in triumph. "They hoped their king would come back to life!"

"Exactly." Juan nodded.

"So, what did they do?"

"The Spaniards baptized him then strangled him, just as they promised." Juan's voice quieted, and his eyes turned away. "Then, after he was dead, they burned his body anyway."

"What?"

"It demoralized the people, and the Inca Empire began to decline from that point on. In fact, burning the king's body worked so well, the Spaniards decided to burn all their dead. They burned the royal mummies and started to enter people's homes to take family mummies. They also took the mummies' gold." At Jonathon's obvious puzzlement, Juan explained. "When an Inca died, his money and possessions stayed with his body. It was not passed on to the family. The gold stayed with him when he died, so he could use it when he returned to life. All the gold the people brought to buy their king's freedom was owned by *living* Incas. They did not touch the treasures belonging to their dead; and the amount of gold kept with the mummies far exceeded the amount that was brought to Pizarro. The Spaniards saw it, and they wanted it."

For a long time, Jonathon stared up at the thin blue sky overhead. Finally he shook his head. "That's not right. I'm not sure I even want to hear the rest."

A smile crossed Juan's face. "The rest is okay. The Spaniards did not get all the mummies or the gold. The Inca Empire heard about their plans and disappeared, virtually overnight, taking everything with them. They left houses, valleys, and temples empty . . . all to protect their dead ancestors."

Jonathon stared at his friend. "Where did they go?"

"One small group fled to Vilcabamba where they were eventually enslaved by Spaniards and forced to work in gold and silver mines until they died; or until smallpox, a disease the Incas had never known, claimed them. Eventually all the Incas at Vilcabamba died."

"But you said only a small group went there. Where did the rest go?"

Juan smiled, pleased with Jonathon's question. "No one knows for sure. That is why they call it the *lost* Inca Empire." Juan shifted in the breeze as he spoke. "Most anthropologists like to claim the majority of Incas fled deeper into the jungle and died there, but they forget, the Incas tamed those mountains. They knew how to survive in them."

"So what do you think happened?"

Juan shrugged. "There are stories . . . ."

"About what?"

"Of the empire escaping through secret tunnels in the mountains."

"Secret tunnels? That's impossible."

"Not really. The Incas built more than twenty thousand miles of stone highway, much of which still exists today. If they could build tremendous roads and carve giant stones above the earth, it stands to reason that they could have mastered the technique of carving stones *below* it."

On the bench, Jonathon opened his mouth to speak, but no words came. Stunned, he shut his mouth. Beside him, Juan continued. "We do know they used tunnels at sacred sites for ceremonies and for the priests to travel unseen from site to site. In other places, they used tunnels for punishing people."

"How?"

"We have writings that tell us they would toss a criminal inside tunnels, put in a basket or two of poisonous snakes or spiders, maybe add some hungry jaguars and leave the victim in the dark maze to die."

"That's awful!"

"That is history. And to the Incas, the worst criminal was one who denied help to his family or in other ways disrespected his family. Family was the foundation of their empire. If you failed your family, you failed the empire. So they would cast out the rebellious or slothful family member and place him in eternal darkness—inside the tunnels—to die there, alone and without the family he failed to value."

Jonathon shifted, feeling uncomfortable. Juan picked at some slivers protruding from the wooden bench and redirected their conversation. "Most researchers think the tunnel system was small—used in just one or two areas by the priests or for punishment."

"What do you think?"

Juan pressed his lips together and nodded. "There are legends all across Peru claiming the Incas built underground tunnels to connect Machu Picchu to Lima on the coast and Iquitos, to the north."

"But those cities are hundreds of miles apart!"

Placing his elbows on the back of the bench, Juan shrugged. "I am just repeating the legends but, as you know, there is some truth to every legend. Every once in a while, the rumors resurface. You will hear stories of people falling into the tunnels and being found days or weeks later, sometimes hundreds of miles away. One American, found in the desert outside of Pisco, said he got lost in a tunnel he was exploring near Cusco. It had air holes and aqueducts, and he followed it until he found a way out, but they could never verify what he said. Of course, some people supposedly fall into them and are never seen again."

Jonathon shook his head. "Have they ever found a hidden tunnel?"

Turning his head to the breeze, Juan seemed lost in thought for a moment. When he spoke again, his voice sounded sad. "Officially they claim no."

"That doesn't sound like a real answer to me."

Now Juan laughed. "Official answers often are not real answers."

"So what's the real answer?"

"A few years ago the Peruvian government capped the entrance to some tunnels not far from here, near the ruins of Sasquayhuaman."

The revelation stunned Jonathon. "You're kidding? Then the tunnels *do* exist!" Anxious for more information, he rushed forward. "Where do they go? What's in them?"

A frown crossed Juan's face. "Apparently they are filled with artifacts. Tourists were going inside and retrieving the items for themselves. Some people were getting lost and not coming out again, so the government capped them."

"Didn't the government explore them first?"

"Officially, no, but they did send in one group of soldiers. Of the seventeen that entered, only two made it back out alive and they had gone *loco*, terrified with fear over whatever they had experienced inside the tunnels. So the government had the tunnels capped. Now the government seals all the entrances they find."

"Why?"

"Obviously they want the tunnels left alone."

"So why did the soldiers go crazy?"

"It could have been many things, the darkness, watching their comrades die."

Jonathon didn't want the story to end. "Didn't the soldiers say?"

"Oh, they babbled things about an evil presence and mummies but no one listens to crazy men."

"Did the Inca Empire really escape through the tunnels?"

Juan frowned. "I do not know what the government thinks. They have stayed silent."

"I'm not asking about the government. I want to know what you think. Do you think the Incas used secret tunnels to escape?"

This time Juan bowed his head. "An entire civilization disappeared without a trace, almost overnight. More than a hundred thousand people and their livestock—gone. Mummies and gold—vanished. To flee overland that quickly would leave a very big trail, but no trail was ever found."

Leaning forward, Juan rested his forearms on his knees and nodded up the road. "You remember those two women speaking *Quechua*? I told you it is the ancient Inca language. It still exists." He glanced at Jonathon. "Explain its existence if the empire was destroyed at Vilcabamba or they all died in the mountains somewhere."

For a moment, Jonathon stared up the road. "A language doesn't survive if there's no one left to speak it." His voice strengthened with conviction. "The Incas had to have survived because their language did!"

Juan smiled and gave the boy a nod. "Now you are thinking as I do. Yes, I believe the Incas survived and, even though I have no proof of where they went, I believe the tunnels do exist and I think the Incas used them to flee to safety."

At Juan's admission, Jonathon felt excitement grow within him. "So why don't you bring a team up here and search for the tunnels? There's sonar equipment you can use to find them and museums to fund you with grants and supplies . . . ." His voice climbed with enthusiasm. "You could get private backers to finance you and even contract with them to take a large cut of the profits. Interviews and book contracts could come next, maybe even a film deal. You'd be rich! Think of the money!" When Juan did not react, Jonathon rolled his head in frustration. "Juan, I thought people went into these careers to make new discoveries!"

"Or learn the truth."

"Truth?" When Juan's gaze did not waver, Jonathon frowned in frustration. "Okay! If you found the tunnels think of all the new 'truths' you could learn. Think of what the whole world could learn! You'd be famous, then you'd be rich!"

Juan smiled. "Jonathon, I am not interested in being rich or famous. Some people, like your father and I, are more interested in preserving things and keeping them from being destroyed." Pushing off his thighs, Juan stood. "Besides, I do not think the tunnels need to be discovered. I think the mountain people know exactly where they are but, for reasons I do not understand, they will not speak about them."

"Why not?"

Juan stood silent for a moment before answering, his gaze again shifting out over Cusco. "They seem frightened, Jonathon. I do not know if it is because they do not trust outsiders or if there is another reason for their fears, but I believe they do not *want* the tunnels found."

"But what if the lost Inca gold is still inside them?"

"What if the mummies are?"

Before Jonathon could respond, Juan continued. "Yes, bringing the tunnels to the attention of the outside world might provide tremendous fortune for a few and bring forth some interesting facts, but we need to remember that those who know about the tunnels are staying silent. Surely they must have a reason."

Seeing a look of frustration on Jonathon's face, Juan reached out and gave Jonathon's shoulder a squeeze. "Relax, Jonathon. One day, when the time is right, we may learn the truth about the tunnels. Until then, I do not think the gold or the mummies are going anywhere."

◆　　　◆　　　◆

Night came to the mountains. Creeping between broken crags and steep peaks, it moved across the valley, driving away the sunlight and burying the earth in blackness.

Entombed in the moonless night, Severino swallowed hard, trying to release the thick lump lodged in his throat. Fear pounded through his veins. He needed to clear his mind and focus on his next move.

Severino let a breath ease silently into the stillness. With only the smallest *snick* of sound, he opened the chamber on his rifle and carefully inserted a single round, letting his finger ease the cold brass into place. Evil had entered the valley. He knew it existed. He had seen it. He knew too that if evil discovered him, one bullet would not be enough. He would die just like the drunk yesterday, and just like his father had three years ago—suddenly, with no time to react.

The memory of his father's death jumped into Severino's mind. He saw the lifeless eyes open in shock; the mouth attempting a startled protest that never had time to escape. Most of all, Severino remembered the blood puddled on the cold floor around him. Kneeling in his father's blood that day, he'd vowed to stop the evil—even if it meant dying himself.

Replacing the image with resolve, Severino sealed the bullet into the rifle's chamber. Live or die, he would make sure he found time to react first. Then the teenager moved into the waiting crypt of night.

FUR

THE TRAIN SWAYED and rocked over rails bathed gold by morning's glow. Beneath the train's passenger cars, wheels clacked out a staccato rhythm on iron tracks. Beyond the oversized windows, mountain terrain—just waking to the new day—peeked through the shadows as the train clattered by. Sometimes the windows looked over an entire valley. Other times they presented only views of jungle foliage. Always the windows invited glimpses of the mountain morning.

Loaded with tourists and natives, the train labored to make the climb from Cusco to the famed mountaintop ruins of Machu Picchu. Yet, despite the unique destination and noisy activity of the crowded cars, Jonathon didn't notice. He stared out the window. His PSP and extra batteries lay untouched inside his backpack.

Through the cool glass, daylight and shadow alternately flickered across his face. They were like the thoughts crossing his mind. Why couldn't his father be more like Juan? Jonathon enjoyed talking to Juan. Juan knew so many things and told interesting stories about mummies and lost civilizations.

His dad, on the other hand, only made things boring. He talked about chiseled walls and broken pottery.

Jonathon sighed. He knew he should develop a better relationship with his father but he wasn't sure how. Above all, he wasn't sure he wanted to. What could be enjoyable about someone who found old baskets exciting?

Frowning, Jonathon tried to rub away the mental struggle with his hand. It wasn't always so difficult to enjoy his father. When he had been younger, he had loved to go with his dad to the museum. His dad would show him amazing things—things most people never knew existed. Jonathon had held ancient weapons and tools in his hands, broken toys from centuries earlier, or pieces of ancient cement with the paints still visible on them.

His father had shared so many things with him then, and the stories and possibilities had thrilled Jonathon. He would watch his dad take treasures from their packing and show them to him—some one-of-a-kind discoveries. Jonathon remembered reverently touching those pieces and feeling awe for the ancient people who made them, and respect for his dad. His father knew so much and had such a great love for people and civilizations he had never met.

But now?

Now Jonathon struggled to feel any interest in the things his dad did.

His mother might be right. Maybe he did need to learn to appreciate his father more. He had once before. Why was it so hard now?

Leaning against the cold glass of the window, Jonathon struggled with his thoughts. How could he feel grateful when his father constantly told him to get his homework done, do his chores, help his mother, stop teasing his younger brothers, leave his sister alone, and go to bed by ten? He had to get permission to go out with his friends; tell his parents where he was going, who he was going with, and what they were doing; and if he came in even two minutes late for curfew his father grounded him! His dad tried to control everything.

Jonathon exhaled without resolve. He didn't know what to do or think.

The train rocked and swayed, and its movements broke through Jonathon's thoughts, distracting him. Over the noise, he could hear melodic Spanish from the mountain Peruvians, the rapid, staccato sounds of *Quechua*, and a mixture of other languages. There were a few Japanese tourists on the train, other tourists speaking German, and a couple engaged in a conversation in French. Though he could not understand their words, Jonathon noticed, as he watched the strangers' emotions, he could understand the gist of their conversations.

Yet he could not seem to talk to his own father.

Jonathon's eyes closed with pain. His mother was right. He wanted a good relationship with his father. He just didn't know how to get it.

A sound nearby drew Jonathon's attention. Opening his eyes, he saw Juan step in from the narrow aisle. The man moved in front of Jonathon's knees and settled onto the seat across from him.

Juan smiled, extracting a newspaper from beneath his arm. "Your father will be here shortly. He is talking to the attendants." He examined Jonathon's drained face. "Are you tired?"

Pushing away from the window, Jonathon shook his head. "No."

"Are you sick?"

"No."

For a moment, the train rocked the two in unison. Carefully, Juan read Jonathon's expression. "Do you want to talk about it?"

The train swayed around a long turn, pulling at the pair as they sat. Escaping the study of Juan's dark eyes, Jonathon turned to gaze out the window. A final shake of his head closed the conversation. "No."

Juan watched him a moment more but Jonathon did not return the look. Quietly, respecting the teen's response, the older man opened the paper and began to read. Miles rolled under the train's wheels.

Eventually, Jonathon's gaze moved to the publication in Juan's hands. As his eyes saw the photos and headlines on the paper, he frowned. Black and white images of three dead people covered the front page. Dark pools of blood encircled the bodies.

Juan had already seen the headlines. He turned over another page of the paper. "They were found dead yesterday."

Jonathon lifted his gaze above the headlines to the man. "Where were they found?"

"Your father tells me you can read Spanish as well as you speak it, so why don't you tell me?"

Rolling his eyes, Jonathon did. "Fine. They were killed in Yunka Wa-yuna, but where is that? I don't live in Peru, remember?"

"Yunka Wa-yuna is a valley about thirty-two kilometers north of here."

"That's only about twenty miles away."

"About."

Concern deepened Jonathon's frown. "How did they die?"

Now a teasing smile appeared over the top of the paper as Juan encouraged the youth to use his Spanish. "You can always read some more."

The strategy didn't work. "You can always tell me. How many times will you *actually* have a teenager ask you to tell them anything?"

Jonathon's question brought laughter out of Juan. "Very few times, you are right." Then Juan grew somber, his laughter fading as he recalled the article. "They died in the Valley of Death. That is what *Yunka Wa-yuna* means in Quechua, 'the place where you die.' There have been several deaths there recently and each murder has been the same: their throats have been crudely slashed."

Shock brought a grimace to Jonathon. "Have they caught the killer?"

"No."

"Do they have any idea who it is?"

"My guess is that they were killed by terrorists, members of The Shining Path."

"Do you have many terrorists around here?"

"Some, but not as many as before. Most have disappeared into the mountains."

Jonathon glanced out the window at the steep peaks surrounding their train. "Juan, we *are* in the mountains."

"*Sí.*"

Jonathon looked at the photo. "Are there terrorists here, near Cusco and Machu Picchu?"

"There is always someone—or something—around that will terrify you."

"That's not what I meant."

"I know, but I cannot answer your question any better. I do not know."

Just then, a bottle of yellow liquid dangled in front of Jonathon's face. He shifted his gaze to see who wanted to sell him a bottle of pop.

His father smiled down at him. "Have you ever tried Inca Kola?"

"Soda this early in the morning?"

"Sure. Just don't tell your mom."

Juan slid over, giving David room to sit. Lowering himself to the seat next to Juan, David extended a bottle toward his son. "You should try some," he encouraged.

"Where'd you get it?"

"I asked the attendants if they had any you could try. It's pretty good. I drank it all the time when I was a here on a student dig."

Jonathon took it, though he remained skeptical. "It looks like vegetable oil."

David passed a third bottle to Juan before staring at the rich, yellow-colored drink in his own bottle. "I thought the same thing, so one time, when one of my roommates wanted a pop, I decided to fill an empty Inca Kola bottle with cooking oil instead. He didn't notice it was oil until he took a big swallow."

The story brought a grin of surprise to Jonathon's face. "You actually did that?"

David's expression brightened at his son's interest. "Hey, I had a sense of humor before I had kids, but when you become a parent they make you trade it for diapers." He nodded to the drink. "Go on," he challenged. "Try it."

Feeling unsure of his father's intent, Jonathon slipped a finger into the neck of his bottle to test the slickness of the liquid.

David smiled over the glass lip of his own bottle. "Don't trust me, huh?"

"Should I?"

"I'm your father."

"That's what worries me." Jonathon's finger told him the liquid was not oil.

David took a swallow of his pop then spoke. "Actually, you don't need to check for cooking oil. As long as I'm within spitting distance of you, you're fine. I learned that the first time around. When my roommate realized it was oil, he spat it out. It sprayed everywhere. I was standing right in front of him when he did too." David chuckled. "He ruined my lucky dig shirt." Nodding to his son, he encouraged him. "It tastes like Juicy Fruit gum."

With a hesitant look, Jonathon raised the bottle to his lips and took a small sip. As the carbonated drink bubbled down his throat and into his senses, he lifted a brow in surprise. "It's not too bad." Tipping the bottle away from him slightly, he examined the golden drink before lifting it to his lips again and downing another mouthful. "Actually, that's pretty good. They ought to sell this stuff in the States. Someone could make a fortune."

"See, I also had good taste before I had kids . . . but I had to trade that in also."

"For more diapers?"

"No, for macaroni and cheese."

Taking another swallow of pop, Jonathon glanced at his father, and, for just a brief moment, a flicker of appreciation passed through him. Cooking oil in a soda pop bottle? Jokes about diapers and macaroni and cheese? Maybe his father *did* still have a sense of humor.

Sitting behind his paper, Juan saw the exchange between Jonathon and his father and a soft smile crossed his features.

◆   ◆   ◆

Inside the mud home, Severino rubbed hard, calloused hands over his face. Fatigue ate at his body. He'd been up all night, and now he needed to complete the chores of the day. He sat for a moment, his face buried behind his hands, elbows pressing onto the worn table. Across his thighs, he felt the weight of his rifle. The bullet he had chambered hours ago lay on the table's surface.

Severino kept his rifle close at all times, in case he needed it.

He hated that need.

In the dark closet of his hands, recent events played through his mind, haunting him. The horrible images gave him nightmares every night, and now they were starting to taunt his mind each day. He found it harder to relax and to sleep; he had seen too much.

Severino struggled with his thoughts. He worried about his sister. He knew she was frightened about the mummies. No, it was more than fear—she was terrified. She had heard things, seen things. In recent weeks Death had entered their valley and men were dying. They were being brutally murdered, their throats slashed. Three more had been killed just last night, including a woman.

Pressing his eyes shut, Severino felt sickness roil inside him. People were dying because of the mummies, and so far he had been unable to stop any of it. Furthermore, he knew that if he wasn't careful, the horrid power would leave him—like his father—facing heaven in a pool of his own blood, his rifle unfired at his side.

FIVE

STEPPING OFF THE TRAIN and onto the platform, Jonathan found himself wrapped in a sudden press of tourists and vendors. They closed around him, instantly impeding his movements, jostling and funneling him to paths he didn't want to take. He couldn't stop the wall of people. Caught in the crowd's hold, Jonathon felt himself being propelled away from the train.

A presence, an emotion, moved against his shoulder. Glancing behind, he saw his father creating a protective wall behind him. His dad met his gaze and gave him a gentle smile, a nod of encouragement, and Jonathon felt comforted.

Juan joined the pair, and the two men moved Jonathon through the crowd with skill, sidestepping vendors, moving around tourists, and nodding to the natives. They had experienced these masses before.

The trio moved through a market area. Vendors displayed jewelry, T-shirts, tapestries, and alpaca rugs. The musty scent of unwashed hides and wool, mingled with the strong odors of diesel fuel, filled Jonathon's senses. All around him were noises, smells, and sights unfamiliar and overwhelming, but the press of so many people didn't seem to bother his father or Juan. They moved through the crowd with ease, smiling at those around them—greeting many in Spanish, all in kindness. The people returned their kindness with smiles of their own, and the wall of bodies opened before them. Jonathon watched Juan and his father. They were comfortable here, in this crowd of strangers.

Moving away from the main market and down a flight of stone

steps, they saw a Peruvian woman seated in the dirt, near an old set of railroad tracks. She beckoned to them, her face showing a toothless smile. Spread out at her feet, on a dirty blanket, lay a collection of fruit. Jonathon felt repulsion at the display and the woman's appearance, but David and Juan moved toward her. Stopping at her blanket, they visited with her, brightening her day with a few minutes of their time. She helped them select the best of her fruit and thanked them, graciously, for their extra pay. Now, with Jonathon's backpack carrying an assortment of native fruit, the three left the crowd of vendors and moved to an ancient wooden foot bridge. It crossed over the Urubamba River, flowing green and cold over giant rocks and boulders below. Above them towered the clouded mountain peaks.

Viewing the steep mountains overhead, David's expression filled with memories. "It's been almost twenty years since I've been here. Everything is so new to me."

Looking between the wooden slats at the river rushing below, Jonathon shouldered his backpack. "It all looks ancient to me." If the trip to Machu Picchu was going to be anything like the vibrating bridge he was walking across, it didn't look too promising.

With a mischievous smile, David motioned his son toward the bus terminal. "We'll need to buy our tickets. The buses leave as soon as they're full."

They moved toward the line and purchased three tickets. David passed a slip of paper toward his son and winked. "They said the ride will take about half an hour . . . *if* all goes well."

"What's that supposed to mean?"

Juan laughed. "It means they are hoping the bus does not break down or slide off the road. But, if it does, there will be another one along in about twenty minutes, or you can climb to the top of Machu Picchu, just like the Incas did."

Returning his gaze above them, Jonathon tried to see the top of the famed mountain. The sides appeared vertical. They disappeared into the gray clouds of mist hugging the summit. Rain threatened to fall from the moist, chilled air. "How could they climb that? It must have taken days."

Beside him, Juan shook his head. "You would be surprised at how fast some of the natives can make the climb."

The three handed their tickets to the driver and climbed onboard.

Juan found a seat by a window and sat down. Jonathon dropped into the seat just in front of him. Both peered through the window at the brown road, which rose and twisted up the steep jungle mountain.

"On foot you can head straight up the old Inca trail. And it is almost straight up." Juan showed the slope of the climb with his hand. "There are even ancient stone stairs carved right into the mountain. If you watch, you will see peasants entering and leaving the jungle all up and down the road. They are taking the Inca trail." Juan settled back into his seat. "Some of the local boys will run the trail for money. They like to bet the tourists at the top that they can beat the bus to the bottom. They even agree to give the bus a head start."

"They race the busses?"

"All the time."

"And do they win?"

Juan smiled. "All the time. This afternoon you watch. Up on top, the runners will make their bets with the tourists, wait until the bus leaves then start down the old Inca trail. Every time the bus turns a new corner in the road, the runners will be there ahead of it, waving with grins as big as the Urubamba River. After the bus goes by, the runners disappear into the jungle and run down to the next level and wait for their bus. They do that all the way down. At the bottom they collect their winnings. The tourists love it."

David laughed. "They don't know that they could do the same thing, if they wanted." More people climbed on the bus and filed past, taking their seats. The bus rocked with each new addition.

"The government built a walking path down the mountainside for tourists. It's not the original Inca trail, but most don't know that," Juan answered. "The new trail takes about forty-five minutes to descend."

"What about the old one? Does it still exist?" Jonathon leaned back, drew his knees up, and pressed them against the seat in front of him.

"You mean the original Inca trail?" Juan asked. "Yes. It is still here, but most tourists will not find it. If you hike straight down the original trail, without stopping to wave at the passing buses, it should only take you about twenty minutes."

David unzipped his jacket. "When we were here as students helping uncover more of Machu Picchu, on our last day a few of us decided to take the original Inca trail down, but it took us longer than twenty minutes." David settled into the seat. "The day before we went down, a tourist was bitten by a snake. It had been lying on the trail and looked like a vine. The guy died. We didn't want to be the next victims, so we took our time and tested every vine lying across the trail with a long stick. Let me tell you—there are a lot of vines lying on that trail!"

Juan nodded "Most likely he was bitten by the *fer-de-lance*. One bite is enough to kill several men. In fact, *Urubamba* in Quechua means Valley of the Snakes."

"Are there lots of snakes around Machu Picchu?" Jonathon's nerves tingled.

Juan laughed. "Enough, but you do not need to worry about the snakes. Here more people die from falls every year than anything else. The steepness will get you before the reptiles do."

A nod of agreement came from David. "It is steep, but I'm proud of myself. I didn't fall once the whole time we were at the ruins. Even going down the Inca trail I kept my balance. However, as soon as I got to the bottom and stepped out onto the flat, I felt like I had sea legs under me and fell flat on my face. The other students teased me about that for the rest of our time in Lima. They called me *torpe* . . . the clumsy one."

Next to him, Jonathon gave a youthful snort. "*Tor-pay* sounds like twerpy to me."

David smiled. "Twerpy . . . *torpe*, I would have answered to either one. Still will."

Two seats ahead of them the driver accepted the last passenger ticket, shut the door and put the bus into gear. The machine gave a lurch and headed away from the terminal toward the dirt road. Laying his head on the back of his seat, Jonathon shifted his gaze out the window to the vertical slopes overhead. Snakes, falls, ancient ruins— above him, the jungle-covered peaks vanished into the ominous, gray mist. Jonathon wondered what he would find on top of the world.

◆　　　◆　　　◆

From his view—seven thousand feet up—the valley spun away. It fell in a dizzying drop through the clouds to the swift and deadly Urubamba River below. Peering cautiously into the distant valley without the security of a guard rail, Jonathon felt as if a fall from the steep peaks would put him straight into the river without a single bounce or roll on the way down. How did people have the courage to live up so high, so close to a deadly misstep?

Moving away from the overlook, Jonathon left the press of bodies that filled Machu Picchu and hiked across the verdant mountaintop. His lungs burned at the effort. Oxygen proved more scarce here than in Cusco, and he felt the lack in each labored breath he took. They warned tourists not to overexert themselves by staying on top for too long. Altitude sickness and severe headaches were common souvenirs for many.

Jonathon's father was scheduled to stay here all day.

A cold breeze whipped across the mountaintop, taunting Jonathon into zipping up his jacket. Slowing his pace to alleviate the strain on his lungs, Jonathon worked his way around the ruins alone and headed for the Inca trail that marked the path to the highest point on the excavated citadel—the famed Gate to the City.

For an hour, he hiked the narrow trail, passing the occasional tourist coming back down or moving up the trail more slowly than he did. Even so, reaching the gate took him longer than expected. He had to stop often to try and fill his lungs with gasping, ineffective breaths and wait for his legs to stop aching. He'd always considered himself to be in pretty good shape, but the effort it took to move at high altitudes surprised him.

Finally reaching the Gate to the City, Jonathon turned toward the ruins. The panoramic sight caused him to draw in a surprised breath. Machu Picchu stretched out all around him in a gray and emerald design more stunning than the photographs.

"Wow!" he managed. Slowly he lowered his laden backpack from his shoulder. With that view before him, Machu Picchu captivated his mind, and his emotions.

Backing against a stone wall, Jonathon leaned on its cold strength. His eyes remained fixed on the image before him. Standing where photographers came to capture the world-famous image of Machu Picchu, he realized no photograph could ever replicate the vivid colors and ancient beauty he saw below him. For the first time since coming to Peru, Jonathon felt complete awe at being there.

Amazed, he hoisted his body up on the stone wall. The ancient effort it took to build Machu Picchu humbled him. His light brown eyes studied the rich patchwork of gray stone and verdant terraces.

Lush plazas, like brilliant green tapestries, wove themselves around stone temples, homes, and storehouses.

For half an hour, he watched the ancient city, fascinated by every billowing shadow from passing clouds, every play of light on the gray stones and brilliant lawns.

Most of the tourists, he knew, kept to the lower ruins, following tour guides, climbing or ascending the steep, narrow walkways, or poking their heads inside roofless buildings. Few tourists ventured up the long, unguided trail to where he was, and Jonathon enjoyed the view mostly by himself, in silence.

At Machu Picchu lawn mowers were not used to keep the grass manicured. Instead, the Peruvian government used a small herd of alpacas and llamas. They kept the lush, green growth cropped short and pleased the tourists at the same time. From his perch Jonathon could see tiny tourists gathered around the animals as they grazed, petting them and posing for pictures. One white alpaca, his neck fully stretched out, eagerly searched for treats in a nearby backpack. The sight reminded Jonathon he had some cookies.

Reaching behind him, he drew his pack to the front and unzipped the largest pocket. Inside he found a packet of cookies and some apple-bananas. He opened the package, removed two of the cookies, then lifted a three-inch banana from his pack. Eating slowly, he enjoyed the flavor of the shortbread and the delicate, applelike taste of the tiny banana. Jonathon finished the miniature banana in two bites and placed the empty peel in a bag. He then let his gaze rise from the scenery below to the mountains reaching above him.

Through the misting gray clouds, his eyes sought out the ruins of a second Inca city which rose even further into the heavens. Huayna Picchu laid its foundation far up on a second, narrower peak. Adventurous hikers only reached the lesser-known ruins by ascending Inca stairs carved almost as a vertical ladder. Many hikers clung to a chain sunk deep into the stone cliffs along the steps. Because of danger and difficulty, some climbers never finished the ascent to the lonely, more isolated ruins. Fear, falls, injuries—even death—halted many who tried to brave Huayna Picchu's heights.

Jonathon tried to view Huayna Picchu's summit through the misty cloud that encircled its peak. Earlier he'd heard one guide tell a small group the most difficult thing about Huayna Picchu was finding the bodies after the hikers fell. Jonathon didn't know if the guide had been joking, but the distant city and its dangerous path interested him. Who had once lived at the top of that mountain? What type of person would have made the dangerous trails and narrow terraces of Huayna Picchu their daily home?

In fact, Huayna Picchu intrigued him more than tourist-saturated Machu Picchu; that's why Jonathon asked the guide how to get there. The man told him the trail to Huayna Picchu started just beyond the Sacred Rock—but they only allowed four-hundred hikers to try the ascent each day. With the slow and dangerous climb, no trekkers were allowed to leave for the higher citadel after lunch.

Jonathon glanced at his watch. It was just before lunchtime now.

Returning his gaze to the misted city, which sat an additional half mile higher than Machu Picchu, Jonathon wondered about its dizzying summit. What could he see from there?

Another minute slipped by.

Again he checked his watch, debating. He still had time.

He'd never have a chance like this again.

Huayna Picchu.

His decision made, Jonathan quickly shoved the last of his things deep into the backpack. Zipping it closed, he swung the pack onto his shoulder. If he hustled, he just might make it.

Finding his father near one of the ancient fountains which still flowed with pure, Andean rainwater, Jonathon rushed toward him. "Dad!" His rapid descent and maneuvers through the crowd had left him breathing hard.

David turned and smiled. "What?"

"Can we go Huayna Picchu?"

Stunned by the request, David turned to peer at the higher city. "Why?"

"Why not?"

"I was sent to study recent masonry findings at Machu Picchu."

"But there's lots of masonry work at Huayna Picchu and over there a lot of it's still not documented. You could be the first one! You might even discover something new."

A sigh left David. "Jon, they didn't send me here to discover new things. I'm here to record some of the things that have already been discovered. They want to improve their records. Hey, did you know legend says the Incas used a magic plant to dissolve rock? Apparently it ate through solid granite like a teenager eating through a new supply of groceries."

The effort to distract Jonathon didn't work. "Ha, ha. Very funny. Dad, I don't care about magic plants. I want to see Huayna Picchu. We'll never get another chance like this, and the gate to Huayna Picchu closes in ten minutes."

"Well, I'm sorry but we can't."

"Come on, Dad!"

"I said no."

Complete frustration escaped Jonathon in a loud exhale. He stared at the distant peak, wanting to see Huayna Picchu even more now.

Just then a new idea brightened his mind with hope. He turned back to his father. "Can I go without you then?"

"No!"

"I wouldn't be alone. There'd be others on the trail too."

David's voice grew firm. "Jonathon, this is not a place to goof off."

"I wouldn't be goofing off!" Anger rose within him.

"Jonathon, it's dangerous. People get seriously hurt every year trying to reach Huayna Picchu—some even die."

"I'm not going to die, Dad."

"I said no!"

"You say 'no' to everything, except the boring stuff!" Irritated, Jonathon waved at the stone wall in front of him. "All I've done this whole trip is wait for you to take pictures of stupid walls that have already been photographed a million times!"

"Well, I'm sorry, but that's my job. You knew I had certain requirements to meet when I came here. I've got to take these pictures and then go talk to the archaeologists, but if you want to see something new, you're welcome to come with me. They've got an excavation going on the east side that's off limits to tourists and their cameras. Maybe *you* will discover something new there."

"Yeah, more walls. Well, I don't want to see them! I'm sick of rock walls! I'd rather see some of Juan's mummies. And least they're not boring." With shoulders set in anger, Jonathon turned. "I'm gonna go find something to do."

"Don't you go to Huayna Picchu."

Jonathon did not respond as he continued to walk away.

David's voice called after him, firmer this time. "*Do you under-stand?*"

Stopping his departure, Jonathon stood rigid, his back to his father, not answering.

"Do you understand?" David's question came with controlled hardness.

Forcing a response through clenched jaw, the teen managed to spit out the one word he knew his father demanded to hear but the one he didn't want to say. "*Yes!*" Then he disappeared down the stone steps.

Gray mist swirled around the ancient mountain peaks. Grayness filled Jonathon's mind. Why did his dad treat him like a baby? Why wouldn't he let him go to Huayna Picchu? He could take the hike with a group of tourists and be just fine! He didn't need his dad to hold his hand.

Moving through the crowd of tourists, Jonathon's irritation grew. They were all taking pictures and pressing forward to see the same things his dad had been sent to photograph: the same walls, the same sundial, the same doorways and aqueducts. The museum didn't need a trained archaeologist to take photos. They just needed to borrow some tourist's photo album. It had been a waste of money to send his dad here, and it had been a waste of time for Jonathon to come. His mom was wrong. He couldn't develop an appreciation for his father in Peru. He could only see his dad's senseless dedication to a stupid job.

The museum didn't need his dad and neither did Jonathon.

"When he pulls his head away from the camera, he can just look for me down at the train station. I'm not waiting here. I'm taking the bus down the mountain." Giving his backpack an angry tug, Jonathon crossed the upper parking lot and headed toward the cream and red-colored bus.

Moving over the earth in angered steps, he barely acknowledged the cold, moist air falling against his face and hands. Arriving at the bus, he hefted his pack higher onto his shoulder, grabbed the metal pole next to the door, and swung up inside.

In the bus, half asleep behind the wheel, the driver startled at the unexpected arrival. "*Baja,*" he commanded, one hand waving the teen out the door while the other wiped sleep from his face. "Get down. You can't come in here without a ticket."

Halting on the bus steps, Jonathon protested the man's command to leave and spoke in Spanish. "But I have a ticket." He fumbled in his jacket pocket but could not find his ticket.

The driver gave a firm shake of his head, his Spanish thick. "You have to have a ticket to get on the bus."

"My dad must have it."

"Then your dad can get on."

Jonathon scowled. "Come on. How could I have gotten up here without a ticket?"

"I do not know, and I am not going to try to guess. The rules say you must have a ticket to get on. *Ay—Americanos!*"

Jonathon's Spanish continued. "But I paid for a ride up and down!"

"Then show me your ticket."

The boy groaned. "I told you, my dad has the ticket with him."

"Then wait until he is here and go down with him. Now go buy a souvenir," came the gruff suggestion.

Jonathon's angry frustration changed to surprise as the driver pushed the lever and shut the metal doors in his face. For a moment he stared at the bus before turning back to the mountain. He was stuck.

Now that his goal to leave early had been thwarted, Jonathon felt lost. His backpack slipped off his shoulder, and he watched, defeated, as another bus closed its doors to leave. When it lurched forward to wind its way down the mountain, an idea flooded Jonathon's mind. He spun back to the metal doors, banging hopefully.

A scowl came from inside the bus and the driver pushed the lever forward. The doors swung open. "Now what?"

"Can I take another bus?" Jonathon asked his question rapidly, anxious to catch the next ride off the mountain.

From his perch inside the bus, the driver snorted. "*Sí*, if you have a ticket." The doors swung closed again but not before Jonathon heard the driver mutter, "*Estúpido.*"

Jonathon frowned. *I am not stupid*, he thought. More frustrated than ever, he left the bus and walked to a large rock at the edge of the parking lot. There he dropped his pack into the long mountain grass and sat on the cold stone. No matter what he did, he was stuck here. His father had the return tickets, Jonathon didn't have enough money to buy another one and, since he was not going to go back and ask his father for his bus ticket that meant he had nothing to do until his dad decided it was time to go.

That was going to be a very long time.

He cast his eyes toward the parking lot, searching for anyone else as frustrated as he was. In front of him, a different bus prepared to leave. The tourists on this bus spoke rapidly in another language, taking final pictures, purchasing last minute souvenirs from the mountaintop vendors, and slowly working their way onboard. All of them were smiling. Their smiles and laughter only increased Jonathon's frown.

A few native boys approached the tourists, pointed down the steep mountain, and then gestured at the bus. From his perch on the rock, Jonathon couldn't hear what they were saying, but he understood their actions. A smile worked through his anger and he remembered Juan telling him how boys often raced buses down to the lower parking lot. This small group of youth obviously had that intent.

Fascinated, Jonathon watched the tourists understand the challenge and accept with laughter and nods. When the last tourist boarded the bus, the native boys smiled and waved, waiting for the bus to begin its descent. The bus lurched forward on its rattling departure from the parking lot and, as it did, the boys turned on worn shoes and tire-tread sandals. Racing to the place where dirt and thick jungle foliage were sewn together, the youth disappeared into the trees, vanishing from sight.

Curious about their descent, Jonathon picked up his pack and slid off the rock. He walked past a new sign marking a trail to the valley and moved toward the thick foliage several hundred yards from the parking lot. He hoped to catch a glimpse of the original Inca trail and the boys as they raced the bus down the mountainside. Next to him, a peasant woman with a blanket full of woven purses strapped to her back moved off the parking lot terrace and descended the trail after the boys. He watched her vanish into the green curtain and shifted his position to try and get a clear view of what lay further below.

Trees and bushes grew together in an emerald tangle, but stitched through the middle, he saw a small trail of brown. Amazement filled him, and a sense of excitement grew within. "The Inca trail," he breathed. "That's the original Inca trail." He watched it snake its way into the foliage.

Jonathon glanced around to see if any of the tourists noticed the ancient trail, which had existed for almost a thousand years. Nobody looked in his direction. "They don't even know it's here." His gaze returned to the trail. "Dad took it once." Jonathon bit his upper lip. "Juan said it doesn't take long to go down."

Looking around him again, he saw two policemen nearby, but they didn't approach. Nor had they stopped the boys or the old woman from stepping onto the trail. "Maybe it really is okay if people walk on it."

Jonathon took a firm grip on the strap of his backpack. "It would get me off this stupid mountain, and I wouldn't have to wait." He tried to penetrate the jungle with his gaze and see the trail further ahead but could not. "That old woman went down. If she can handle it, I can too." For a moment, hesitation filled him. He chewed on his bottom lip. "It's a once in a lifetime opportunity. If I don't go down now, I'll never have another chance. I mean, it's not like I can just hop on a bus at the mall next Saturday and come back."

Still, he hesitated. What would his father say?

"He'll probably chew me out for taking it." Jonathon scowled down the slope at the thought. "But he took it once, and it's safer than Huayna Picchu. If I can't go there then I'll walk down the original Inca Trail and I won't *fall* when I get to the bottom!" His decision made, Jonathon stepped off the parking lot into the jungle.

As the thick, green world swallowed his view, a shudder passed through him—a wave of second guessing. *Maybe I should tell Dad what I'm doing*, he thought. *Or at least tell the bus driver so they'll know where I am.*

But just as quickly as the thought came, Jonathon drove it away. That would be wasted time. His dad was too busy with useless work to be bothered by his son's plans. They'd figure it out, anyway. There were only two places on this mountain: the top or the bottom, and if Jonathon wasn't at the top then it wouldn't take much intelligence to realize he'd be at the bottom, or at least headed that way.

Besides, he couldn't get lost. He would stick to the trail and reach the bottom before anyone even noticed he was missing.

SIX

WHEN THE DISK could hold no more pictures, a red light
flashed. Straightening, David pushed the button to eject the
digital record. His eyes swept the mountaintop and noticed the sun's
position. Glancing down at his watch, he checked the time. They
should be heading to the bus.

All around him, tourists picked their way through the ruins to the
waiting coaches. From across the distance, he saw Juan and waved.
The Peruvian returned the gesture, and David shouldered his camera.
One day at Machu Picchu was just not enough. He could easily spend
a couple of weeks here getting reacquainted with the ruins, studying
the recent findings, but they had a bus to catch and a long train ride
ahead of them. Besides, he'd promised Jonathon he would finish his
work today, and he would keep that promise.

Reaching down, David retrieved the leather camera bag and backpack that held his notebooks. He needed to find Jonathon and get
back to the bus. They had some things to do together. The thought
of spending time with his son brought a smile to his tired face. David
looked forward to that. He hoped his son felt the same way.

◆　　◆　　◆

Jonathon carefully worked his way down the steep mountain trail.
Using his pack to balance him on the slicker parts, he rarely lifted his
gaze. Juan was right, the mountain terrain was very steep. Jonathon
worried about falling with each treacherous step. In addition, he kept

remembering his dad's story about poisonous snakes that looked like vines and, unfortunately, the jungle floor held a thick littering of vines and branches. "Why didn't I remember the snakes before I started?" he grumbled.

In an effort to escape the shadowed world with its vinelike snakes and unknown dangers, Jonathon hurried his step. The descent dropped so vertically at times that he used the tall, narrow stairs embedded into the earth as stone ladders. He wondered how the Peruvian teenagers could run the trail. He struggled just to walk it.

Jonathon peered at his watch. He may not make it down as fast as the Peruvians, but he definitely needed to make it down before the last train left for Cusco.

The thought caused a shudder of cold to trace through him. Maybe the trail took longer than his father remembered. "Don't worry," he told himself. "The runners can make it down faster than a bus. They even stop to wait for the buses so they can wave at the tourists. Besides, it's all downhill. I can jog the easy parts." Still, as he gazed around the thick jungle, Jonathon realized he would hate to be left alone on the mountain at night.

In light of his growing fear, Jonathon quickened his pace. Moving as fast as he dared through the semi-light, Jonathon slipped twice and then fell. "Great. Now I can't brag to Dad."

After a second fall, he stopped to have a mental debate, brushing his jeans clean. Maybe he shouldn't have tried this. He could still be a long way from the bottom. In fact, how did he know where the bottom was?

Jonathon hesitated and glanced up the slope. He wondered about turning around and climbing back to the top. Maybe he should leave the Inca trail to runners and little old ladies.

The last thought set his resolve. He couldn't have little old ladies beating him to the bottom! While he didn't know how far the trail went, he did know it would take him at lot longer to climb back up. He needed to continue down the path. It had to open up in the parking lot because that's where all the runners collected their winnings.

Jonathon again looked at his watch. He had time. The last bus still hadn't left the upper parking lot.

✦　　✦　　✦

David Bradford leaned into the door of the red and cream-colored bus. "Did you see my son?" he asked the driver in Spanish.

"*Sí, señor,*" the man responded. "He was here earlier. He wanted to go down then, but he did not have a ticket. I told him he had to wait for you."

"Did he say anything else?"

The driver gave a nod. "He asked if he could ride down on another bus."

"Did he find one?"

The driver shook his head. "I do not know. I told him he needed to buy a ticket for the other buses, and he just walked away. I thought he would return later with you, but maybe he purchased another ticket."

David turned to Juan. "What should we do?"

From inside the bus, the driver spoke again. "The buses have radios. I can contact the other drivers and see if he rode down with them."

"Yes, please. I would appreciate it."

The driver responded by unclipping his radio.

Turning away from the bus, David frowned. "I wish I knew where he was."

Juan offered encouragement. "He is a teenager. He probably lost track of the time and is busy playing his PSP somewhere."

Behind them, the radio crackled with Spanish. In front of them, the mountain showed signs of lengthening shadows, and the air grew colder all around them.

Soon the driver leaned toward the men. "*Señores,* the drivers all said no boy like your son rode down the mountain with them. He must still be here on top, somewhere."

Frustration filled David. "He's not. We've already looked."

Beside him, Juan frowned. "Maybe he hiked down."

At the mention of it, David turned. "Do you think he would?"

"*You* did once. And he *is* your son."

Behind them the driver started the mighty engine. "*Lo siento, señores.* I am sorry, but I must return my other passengers to the bottom or they will miss their train. We must leave soon."

Anxiety mounted, and David turned to scan the mountainside around them. Juan placed a hand on David's shoulder. "Listen, you take the bus down. I will continue to look for him here. If he is already down at the lower parking lot waiting for us you can phone me at the guard shack. There are always guards on duty at night up here."

"But how will you get down?"

Juan shrugged. "If he is there, I will take the next bus down. If you do not find him at the bottom, I will walk the trail and see if he decided to go that way and lost track of time. Maybe he is talking to some Peruvian youth along the path."

David sighed. "He wouldn't be talking to them. He doesn't talk to anyone anymore." Another sigh came, this one sounding more like a growl. "We've got a train to catch. He knows that."

"If we miss the train, there are hotels below in Aguas Calientes. We can always take a room for the night."

Dissatisfaction showed on David's face. He didn't like any of the suggestions, for none of them solved the problem—none of them told him where is son was. David swallowed, fighting his real concern. He didn't know where to find Jonathon and, behind all his frustration, he was truly worried.

Juan took David by the arm, gently pressing him toward the bus doors. "Go on. Go down the mountain and look for him there. I will search here and ask one of the guards to wait in the shack for your call."

"But what if we don't find him?"

"We will find him, and he will be fine. Go, he may already be down below waiting for us."

Heaviness filled David's voice. "Okay, but if you find him before we get down—"

"We will radio the bus."

"Thank you." Then, with worry weighting his heart, David climbed onto the red and cream-colored bus.

◆　　◆　　◆

Jonathon frowned. Increasing darkness made it harder to see the trail. In fact, he wished he hadn't taken the trail at all. It twisted and snaked its way down the mountainside, and there were many places where it seemed to disappear into the thick jungle altogether. At times, Jonathon thought he'd lost the path, only to stumble forward a few steps and see it reemerge in the shadows ahead. More overgrown than he thought it would be, he wondered how peasants and runners traveled up and down it everyday.

Angered, he stopped in the middle of the narrow trail. Just where were those peasants and runners? He should have caught up with the old woman by now.

Then Jonathon realized he had not seen or heard anyone. He should have at least heard the noisy engines of tourist buses. After all, didn't the Inca trail cross the road? Wasn't that why the runners were able to stop and wave to the tourists at each bend?

Realization began to creep, like cold air, into his mind. The Inca trail should have been taking him almost straight down, across the dirt switchbacks, not weaving through the jungle like this one. Jonathon's heart began to pound. He hadn't crossed *any* roads. He hadn't seen or heard any buses or people or runners go by. In fact, he wasn't anywhere near a road!

He spun around and stared up the mountainside. In the growing darkness, the trail twisted then vanished from his gaze only a few feet away. That was why the trail seemed overgrown and hard to find. He wasn't on the right trail at all!

Somehow, he had stepped off the Inca trail and wandered onto a new one!

Panicked, he scrambled up the slope—retracing the way he had come—but the earth crumbled, and he slipped, falling against the face of the cold, dark mountain. He didn't feel the dirt coat his face and hands. He climbed again, calling out as he rushed to undo his folly. "Hello? Can anyone hear me?" But only the birds and the sounds of the jungle answered.

◆　　　◆　　　◆

David called the guard shack and talked to Juan. He had not found Jonathon waiting in the lower parking lot. Though David didn't say much, concerns filled his mind. He knew the last train left in half an hour. If they didn't find Jonathon before then, they'd have to spend the night at a mountain hotel. And while that wasn't a problem, David faced a deepening fear. Jonathon may have tried climbing the steep, dangerous trail to Huayna Picchu and fallen among the ruins, or worse, fallen over the side. David also knew with darkness coming, risks grew as well. Jonathon could take a misstep and become hurt if he wasn't already. And if he was hurt, the growing cold would make things much worse.

Juan felt the same fears. If Jonathon wasn't on top, or at the bottom, he hoped to find the boy somewhere in the middle. Promising David he'd hike the trail, Juan hung up the phone and turned to the guard. He extracted a promise that they would call down below if they found Jonathon. Then he moved across the parking lot to where the new sign pointed out the tourist trail. Its well-marked path descended into the jungle. If he hurried, it would take him about half an hour to descend. Hopefully he would find Jonathon along its path, and hopefully the teen wouldn't be hurt.

◆　　◆　　◆

Jonathon didn't know where to go or what to do. The slickness of the steep mountainside made it impossible to climb up the way he had come, and the growing darkness took away a clear view of the trail dropping below him. Covered with mud and decaying leaves, scraped and cut, he moved beneath the thick and tangled foliage, calling for help until his throat became hoarse. There was no trail before him now.

Pushing through the thick growth, he tried not to notice the darkening shadows or listen to the unfamiliar sounds. Above him, through occasional breaks in the trees, he could see daylight leaving the sky. He didn't want the sun to set; he wanted it to stay until he could find his way out of the jungle. The coming night worried him.

Climbing a tree to search for a road, Jonathon's eyes found nothing from his windy perch except an undulating sea of green. Discouraged and more worried than ever, he lowered himself to the jungle floor and sat amid the leaves and vines, his back to the rough trunk of the tree. He did not want to spend the night in a mountain jungle with all of its unknown creatures. The thought truly frighten him. Jonathon needed to find his way out before dark. Rising to his feet, Jonathon again shouldered his pack and moved forward, through the wall of green.

Twenty minutes later, the thick jungle spat him up against a solid granite cliff. Angered at the wall, he looked above him. He knew the red and cream-colored bus had long since arrived at the lower parking lot and that the train would be leaving the station in just a few minutes. As the thought ate into his mind, he groaned in frustration, tipping his head to the sky. "Why didn't I tell Dad what I was doing? I should have told him, or someone."

Growling at himself, he brought his gaze back to the granite wall in front of him. "Well, I didn't tell anyone, so now I'm the only one who knows where I am—not that I know where I am—but I'm still the only one who can get me out of this mess."

Determined, Jonathon climbed up the rock face to a ledge, hoping to get high enough to see above the trees. Ferns and moss grew across the narrow mantle. His athletic shoes, damp from the jungle moisture, kept slipping as he moved along the mountain face.

"If I can find the Urubamba River, then I can follow it to a town or something." He slipped again but caught himself. "Actually, if I can just find a stupid stream I can follow it to the river and then follow the river to civilization." Angered and overwhelmed, he shouted at the trees. "Where are the stupid streams? *Where are the people?*"

The outburst caused his body to shift and, with horror, Jonathon slid from the rock ledge. He grabbed for handholds but failed. His body tumbled backward through trees and brush and he crashed to the jungle floor ten feet below.

When the dead leaves and branches stopped raining down around him, Jonathon opened his eyes. Above him the dark trees stood silhouetted against a dimming sky. Slowly he exhaled. "Ouch!" he said out loud. "That hurt." Lying on his back, his pack twisted to the side, Jonathon watched the fading light through the trees above him. For the first time, tears of frustration burned in his eyes. He didn't want to be here.

His discouragement grew. Still lying on his back, he vented his frustration to the jungle. "How come there are so many stupid trees around here?"

Because, this is a jungle, his mind responded. *There are supposed to be lots of trees here.*

Jonathon rolled to his knees, brushing leaves and dirt off his jacket. He could feel dampness seeping through his clothes and frigid air penetrating his body. He didn't know a jungle could be so cold. Reaching forward to push off the earth, one hand descended on something long and round. It moved beneath his mud-encrusted palm and Jonathon lunged backward. *Fer-de-lance!*

"Snake!" he cried out, scrambling away and knocking at his clothes. The horrible thing uncoiled at his feet and then lay still. Jonathon blinked. It was only a vine, twisted beneath him by the fall. Filled with temporary relief, he remembered some long-lost fact from his science class—a fact he did not want to recall now! The deadly *fer-de-lance* hunted at night.

Closing his eyes, Jonathon realized it might be a very long night.

Just then a giant bat erupted through the foliage. It swept by him in the deepening shadows, so close he heard the sound of its passing and felt the rush of wings skimming the air. Jonathon's heart and stomach lurched inside of him. A lot more than snakes came out at night! Alone on the mountain and fighting his nerves, he acknowledged he was lost. Scout training said to stay put, but the thought of sitting still in the jungle frightened him more than moving through it. At least by moving, he would be making noises and not hearing them! Besides, in the thick-foliaged jungle, help might be only a few more yards ahead. He might find a trail, a road, or a person. He'd never find that by sitting still.

Returning to the rock wall, Jonathon lifted his body back onto the ledge. He doubted snakes hunted on rock ledges. He'd follow this rock wall as long as he could.

Using care, he continued to inch his way, once again, between tree and stone. In the branches behind him, a bird screeched its call to the coming night. Jonathon jumped. When the cry died away, he shuddered and moved on, aware of the pounding of his heart. He hated to think what could be near him, just a few feet away in the tangled jungle, hidden by leaves and vines . . . watching him, or getting ready to grab him.

Even more reason to keep moving, he thought.

Growing darkness took away the color of the world around him. It also forced Jonathon to move along the rocky outcrop by feel. In the dim light, his foot slipped on a damp spot, pitching him forward. His face slammed against the granite wall, the pain throbbing. For a moment, he rested. His body hurt; his mind hurt.

He hated the entire situation.

Drawing in a determined breath, Jonathon pressed forward again. Another slip slammed his body into the rocks, and he pressed his eyes closed. Fury began to overtake his fear. He wouldn't be in this mess if it wasn't for his dad! "It's all your fault!" he growled. "If you had just let me go to Huayna Picchu or stay behind in the States, I wouldn't be here!" His words came through clenched jaws. "But no, . . . *you* wanted me to do things *your* way. Well, guess what, Dad? Your way stinks!"

The more he voiced his anger, the angrier he felt. Bruised and pressed against the rock face, he spat out his words with less remorse. "You're always telling me what to do. *Don't do that. You can't do that. You're not doing that right.* You always treat me like a baby. If you'd treated me like a grown-up, I'd be back in the hotel room—resting after a safe climb to Huayna Picchu."

A bug landed on his face. He slapped at it. Why were there so many bugs in the jungle? He wished they'd all go to his dad's hotel room!

Another insect landed near his left eye. Jonathon shook his head to dislodge it, hissing in anger as it zipped by his face and landed on him again. Two more times he failed to swat it away. Roaring his voice to the jungle, Jonathon expressed complete frustration. "I hate it here!"

Instantly the jungle filled with the chattering call of startled animals. Above, below, and behind him they erupted from their perches, escaping the noisy intruder. Leaves and debris fell on Jonathon and pushed his heart into a fit of wild pounding. He didn't realize so many animals were so close.

Then another thought came to him. His voice had frightened them away, scattering them deeper into the trees. He wanted them to go—to leave him alone—and if his yelling would chase away the insects that would be an added bonus. Jonathon continued shouting his anger to the trees. "Know what? I hate jungles too. That's why I live in the United States. *We don't have any jungles!*"

The inner voice cut through his tension. *You live in the United States because you were born there, and you're in this situation because you walked here. You created your mess . . . not your dad.*

Just as quickly as the thought passed through his anger, Jonathon drove it away. "I'm in this mess because of Dad. 'Go to Peru and get a better relationship with him,' Mom said. Well, I did, and you know what?" His voice rose as he cast his gaze and his anger across the jungle, wishing his father could hear him. *"This relationship stinks! I hate it, and I hate you!* If you had been more worried about a relationship with me back home in the States rather than your dumb rocks, I would never have had to come here in the first place!"

You are just as responsible for the relationship, the voice returned.

Jonathon didn't like the voice, and he especially didn't like it being right. "Oh, shut up." Against the wall, he angrily stepped forward, shoving his foot down on a tapestry of dead vines and branches. In horror, Jonathon felt his foot shatter through the decayed weaving and disappear into a cavern. Before he could react, he lost his balance. Forward momentum sent his body tumbling through the aged foliage, and Jonathon found himself falling into a black abyss.

SEVEN

DROPPING INTO THE OPENING, Jonathon roared his surprise. Dirt, rocks, dead leaves, and vines cascaded down. He fell with the mixture, rolling and bouncing off unseen surfaces. His shoulder jolted hard against a boulder. The force spun his entire body in the opposite direction. Crying out with the pain, he somersaulted deeper into blackness.

In the tumbling descent, he collided with a wall of stone and started to slide. The chute dropped beneath him at an almost vertical pitch. Clawing frantically, Jonathon tried to stop his skidding fall, but the rocks took the skin from his palms and refused to give him anything to hold. The chute ended abruptly, and the earth dropped away again.

This time no rocks interrupted his spinning fall through a black void, five feet, ten, then almost twenty. His body slammed into cold, hard earth like a flattened ball. He tumbled, rolled several times down an incline, and lay still. Dirt and rocks rained down around him, but he didn't notice. Knocked unconscious, his mind and eyes did not experience the filthy downpour nor see the darkness of his new world.

But some eyes were not closed. Here in the underground world, they watched him.

◆　　◆　　◆

Standing in the valley next to an empty bus, David watched the last light of day disappear behind the steep mountains above. Cold gnawed at the valley, and a deeper chill ate at his heart. He saw Juan move up the cobbled street, and David's heart and stomach lurched inside him. Juan was alone. Breaking into a run, he approached his friend. "Where is he? Did you see him?"

Juan shook his head. "No. I met a couple of natives, but they have not seen anyone either. I am sorry. I do not know where he is."

A policeman, dressed in a khaki uniform and hat, stepped forward. "*Señores*," he spoke in Spanish. "It is growing late. If he is still on top, among the ruins, I am sure he will appear tomorrow morning. Most of the people lost there are found by the next breakfast."

"*Most* of the people? What about the others?" David put forth a barrage of questions in rapid Spanish. "What if you don't find my son tomorrow morning? What if he left the ruins and is lost in the jungle?"

The policeman responded with a shrug. "If that is the case, a local will most likely find him. They are good to help any lost tourists."

The answer still did not give David his son. "What if nobody finds him? Isn't there anything else we can do?"

The officer hesitated. "Well, if he is truly lost, we do have a dog trained for this kind of thing—"

"If he is *truly* lost? What is that supposed to mean? He *is* lost."

"We do not know that yet, *señor*. We have no proof—"

"Proof? He's not here! What more proof do you need?"

"*Señor*, you said he speaks Spanish. It could be he made friends with a local youth, and they are playing together." The officer smiled, "or maybe he found a lovely *chica* and has just lost track of time."

"My son is not playing, and he did not lose track of time with some *chica*!"

Realizing his error, the officer apologized. "I *am* sorry, *señor*. It is probable he is merely sleeping, then. The thin altitude here makes many people tired."

"I don't want excuses. I want my son, and I want that dog here to help us find him. Go get the dog and start him searching."

The policeman's face showed his unease. "The dog is in Cusco, *señor*. The soonest we can bring him here is on the train tomorrow morning . . . that is, if he has not been sent away to another province to help there."

Sensing David's hopelessness, Juan put an arm around his friend and guided him a step away. "Let us stay here tonight, in a hotel. The guards on top told me they will search for him tonight during their rounds. In the morning, if we have not found him, we will request the dog."

"I don't want to wait until tomorrow. We can pay someone to bring the dog to us tonight and we can go search for him ourselves." David's voice held anxiety.

The officer, still a pace away, overheard David's raised voice. "Search where, *señor*, in the *selva*?" His question reflected surprise.

Turning on the uniformed man, David snapped his reply. "Yes, in the jungle!"

"Ah, but the *selva* is dangerous."

"Do you think I'm afraid of the jungle right now? The only thing I am afraid of is what may have happened to my son." David's eyes burned with tears and anger.

Again Juan's voice came, calm and quieting. "David, listen to me. The officer is right. There is not much we can do in the jungle when it is dark. We could be hurt or lost ourselves and then we would be of no use to Jonathon. We must let night come and take its turn on the earth. Then, when the sun rises, we can go and search again."

"I don't want to wait until morning. I want to find him now!"

Juan understood David's frustration but recognized the need for prudence. "We will search better tomorrow and cover more ground if we are rested. Come, let us get a room. We can contact some people to organize a search, and then try to get some sleep. In the meantime, the *guardia* and policemen are alerted. They know he is missing and are searching for him. They will notify us if they find anything, I promise."

◆ ◆ ◆

In the blackness, something stirred near Jonathon. Something moved over his open palm. Jonathon's fingers twitched at the intrusion, but the invader did not stop. It continued onward, moving up his wrist. Intent on its course, the unseen pest traced a path up Jonathon's forearm, over the elbow, and onto Jonathon's shoulder. Onward it continued, over the strap of his backpack and then across his neck.

As the intruder crossed onto his cheek, consciousness returned to Jonathon. Within the sightless world, his eyes flew open in the blackness and he hurled himself away from the unseen presence even as both hands slapped at the trespasser. With an audible *pop,* it flattened into a moist lump against his face. The size of its remains horrified Jonathon, and he pushed against it with his bloodied hand, aggressively wiping it off as he sat up in the darkness, his cheek moist and his heart pounding.

His rapid movement caused intense pain to explode through his body. Doubled over in the darkness, he couldn't move, couldn't release himself from the shooting agony. Throbbing torment held him prisoner. His mouth opened, and he gasped for relief, fighting to control the excruciating pain, but the intensity overwhelmed him. He inhaled sharp, short gulps of air trying to stop the pain, yet each breath caused fire to fill his lungs. He had to have broken something, maybe a lot of things.

Slowly his mind claimed control, and as he did, the agony subsided but the darkness did not. Where was he? What had happened? Blackness surrounded him, so thick it seemed tangible.

Then Jonathon became aware of movement across his body. His clothes, his skin, even his hair tingled with the scurrying of invisible creatures.

He twisted to escape them, crying out in horror and pain at the movement. He batted at his hair, slapped at his chest and arms, and swatted at his legs. Fear brought Jonathon to his feet in the sightless world. He tried to flee from the living things crawling over him, but a crack of pain against the back of his head filled his mind with white, hot light and sent him staggering forward. Stunned, he collapsed to his knees, his body numb. Blood began to run down the back of his neck. Blackness overtook his mind, and Jonathon sank to the cave floor, once more unconscious to the creatures around him.

◆　　◆　　◆

In his hotel, David paced the length of his room, his heart and voice crying for answers. "Where is my son?" he groaned. "He couldn't have just dropped off the face of the earth. He has to be out there, somewhere!"

"He is, David." Juan spoke quietly.

"He's hurt, Juan. I can feel it. Something is very wrong, but I can't get to him. Do you know how helpless that makes me feel?" David's voice lowered in pain. "He's my son. I'm supposed to know everything about him and I don't even know where he is right now!"

Pinching his tear ducts with his fingers, David tried to fight the grief. "Ever since his birth, I've only wanted the best for him . . . the *very* best." He lifted his gaze, staring at the far wall without seeing it. "When he was a newborn I wanted him to have the best night's sleep he could have, so I gave up my sleep to hold and rock him when he cried. As he got older, I gave up money for my clothes to buy him new shoes or a new pair of pants. I gave up opportunities I wanted, just so he could have things he wanted. He got braces and computer games, he joined soccer teams . . . ."

Emotion caused David's words to lodge in his throat and, for a moment, the room grew heavy with silence. Then, when he spoke again, he could only whisper. "I did it all for him, and do you know what, Juan? I didn't mind. In fact, I gave it all up, knowing full well that I could never give him as much as he had already given me."

David turned tear-filled eyes to his friend. "From the moment I first held him in my arms, he gave me joy and a purpose I'd never felt before. He gave me *life,* and I knew then that I'd give up my life for him." A tear slid down David's cheek. "Now I can't. I love him, Juan and I can't help him. I've failed as a father. I've let him down."

"If what you have told me is true, you haven't failed him. You have loved him with all your heart, and that is never a failure." Juan watched David absorb his words. "I know you are worried—we all are—but you must try and rest—for Jonathon's sake. We have called together a search party. They will be here in the morning, along with the police and their search dogs and many other locals. Until then, there is nothing more we can do."

David moaned from deep within. "Yes, there is. There is one more thing." He turned saddened eyes toward his friend. "I have to tell his mother."

❖ ❖ ❖

Jonathon's eyelids flickered then opened. Black greeted his vision so thick and complete, he wasn't sure he'd opened his eyes. With his face resting on the cold stone he blinked—hard. The darkness remained. He shut his eyes tight then opened them wide, feeling the sensation of his moving lids. Still he saw only a thick, black veil. Lifting his hand to his face, Jonathon placed it over his eyes and blinked again. He could feel his eyelashes brush the palm of his hand, telling him his eyes were open. The darkness was real. He had been buried alive in a tomb.

The thought caused Jonathon to shudder, and he closed his eyes. "This is not a tomb," he told himself. "It's just the middle of night."

Lying on the cold, hard floor he turned his mind away from the impenetrable blackness to his body. The creatures no longer crawled on him. For that much, he felt grateful.

Face down on the floor, he felt the chill through his clothes, feeding on his body. His limbs, muscles, and bones throbbed with cold. It hurt to breathe deeply. His head ached. When he shivered, it felt like a jackhammer pounding his skull and a knife cutting through his chest. He needed to break contact with the ground and find a warmer place to sit.

Jonathon pushed off the floor but pain exploded throughout his body. Crying out, he collapsed to his chest. The movement drove the breath from his lungs and left his brain spinning in dizzy circles. Lying again on the cold ground, Jonathon sucked his breath and gritted his teeth against the pain. His eyes were shut tight against the pain. *Why does everything hurt so much?*

This is not good, he thought. *If I'm hurt too badly, I'll never be able to get out of this place, whatever it is.*

He winced in agony.

Why does it feel like my head is split open? His memory cleared. *Oh, that's right. I hit my head on something—hard.*

Jonathon shifted his weight to reach the back of his skull but immediate pain sliced through his chest, driving the breath from him. It felt as if constricting bands had been placed around his torso. He couldn't breathe in, he could only exhale and he wondered how many ribs he'd broken. At the awful intensity attacking his body, Jonathon wanted to curl up in a ball and curse. Instead, he held still, taking only tiny breaths until the pain subsided. He did not want to be here!

Swallowing hard, Jonathon whispered to himself in the dark. "I've got to figure out what's broken."

He knew his left side was damaged. Carefully, Jonathon managed to move his left arm toward his rib cage, applying pressure to it as he rolled his body. He wanted to vomit from the pain, but wisdom told him not to. He knew he couldn't take the pain vomiting would bring.

Shifting into a more comfortable position, Jonathon managed to move his right hand to the back of his skull, where he felt a mass of dried blood matted to his hair with dirt and debris. The back of his shirt and jacket also felt stiff with dried blood, and Jonathon recognized a hardened coating on the side of his face where blood had flowed. He must have bled a lot.

Gingerly he touched the wound beneath, wincing as his fingers probed its long surface. He was grateful the wound felt dry now. Apparently the bleeding had stopped. Jonathon sighed with relief.

I wonder if there are creatures down here attracted to blood.

The thought sent a chill through him. He didn't know the answer and, just in case they would crawl across the floor to find him, he didn't want to be lying down.

Slowly now, slower than before, he rolled to a sitting position, pressing his right hand over his head wound to reduce the throbbing. His left arm, feeling numb and a bit useless, pressed against his side, bracing his ribs against the pain as he moved. This time he managed to sit up.

Wary of his unseen surroundings, he moved with caution. He did not want to hit his head again on a low overhang—or worse, shift wrong and fall into another abyss. But only blackness seemed to hang above his head, and the earth felt solid beneath him.

Sitting on the cold, hard floor he mentally assessed the rest of his body. Everything hurt: his ribs, his left shoulder, even his knee, but his headache felt bigger than Machu Picchu.

He knew he had to have fallen into a cave or crevasse of some type. In the darkness, he tried to gain his bearings, to understand where he might be.

Definitely not the mall.

Jonathon ignored the negative thought and carefully turned his head through the pain, searching as far as he could. The movement brought spinning dizziness, and he closed his eyes.

What are you looking for, the voice taunted. *A lighted EXIT sign?*

Jonathon felt anger at the pestering thoughts but irritated too because he had been looking for something . . . a ray of light, a shaft of moonbeam—something, anything—filtering down through the hole that swallowed him.

When the spinning subsided, Jonathon slowly opened his eyes. But he found only blackness—total and complete impenetrability. He couldn't even see his hands in front of his face.

Maybe he could call for help.

Despite the tremendous pain that arced through him, Jonathon took a shallow breath—just enough to sustain his voice—and yelled through the darkness. "*¡Ayuda!* Help! Is anybody there? Can anybody hear me?" The effort left him racked with agony, sucking in ragged breaths until he gained control again.

What are you doing? This is a cave . . . not a freeway. Do you honestly think someone is here?

Jonathon closed his eyes again.

The taunting voice in his mind seemed to enjoy the situation. *Besides, you may not want to call for help. If anybody is here they're probably not somebody you want around. This is a cave, remember? It may be a mass murderer who hears you or a crazy hermit who hasn't had anyone to eat—meet—in years.*

"This is ridiculous." Jonathon hissed through gritted teeth. "There are no mass murderers down here."

How do you know? It's not like a mass murderer let anyone out of here to go broadcast his presence to the rest of the world.

Jonathon pressed harder against the back of his head, trying to stop the pain and the thoughts, but the inner musing continued against his will.

There could be a dead person down here, right next to you . . . only a few feet away. What if you touch him in the dark?

Jonathon retracted his limbs, drawing them close.

What if he reaches out and touches you? Or grabs your neck?

The thought that something might come out of the darkness to grab his neck unnerved him. Despite the pain in his shoulder and ribs, Jonathon wrapped both hands over his neck and closed his eyes. He didn't want to be thinking these things!

Yet, in the darkness, he couldn't stop the growing worry that maybe someone else *had* fallen down this same hole years ago and died, rotting into a decomposed collection of bones, close enough to touch.

The image wouldn't be ignored. Legs drawn up, hands covering his neck, he tried to hold as steady as he could. He didn't want to bump into *anything*.

There could be monsters down here . . . or vampires.

"Shut up. There are no such things."

But what about mummies? The voice taunted. *They* **do** *exist. You even saw one yourself.*

With his hands still covering his neck, Jonathon positioned his arms to cover his ears. "I don't want to hear this!" he groaned, "Somebody get me out of here!" His anxious voice echoed off the rocks, then disappeared into silence.

Nothing.

No response.

Only blackness.

Jonathon began to rock back and forth, ignoring the pain. "Somebody, help me!" he yelled again into the tomb-like world. "Anybody!"

But only the rocks and the darkness felt his presence.

Jonathon knew he had to relax so the pain would lesson. He also had to control his thoughts or he'd go crazy. He couldn't be thinking about dead bodies, vampires, or mummies down here in the dark!

Leaning forward, he pressed his forehead against the surface of his knees, his hands still protecting the back of his neck. He didn't like the pain or this sightless world which refused to yield its secrets. It filled his mind with too many disturbing thoughts.

"They're probably looking for me by now. I'm sure they know I'm missing." He spoke carefully, trying to avoid the pain yet needing to create the comfort of hearing his own voice in the darkness. "I wish I knew what time it was!"

Then he remembered his watch. It had a light up dial.

Jonathon released his neck and eased both arms around to the front. His fingers found the watch still wrapped to his wrist and he depressed the tiny button. Instantly the world before him became bathed in pale blue luminosity—the first light Jonathon had seen since his fall. Avoiding any other sights now visible around him, his eyes squinted to read the time. "Two-thirty?" The time stunned him. "My watch must have broken in the fall." But the minute hand swept its way around the watch face and Jonathon realized the watch still worked. It must be the middle of the night.

With a soft groan, Jonathon released the button and closed his eyes. He must have been unconscious longer than he thought. "Well, that explains why it's so dark down here. It's night." Strangely, the thought cheered him. That meant the darkness would last only a few more hours. In three hours, maybe four, the sun's light would filter down the opening. Then he could better view his situation, find a way out, follow a stream to the Urubamba River, and from there it would be a cinch to find his dad.

Oh, he wanted to be with his dad.

A smile pressed across his face. "That's probably a first."

Just as quickly, however, his mind grew serious. "I really don't want to have to wait until morning. I don't want to be stuck down here any longer than necessary."

Lifting his head against the pain and dizziness, he peered into the inky blackness, trying to see the chute he had descended. Maybe he could see stars peering down through the hole.

There were none.

Exhaling in defeat, Jonathon slowly returned his head to his knees and closed his eyes. He couldn't see a thing.

You could use your watch to see.

This impression was quiet, softer than the taunting voice of earlier. Jonathon lifted his head at thought. When he'd checked the time, the watch had illuminated the ground around him. Maybe he could use it to find his way out.

Or find a dead body! The harsh thoughts returned.

Jonathon hesitated. What if he *did* see a corpse?

Dread pounded into every nerve. What if he saw something *approaching* him?

The battle in his mind continued until Jonathon concluded that *not* seeing might be even worse. Drawing in some air, he found the button on his watch and pressed it. Once again, the cave took shape beneath a pale, blue glow, and Jonathon jumped. Dark shapes loomed, and then he saw that the shadows came from the rocks around him. He exhaled, relieved. For a few feet, at least, there were no more holes and no dead bodies.

Licking his lips, he took another breath and extended his wrist in front of him, casting the eerie blue light further out to the darkness. Jonathon let his gaze explore the cave. As the light met with the deeper recesses of his cryptlike world, he became aware of movement, horrifying . . . on the walls, the floor. Waves of spiders and insects scurried to hide from the light, vanishing into cracks and crevices. He roared in horror and let go of his watch. The cave dropped into darkness. Terrified, Jonathon kicked into the unseen, trying to rid the area of a million fears. "Get out of here!" he cried. In the cave's inky hold, he wasn't sure seeing had been a good thing. Now he knew the walls were filled with creatures—he just didn't know what types.

His imagination sent them crawling up his spine and over his body in cold chills. A lock of his hair shifted and brushed against his forehead. Jonathon jumped. He knocked it away then rushed to wipe his hands clean on his clothes. Pain and terror controlled him. He envisioned large, hairy jungle tarantulas like he'd seen in movies, or fast moving and deadly centipedes. Perhaps they were waiting to leap on him from the walls. Maybe they were slowly lowering down on spinnerets from the ceiling. Or, worse, they could already be clinging to his back like in the Indiana Jones movie he had seen.

With a roar, he scrambled across the floor away from his fears, swiping at his back. His hand hit something large behind his shoulder. He convulsed with horror, bolting to his feet without any thought of low ceilings.

The strap on his backpack tugged against him, just below the shoulder blade, and its weight ended his flight. His hand had not brushed against a giant spider, only bumped the strap of his backpack!

"My backpack! I forgot about my backpack." He exhaled slowly. "That was stupid." Bending over in the darkness, Jonathon gripped his torso in pain, the sharp agony in his head pounding. He swayed and his knees buckled, but Jonathon managed to stay upright. Fighting another curse, he pressed a hand against the back of his head, trying to force the throbbing to subside. "I really don't like it here."

Several seconds passed before the pain lessened its grip. Straightening with caution, testing the reaction of his body and what may be above him, he managed to come fully upright in the darkness. With that victory, Jonathon swallowed. "I don't care how much it hurts, I am *not* going to sit down for the rest of the night. I don't want anything crawling on me. I don't even want *think* something is on me."

Again, he illuminated his watch. Less than two minutes had passed. Jonathon sighed out loud. "It's going to be a long night."

With his watch still casting a blue glow, Jonathon braved another look around the dimly lit cave. This time the walls did not move, their occupants still hiding from the first invasion of light. "Good. Just stay there," he ordered. "I'll keep this watch light on all night if I have to."

With the limited view provided by his watch's glow, Jonathon tried to find a way out. He really didn't want to spend the night here.

Moving the light across the cave walls, the pale illumination cast strange shadows into the darkness but it revealed no openings above him. Turning around, Jonathon sent the watch's light behind him.

He froze.

There, silent and ominous, gaped the dark entrance of a tunnel.

EIGHT

JONATHON'S body chilled as he stared at the dark opening—its gaping mouth ready to devour him. The darkness of its core told him the tunnel extended far deeper than he wanted to consider. As his mouth went dry, he knew the unknown creatures on the walls did not frighten him as much as the foreboding portal.

What if something is hiding in that tunnel, waiting to come after you?

Unable to turn away, Jonathon's senses prickled at the thought. "This is stupid," he told himself. "You've seen way too many movies." Yet he watched the opening, straining his hearing, listening for movement.

He heard nothing.

He tried to see, or sense, motion in the hole, yet his eyes registered nothing.

Still—

"Hello?" Jonathon called out hesitantly. "Is anyone there?"

Oh, that's real good. Just announce your presence. Here zombie, zombie . . . come here, boy.

"Shut up."

Why? You didn't. Now, thanks to you, something could be coming here. It could be approaching closer and closer . . . .

Jonathon tried to ignore the voice—but his heart raced with fearful thoughts. On his watch, a second passed, then two.

"This is stupid," he muttered. "What if that's the way I came in?"

Oh, come on. That hole is downhill from here. Don't tell me you honestly think you rolled up the incline to get here!

"If the fall was hard enough."

If the fall was hard enough, the voice mimicked sarcastically. **Great. Not only are you yelling to zombies but you're also stupid.**

"I am not stupid. I've yelled before down here and nothing came. That's because nothing can live down here . . . well, besides me and the things in the walls."

Zombies aren't living . . . .

The sudden thought drove Jonathon back a step. Though he didn't really believe in zombies, he also didn't want to think of those kinds of things while staring at the sinister opening. It seemed evil, and evil, he knew, was real.

◆　　　◆　　　◆

Rubbing his hands over his face, David sunk into a chair, defeated. Juan questioned his friend. "How did it go?"

"Not good. She's very upset." He closed his eyes. "She's taking the first plane down. I hope we find him before she gets here. I just want him home."

Opening his eyes, David shifted his gaze toward Juan, his voice serious. "I don't care what people may think. No matter how much he may hate me or be mad at me for this afternoon, he didn't run away. Jonathon is not a quitter or a runner."

"I know that." Juan's gentle voice softened David's pain. "I also know he doesn't hate you. What Jonathon hates is the fact that he is getting older and has to remake his relationship with you. He misses what he had when he was a boy and he is worried about not having that closeness with you as he grows into a man. That's what he hates. It's not you."

Emotion choked David's voice. "Thank you, Juan. I worry about our changing relationship too, but right now I'm worried about never having *him* again. He's not here, Juan. He can't be. I can feel that. My son is alive and in trouble." David struggled with his words. "He's trying to get home and can't."

"If he is hurt and cannot move, the dogs will find him tomorrow."

"That's not what I mean." David paused for a moment, fighting his greatest fear. Leaning forward, he locked an anguished gaze onto Juan. "I'm worried about terrorists, Juan, and I want to know the truth. What are the chances they may have kidnapped him?"

Juan didn't respond. Silence filled the hotel room. David watched and waited, his emotions intensifying.

Finally, with a sigh, Juan gave a cautious answer. "There are many people at Machu Picchu every day. The odds that the terrorists would take *your* son . . . ."

"But of all the people at Machu Picchu today, *my* son is missing!"

More silence followed David's forceful words and, for a full minute, only the clock ticked. When Juan spoke again, his voice was quiet. "I don't know if terrorists took him, but I will be honest with you. Yes, it is possible. There are terrorists here, in these mountains."

"Why would they take him?"

Uncomfortable, Juan struggled with the answer. "I do not know. If they did take him, they may only want a ransom . . . ." His strained voice hesitated as he battled his next answer. "Or they may want more."

"Like what?"

Juan regarded his friend, hating the answer he had to give. "They may want to use him as an example, to prove to the authorities just how serious they are about their demands." His eyes met David's. "And if that is their purpose, I fear no ransom will buy him back."

Sick to his stomach, David closed his eyes.

✦   ✦   ✦

Once again, Jonathon looked at his watch: 8:30. He had waited for six hours for morning to come, but no light pierced the blackness, no ray of sunshine beckoned to lead him out. The time on his watch meant he had missed at least one cycle of daylight deep inside this tomb with no evidence of its passing besides the ticking of his watch.

He'd been buried alive.

The blue glow from his watch flickered then dimmed, and Jonathon knew he had pushed the illuminating feature so many times the battery would soon fail. He didn't want to be trapped in the pit's darkness forever. "There has to be a way out," he stated firmly to the darkness around him. "I fell in somewhere. I just need to find out where before my battery dies."

Turning to the wall he felt most comfortable with, he illuminated its surface again. Holding the light up as high as his battered body would allow, he searched for a hole he may have fallen through, but he only saw more darkness. Walking with caution, Jonathon began to trace the upper perimeter of the chamber, searching for any opening that may lead to the surface.

His slow path took him toward the darkened tunnel. As he came close to its opening, he hesitated, nervous. Maybe the opening he fell through *was* just inside the tunnel.

In the dim light, he stared at the cave's leering mouth. He didn't want to go inside. Maybe it was his imagination, but he sensed a presence in that dark corridor, one of death, and he didn't want to meet it.

Stepping away from the opening, Jonathon continued to the other side of the chamber. He noted it was getting easier to move and a little easier to breathe, and for that he felt grateful. *When I find the opening,* Jonathon thought, *I just might be able to climb out.*

Feeling his hope increase, he lifted his arms higher to illuminate the ceiling. A few more steps around the stone cavern and he felt something wisp against his hands and face.

Spider webs!

The sensation startled him. Jerking backward, his fingers slipped and his watch went black. Jonathon was horrified as his wrist and fingers tangled in the web's fine strands. They wrapped around him and brushed against his face. The web was enormous!

Crying out, he struck at the webbing, trying to break free, but the huge weaving held with unbelievable strength. It wouldn't release him. Jonathon couldn't help but picture the giant spider that must have created such a web. He could see its huge legs and fast movements carrying it across the strands to attack. Terrified by the vision in his mind, he yanked and thrashed in his prison, determined to escape before the spider descended. Then the ceiling broke loose and everything lurking above him in the darkness dropped, tumbling down on him. Dust and debris . . . and hundreds of spiders.

Jonathon howled. More and more spiders, some the size of his fist, showered down on top of him, their ceiling home destroyed. They pelted his face, hung in his hair, lodged against the skin of his neck, or fell into his clothing. Panicked, he batted blindly in the dark, his voice crying in sheer horror. With a final jerk of desperation, he broke the web's hold and jumped away.

Wrapped in complete darkness, he struck at the horrors still falling all around him. Chills raked his body. The sound of spiders hitting him and the floor—the sensation of them landing on him—filled Jonathon with fear deeper than any he had known before. The awful noise of the downpour of spiders and dirt echoed through the chamber, then slowed, then stopped. The only sound left in the cave came from his frantic movements and horrified cries as he knocked the remaining creatures away.

The body of a large spider fell against the top of his shoe. With a roar he kicked it into the darkness and found the light on his watch. He dreaded activating it. A cave floor writhing with the movement of live spiders scurrying over and around the debris frightened him, but he was more afraid of having them climb on him in the darkness. He needed to see exactly where they were.

Pressing the button on his watch, the cavern filled with pale blue light. In the hazy air and eerie glow, a few wisps of dust rose from the ground and swirled around him before disappearing into the dark. The displaced ceiling lay in a mound in front of him, but the floor lay still. None of the spiders moved.

Narrowing his eyes, Jonathon intensified his study. They were spiders but they seemed paralyzed, frozen.

Then he noticed their retracted legs, folded over their abdomens in death. He had been drenched in a shower of *dead* spiders.

Horrified by the bizarre occurrence, Jonathon inched closer. Still uncertain, he pushed at the motionless carcass of a giant spider with his shoe. Even folded in death, it equaled the size of his fist. Two dehydrated legs broke from its exoskeleton and fell to the dirt, startling him. Jonathon pushed at another spider with the same result. They were dead. All of them.

He glanced upward. There must have been several hundred dead spiders in that one portion of the ceiling!

With an instinctive swipe over his hair, Jonathon quickly sidestepped the area. As he did, his terror suddenly increased. If there were that many dead spiders, how many more live spiders were still lurking above him?

The thought sent a shudder through his body, igniting the old pains and new uncertainties. Fighting to catch his breath and control the pain, Jonathon closed his eyes in an effort to calm his nerves, which were still tingling from the ordeal. He decided he needed to know what was up there. Carefully, he lifted his lighted watch above his head, shining it into the dark recesses above, watching for movement and webbing. But the ceiling appeared as still as the floor, and he saw no signs of life above him.

Jonathon's gaze returned to the sight beneath him. The spiders must have come from somewhere.

Confusion tumbled through his mind as he examined the dirt mound. This time he saw something unusual protruding from the small mountain of debris and dead spiders. Leaning closer, he toed the object with his foot. It looked like a plant frond. Using his shoe, he scraped away dirt and carcasses, exposing more of the object. Still unsure of what he saw, he touched it with his finger then began to withdraw it carefully from the barrow of spiders. The object moved suddenly, causing the small mountain of spiders to shift and tumble. Startled, Jonathon jumped back and let go. The spiders and dirt lay still. Carefully, he approached again and pulled at the object.

It wasn't a plant frond but part of a woven mat with a fine web of cording attached to it . . . the same cording that had entangled Jonathon. And there were more pieces of the mat and cording scattered beneath the dead spiders.

Lifting his gaze back to the ceiling, he felt confusion until his mind filled with the memory of Juan's story. The Incas had dumped baskets full of poisonous spiders and deadly snakes into secret tunnels. Prisoners cast into the darkness were left to die from the poisonous bites.

This had once been a basket of living, deadly spiders!

The woven container, with a lid to keep the spiders inside, had been suspended above the cavern with some type of fine webbing left dangling beneath it. When a prisoner stumbled into the webbing and became entangled, as Jonathon had, he would pull the deadly basket down on top of him, releasing its contents! In taunting blackness, the prisoner would find himself fending off a shower of living spiders.

This basket had never been released from the ceiling until Jonathon became caught in its snare. The spiders, trapped inside their woven prison centuries ago, had died.

But what about the other baskets? Jonathon's mind filled with cold fear. Could other spiders have escaped from their traps? Could those spiders have survived and eventually reproduced down here in the dark? Maybe their offspring were some of the creatures he'd felt crawling over his body earlier, or seen scurrying into holes and crevices. He could be surrounded by thousands of poisonous spiders, deadly descendants of the originals.

Then came another thought, even more disturbing than the first.

He had stumbled into a trap—one purposely designed to kill. This place was probably littered with booby traps.

As the realization consumed him, Jonathon's heart began to pound and his nerves throbbed. He hadn't merely fallen into a random crevasse. He had fallen into a planned death chamber! Worse, he wasn't the first person to be down here. Hundreds of years ago, this basket had been prepared, then hung, for someone specific—someone sent here to die.

That meant a corpse *did* exist somewhere in the darkness.

Trembling where he stood, Jonathon closed his eyes as horrifying thoughts overwhelmed him. This place had been built to hold the condemned—it had been designed and rigged as an inescapable pit of death.

He stood, trapped, in an ancient Alcatraz.

◆   ◆   ◆

At the bottom of a foliage-entangled ravine, Severino studied the cave only a few yards above him. Moving his hand slowly, he felt the safety on his rifle, making sure it was off. If he needed to pull the trigger, he wanted to be ready. He didn't want to die here. Creeping forward, he kept every sense alert.

A flock of birds erupted from their perches. The noise burst through the trees, startling him. Severino dropped to the brush—every nerve racing. He didn't know if he had frightened the birds or if they were startled by something else.

Crying their warning, the winged flock exploded skyward, seeking refuge in the heavens. As they disappeared over the trees and their alarmed calls died away, Severino remained still. Waiting for his pounding heart to calm, he listened for rustling footsteps. For several long seconds, he held motionless, but no sound reached him. He traced his eyes along the steep mountainside, looking for movement, and saw nothing. The mountain face carried an unnatural stillness. Even the wind seemed to be hiding.

Drawing a deep breath, Severino rose to his feet and began to climb toward the cave's mouth once again, not knowing if sinister eyes watched his approach. He knew the risks of coming here, but he had to. Rumors in town were spreading of a narrow cave—a monster's mouth, they called it—that led to a chamber full of mummies. Those mummies, Severino knew, must never leave the mountain.

So he had come to seal the cave. And, if he died on this slope before he accomplished his job, it meant he had failed to keep the mummies inside.

◆　　◆　　◆

Jonathon fought to control his mind and his fears. He had to get out of this death trap. He needed to find the place where he had fallen in. It was his only hope. Illuminating the cavern, Jonathon resumed his search. His shoes crunched on spider carcasses and the eerie light from his watch bent the stone walls into odd, corpselike shapes. Fighting his fear, Jonathon continued, moving further around the cavern, searching for a hole or fissure that might lead him to the surface, but he found nothing.

The cavern veered to the right, and Jonathon hesitated. Not knowing what might be waiting around the bend, he forced himself to find the courage to move forward. When he did, he exhaled loudly and stepped around the stone barrier. As his watch illuminated the far side of the cave, Jonathon came to an abrupt halt. His stomach churned, twisting inside him while his heart exploded with fear.

In front of him stood another tunnel—its cavernous mouth open and waiting.

For a moment, he felt his body sway. Jonathon looked behind him. In the dimness he saw the opening of the first tunnel then returned his stunned gaze to this newly discovered second opening. Continuing to look back and forth, Jonathan examined them again, comparing the portals in the weak light. Except for their location, they looked identical. Each hideous opening appeared to be the same width and height. Each cavern stood flanked by stone teeth.

The passages moved in opposite directions, taunting him with their dark secrets.

As he compared the two tunnels, Jonathon's mind tried to deny what he saw. He stood between two tunnels so alike in shape and appearance that they couldn't be natural. They had been man-made.

"No," he whispered, not wanting to accept the truth. "Please, no."

Jonathon now knew he stood in a death chamber encircled by the secret tunnels of the Incas.

Hundreds of miles of hidden tunnels.

NINE

JONATHON used the fading blue light from his watch to stare at the gaping holes while his mind sorted through all Juan had said about the tunnels. The ancient Incas cast people into darkened tunnels to die. Every year rumors claimed people fell into them and were never seen again. These tunnels killed people.

"Oh, this is *not* good." Jonathon spoke his protest audibly.

As his heart pounded with fear, a quiet portion of his mind recalled Juan's other stories. People had supposedly traveled through them and lived. Even Juan thought the ancient Incas used the tunnels to *escape* their enemies.

What if that was all true? What if one of these unknown corridors led to freedom?

Jonathon held still, studying them. The dark apparitions beckoned and repelled him at the same time. He peered into the new tunnel, searching its hold for flickers of light, but saw none. He listened, his ears plying the tunnel for sounds of movement. Nothing moved.

Hesitant, Jonathon extended his watch toward the opening, casting its glow just inside the darkened mouth. For the first few feet, at least, the passage was empty.

Forcing moisture down his throat, Jonathon made his decision. He stepped inside the opening of the second tunnel. Lifting his arm as far as the pain allowed, he threw the weak light above him, scanning for openings . . . or baskets of spiders. His gaze traveled over the rocky roof, seeking any place he could escape. Only solid stone met his eyes.

The tunnel's close walls felt confining, and his heart beat strongly. Fear began to fill his mind. The end of the passage funneled into the darkness. He didn't know how far it went or what lay in its hold, but he could not bring himself to explore any further. It was too much.

Seeking security from the chamber he knew, Jonathon stepped away from the unknown. As he did, his heel caught on something and he tripped. Feeling his body pitch backward, Jonathon twisted and threw his hands behind him to catch himself. Pain lashed his torso at the move, and he lost contact with the light's button. Darkness swallowed the tunnel. He stumbled backward and crashed to the ground, making contact with something hard and sharp. Roaring in surprise, he retracted his hands from the object and felt hardness scrape his knuckles, leaving behind the sensation of cut flesh. Rolling to his knees, Jonathon felt the object beneath him.

Groping for his watch, he pressed the button.

A human skull erupted from the darkness at him. Its open mouth and empty eyes sockets gaped only a few inches away. The decayed teeth, in a grotesque and silent scream, showed fresh blood from Jonathon's knuckles. Beneath him, his knees pressed through the broken bones of a human rib collapsed by his weight.

Choking in horror, Jonathon fell backward again, and the cave went dark a second time. He forgot the pain in his ribs and his head as he scrambled to escape the creature, but everywhere he put his hands there were bones and the scent of death. Panic filled him. Moving blindly on his hands and feet, fumbling for the passage opening, he found space and rushed forward.

As he entered the chamber, his hands and feet crunched over the bodies of hundreds of dead spiders and basket debris. Still he fled the thing behind him, not stopping his retreat until he collided with stone, solid and unmoving, smashing open his flesh as his face slammed into the rock barrier. Blood wet his skin as it flowed rapidly over his features, but he didn't notice.

Halted by the solid wall, Jonathon climbed to his feet, pounding his hands on the stone, yelling for escape. Beating at the walls of his tomb, and trapped where others had died, Jonathon yelled for release, but none came. No one heard. He was buried alive in the Andes Mountains.

It seemed a lifetime passed as he called and pleaded for help, but the darkness did not answer. Finally, wrapped in a shroud of fatigue and helplessness, Jonathon sank to the earth. He would die here. Like the remains in the tunnel, he would die and decay in this dark pit, never to be seen—or see—again.

With his body and mind in agony, Jonathon drew his legs toward his chest and wrapped his arms around them. He rocked in the darkness. "I just want to go home!" he choked. Trapped inside a stone crypt filled with horrors, both real and imagined, Jonathon knew he'd go crazy first. His mind would die long before his body. And, as he rocked himself in the darkness, he wondered if it already had.

"No!" Pressing his eyes shut, Jonathon sought to calm his mind. He couldn't think like that. He couldn't give up, not now—not as long as he could still breathe and move. He had to try to find his way out. If there was a way into the tunnels, there had to be a way out.

The idea allowed him to reclaim control over his mind.

In the darkness, Jonathon sifted through a collection of thoughts. He knew the Incas had designed the chamber as a death pit. In order to keep their victim trapped inside, they had most likely disguised the entrance chute . . . the same chute Jonathon tumbled down. That meant Jonathon would probably not find it and, if he did, he wouldn't be able to climb back out of it.

If he was going to escape, he would have to find another way.

He closed his eyes. He couldn't carve his way out. The cavern was solid stone. His only hope lay inside one of those tunnels.

The thought caused his stomach to reel. He didn't want to go inside the tunnels. He didn't even want to move. Every time he did, something awful happened.

Pressing his head on his knees, he felt warm blood seep into his jeans. For the first, time he realized his face was bleeding. He reached to wipe away the flow and recoiled. His hands smelled of death; the scent of ancient bones assaulted his nose. Jonathon shoved his bloody and battered hands under his arms. He didn't want to smell them! He didn't want to remember what he'd discovered inside that tunnel.

Maybe he could try the other tunnel. He could use his watch light and check to see if the other tunnel had a skeleton before he entered.

Jonathon didn't like that idea any better.

Using the bottom of his shirt to mask the smell of his hands, Jonathon pressed at the blood on his face. He felt the painful swellings already beginning. He wondered if his eyes would swell shut. "At least I won't see any skeletons that way," he muttered.

The words didn't comfort him. Even without his swollen face, he knew he didn't have much time. The battery from his watch was dying. Maybe he should just stay put and wait. What if his father was following his trail and would be here soon?

Yet Jonathon knew his father couldn't track his steps. In a jungle that received rain almost everyday, there were no footprints left to follow! Besides, it was one thing to find a missing person above ground in the tangled expanse. It was something completely different to find a person who had fallen off the face of the earth!

No. Jonathon knew if he was going to get out, it would be up to him. He had to try the other tunnel.

Time passed. His facial bleeding slowed, clotted, and then stopped. The pain in his ribs and head subsided to a dull presence. Jonathon exhaled. He didn't have much time left.

Making an apprehensive decision, he brought his injured body back to its feet. Maybe the first tunnel contained the way out. The second tunnel had a dead body in it—obviously not a promising sign.

In the dim light, Jonathon approached the first opening. With his nerves electrified, he searched for a skeleton and found nothing. The light from his watch flickered and caused Jonathon to grimace. Soon it would go out and then he would never get home. He needed to hurry his search *and* conserve the battery.

Jonathon looked at the path in front of him. If he could memorize the terrain then travel that short distance without a light, he might be able to do both. Scanning the ground in front of him, he mentally marked where to place his feet. Then Jonathon let the cave go dark and extended his hand toward the stone wall. As his torn palm made contact with the cold surface, he recoiled. What if he touched something again? Whether dead or alive, neither was good.

Reactivating the light, Jonathon searched the tunnel sides and saw nothing. Head bowed and heart pounding, Jonathon forced his mind to calm down, and again, he let darkness consume the cave. Returning his hand to the wall, he touched it lightly once, twice, and then placed it against the rough surface. Concentrating now on the path he had memorized, he moved forward. In the darkness his feet toed the earth with each step, his hand fingered the wall. Every rock, every clump of dirt that broke beneath the weight of his step or fell from the rocky walls caused him to jump in fear. Progress came slowly.

Two steps, three . . . then finally four.

Jonathon stopped and groped for his watch. He had made it. His fingers found the tiny button, and instantly he sent the dim light into the tunnel. A quick scan told him there were no skeletons or spiders ahead.

"And no mummies. So far I'd say that means things are going well."

He peered through the pale glow, searching for an exit. Nothing. Drawing in a deep breath of air, Jonathon noted that the lower tunnel now began to rise toward the surface of the earth. Maybe it *would* take him to the surface. With his confidence increasing, he memorized his next steps, released the light, and again moved forward in darkness.

Despite his best efforts to remember each obstacle, he scraped his knuckles, banged his fingers, and jumped dozens of times. Often he jerked away as his hand bumped into the unseen. Sometimes the cause of his fear proved to be a solid rock. Other times, he felt the object scurry away. Those instances made Jonathon recoil, shaking his arm and wiping at his clothing. Worse were the moments he tripped or stumbled over something beneath his feet. Each time he feared he would find something hideous—a skeleton or a mummy staring at him through dried eyes.

Thankfully those things didn't appear when he illuminated the tunnel, although sometimes he caught sight of movement on the walls, of something disappearing deep into a crack. He never explored those cracks. He memorized where they were and avoided them. He didn't want to find a large, aggressive occupant.

Yet, despite his fears—maybe *because* of his fears—he continued moving forward. He had to. He knew now it was his only chance to survive.

The light from his watch flickered more often and grew weaker. He didn't have much time left before he'd be unable to move forward or go back. Soon the light only showed three or four steps ahead; then two.

With his battery dying, Jonathon felt discouragement. He sank to the cold ground to rest, both physically and emotionally.

His stomach growled. The last meal he'd eaten had been breakfast at the hotel before they took the train from Cusco. He didn't even know how long ago that was. At the ruins, he'd only eaten a banana and some cookies.

Jonathon remembered his backpack. His father filled it with food and water before they rode the bus to the ruins. It still had food in it.

Reaching behind him with excitement, Jonathon pulled his pack around to the front. In the darkness he found the zipper. The tunnel filled with the sounds of it opening. Shoving deep in the pack, Jonathon's hand passed over damaged fruit and a couple packages of cookies before coming to rest on the solid sides of a water bottle. Freeing it from the pack, he unstopped the bottle and took several long, deep swallows. It flowed down his throat with sweetness. He drained more of the delicious liquid into his body. He wanted to drink the entire amount but he knew he should save some for later.

Why save it? The taunting voice challenged. *You aren't going to live much longer anyway.*

"I might." Exhaling deeply, he recapped the bottle. He really did need to save it. It may have to last a while.

Extracting a small banana from his pack, he turned back the peel and took a bite. It was mashed and bruised, but still edible. He consumed the tiny fruit, savoring each swallow. Two cookies finished his rationed meal, and Jonathon leaned back against the wall. He enjoyed the satisfying sense of water and food in his stomach and realized this was the most relaxed he'd been since falling into the pit. He savored the feeling as hope began to flow back into him. Maybe he could make it.

Several minutes passed before Jonathon pushed the water into his pack and zipped it closed. Intending to conserve the fading light, Jonathon climbed to his feet in the darkness. As he did, he unintentionally smacked his forehead against a rock. In that instant, the painful swelling from earlier split open and once more began to bleed. Stepping backward, Jonathon doubled over and pressed his hands to his forehead. Blood—sticky and warm—dampened his palms. In the dark, he felt his hope drain away, and he shut his eyes to a new flood of pain and frustration.

Forget the water bottle and the bananas. He hated this place!

Just then the cave floor trembled beneath his feet. The tiny ripple rolled up through his shoes and into his legs. Unsure of the sensation, Jonathon lifted his head in confusion.

Beneath his feet, the vibration grew. Then, from deep below, came a sound—a groan which increased until it filled the entire passageway, reverberating off the walls, sounding like a roar of anger. In that instant the entire ground started to shake. He swayed at the movement, trying to keep his balance. The roar increased, and a new sound joined the cacophony—that of rocks and earth breaking loose. Then the floor shifted and began to *tip*!

Horror filled him as the earth heaved upward and the floor canted away beneath him. Before the thought fully registered, his feet started sliding. Sand and grit slipped by as the ground tottered then swung upward in front of him.

Jonathon dropped to his knees to keep from falling. Larger rocks slid and bounced past. His body began to slide backward. Desperate, he lunged forward, groping for something to hold. His backpack flipped over the edge of the rising earth. Still clinging to its strap, he fell onto his face.

The earth continued tilting at an increasing angle. In the darkness, Jonathon slipped down the incline just as the pack lodged on something and held firm. Jonathon's descent stopped as abruptly as it began.

As he clung to his pack the roaring noise continued. Rocks and sand poured past him, and he shut his eyes against the debris. Grit filled his mouth, ears and hair; rocks pelted his body. A large stone smashed one hand, and it went numb, slipping from the pack's strap.

The damaging blow caused Jonathon to lose partial hold and his body swung out sideways—over emptiness. Clutching the pack with his good hand, he tried to force his damaged hand and fingers to help, but they refused to grab. In desperation, he looped his arm through the strap, reclaiming a firmer hold on the pack.

Beneath him in the dark, the new space hungrily swallowed all that had not found anchor. Jonathon felt a belch of cold air burst up from the earth's stomach and envelope him. Rocks bounced past, striking him before they dropped into the opening. The sound of their distant contact below frightened him. The fall would be deadly.

The roaring sound faded and, when it did, the earth stopped tipping. The free fall of rocks slowed then stopped. Jonathon swung and twisted precariously against the stone face which, less than a minute before, had been the floor. He knew he had to climb out of here and over the edge before his pack dislodged or broke.

With his damaged arm still looped through the strap, Jonathon released the strap with his good hand. He had to grab the rim. Sucking in and holding his breath against the pain in his rib cage, Jonathon managed to grip the protruding edge above him with his fingers. Clinging to the lip with his good hand and with his other arm still hooked through the strap, he sent his feet scraping against the steeply pitched earth, trying to find a foothold. There were none, only smooth stone.

His fingers slipped and lost their grip on the precipice. Falling backward, fear and pain ripped through him simultaneously. He cried out as his body jerked hard against the pack. It shifted but held as Jonathon swung from his injured arm looped through the strap. He grabbed the strap with his good hand and roared his disapproval. This was not what he wanted to be doing!

Turning his body to face the rock he felt the pack slip, pulling free of its anchor. He was running out of time. Concentrating on reaching the edge again, he knew he needed to get his good arm hooked over the lip instead of just his fingers. Then he might be able to pull himself up the steep incline.

Jonathon willed his good hand to release the strap at the same time he surged upward. He swung his arm through the air, and felt it pass over the edge. Quickly, he grabbed the lip with his forearm and held on, crying out in protest as intense pain erupted in his side. Pressing his eyes shut, he fought the agony as icy sweat beaded up on his forehead. He wouldn't be able to tolerate the pain much longer. He needed to get a leg over the edge, quick; then he would be able to work his body out of the pit and find solid ground on the other side.

His first two tries failed. He felt his arm weaken and begin to tremble. His lungs cried for air. On the third attempt, he released a quick prayer. Elation filled him as he managed to hook his foot and lower leg over the ledge. Maintaining that same prayer, Jonathon thrust and pulled his body upward, working his knee, then his thigh, over the rim. Inch by inch, he pulled himself from the mouth of the abyss.

Solid ground rewarded his efforts, and Jonathon rolled onto his back, away from the slanted rock. With his arm still hooked through the strap of his pack, he cradled his injured hand, pressing it against his stomach and his arm against his side.

"Thank you," he whispered.

Gasping for each pained breath, he stayed still for several minutes, not daring to move. What had happened? Had that been a subterranean earthquake?

As his breathing came under control and the throbbing in his hand and side lessened, he eased himself upright. Whatever happened, he wanted to get away from the edge in case something else occurred.

This time, to make sure of his path, Jonathon activated the light.

A contorted world met his gaze. Beside him the tilted floor dropped toward a black abyss, yet the rest of the tunnel appeared untouched. The floor hadn't broken apart, as he supposed. Instead it remained whole—a solid stone base that rotated into a slide, funneling everything down to a dark chasm below.

In amazement, Jonathon studied the symmetrical slab, now resting at a steep angle. He glanced at the black opening. Both were perfectly sized.

In the darkness, truth began to lighten his mind. The giant stone had been designed to rotate! It had been cut, fit, and balanced over a deep pit. He hadn't triggered an underground earthquake. He'd triggered a trap.

A tomb trap.

Whoever came this way wasn't supposed to leave.

◆   ◆   ◆

The rocks, stones, and brush Severino placed in front of the cave succeeded in closing the ominous mouth. In the gathering darkness, he studied his work. Nothing would be able to leave the cave now. Lifting his rifle onto his shoulder, he turned and started down the steep slope. Tonight he would tell his sister to stop fearing. The mummies wouldn't be leaving the mountain.

TEN

IT WAS OVER. On the cold floor, completely engulfed in darkness, Jonathon sat in defeat. He managed to work his way back from the convoluted tunnel to the chamber just as the fading light from his watch died. Now, sitting at his starting point with no light to guide him, he couldn't travel any further. He could only sit blindly, with the last of his food and water, and wait for death to take him. He would die here with nothing but stone and darkness to mark his passing. No one would ever find him, and no one would ever know what happened.

Lowering his body to the stone floor, Jonathon let his pack pillow his head while he curled up his body. He tried to forget the inner ache that hurt more than the pain. His own actions had placed him here. He'd gone against the wishes of his father, ignored the prompting to tell someone of his plans, and descended the mountain without permission. Now no one knew where he was.

Buried in the darkness, he realized that his own choices, each of which seemed small at the time, had grown into an overwhelming situation he didn't have the power to correct. Despite his best efforts, he realized that some even small choices ended like that—out of your control.

Closing his eyes, Jonathon spoke to the skeleton. "I guess if I die here I won't be completely alone, will I, Bones? And you won't be alone anymore, either." In the sightless world, he felt sorrow for the unknown person who'd left his skeleton only a few feet away. His voice softened. "Hey, Bones? I'm sorry you had to die down here, away from your family."

Tears burned in his eyes. Entrapped in this tomb, Jonathon felt a grief deeper and quieter than any he'd ever experienced. It was the sorrow of leaving.

He realized he wouldn't miss his friends, his PSP, the mall, or hanging out. He would miss his family.

Jonathon let his thoughts wander to them. They were who he didn't want to leave. He wondered what they were doing. Were they searching for him right now? Were they anguishing over him?

Without seeing them, he knew they were doing both. He also understood they were anguishing because they loved him.

A tear pushed free from the corner of his eye, trickled down the side of his face and dropped in the dirt. Why did he think a good family had to be a 'perfect' family? A good family stayed together despite their weaknesses. A good family loved each other even when they knew the other family members had imperfections. That's what made those families so good.

Lying on the cold stone, Jonathon also knew he wanted to see his father again. He wanted to tell his dad how sorry he was for all the harsh words he'd spoken in the last few years, and for all the times he didn't speak at all. Mostly, he wanted to tell his father how much he loved him.

He didn't want to die . . . not here, not now. If only there was some way out, some way back.

There is. Take the second tunnel.

The quiet thought came with such clarity that Jonathon blinked his eyes. The impression returned, stronger this time. *Take the second tunnel.*

In the blackness, Jonathon turned toward the skeleton's tunnel. Could he have tried the wrong tunnel? Could "Bones" have died only a short distance from freedom and never known it?

Just as hope began to grow, Jonathon remembered the light from his watch had died. He couldn't search the tunnel even if he wanted to. He couldn't even find it.

Use your PSP.

Jonathon's mind exploded. In all his struggles, he had forgotten the PSP in his pack. He'd packed it that morning in the hotel. The game was illuminated and he even had extra batteries! His hands shaking from excitement, Jonathon sat up, fumbling for his pack. Opening the zipper, he rummaged through the contents until he felt the electronic game and pulled it out. Trembling with excitement, he turned it on. The tunnel burst into a warm glow.

"It works!" He shouted his elation to the rocks. "*Yes!*"

Climbing to his feet, Jonathon swung the game around him. It illuminated the world for several feet. The ceiling, the walls, the floor—the game gave more light than his watch! He *could* take the second tunnel! Bending down, he grabbed for his pack and realized he could even set the game aside, use his hands for other things, and not lose his light. Excited, and with a prayer of gratitude, Jonathon collected his belongings, zipped his pack closed, and swung it onto his shoulder. As he reached for the PSP, he froze. Cold defeat washed over him. The first tunnel had been rigged to kill a trespasser. What if the second tunnel was also a trap? He knew he wouldn't escape another time.

The second tunnel is your only chance. You will die if you stay here.

◆　　　◆　　　◆

"That cave is closed."

Severino's announcement brought his sister's startled eyes around to meet him, and her voice trembled. "Are you sure?"

"Yes, Delia. I sealed it myself. Nothing is leaving that mountain."

Delia pushed the clothes into a bucket of sudsy water. "But there are other openings."

Anger escaped his voice. "You know I cannot seal the entire mountain! I risked my life to seal that opening! I could have been killed!"

Tears filled her eyes. "I know. I am just frightened because of the mummies. I have heard stories." Her voice softened, and she shook her head. "I am sorry if I ask too much. You have done so much already. I do not want you killed like *Papá.*"

Her words softened Severino. Putting an arm around his sister's shoulders, he gave her a gentle squeeze. "You do not ask too much. And I will not die like *Papá.* I have a rifle and I will use it."

Wiping away a tear with the back of her soapy hand, she avoided looking at him. "A rifle will not stop them, Severino. You know that. They are evil. They have come to this valley for only one thing, and nothing can stop them, not even your rifle." Delia submerged her hands in the suds.

Severino stepped in front of the laundry bucket, lowering his face and forcing his sister to look at him. "I will stop them, Delia. You must trust me. I will not let those mummies leave the mountain.

◆　　◆　　◆

In the dim light of his game, Jonathon slumped on the cave floor and fought despair. He cradled the two dead batteries he'd just replaced, clicking them together in the palm of his hand as defeat filled him. Even with his efforts to conserve the light, he only had two more batteries left. Soon, Jonathon knew, he would be trapped in darkness forever.

He couldn't understand. When he did not encounter booby traps, he felt so sure the second tunnel would lead him out of this mess. Pushing forward, he let hope convince him an exit had to exist. No one carved a tunnel into solid rock without a reason. The passage must lead *somewhere*. So he'd followed it, losing all track of time, eating his scant provisions in carefully rationed portions, and sleeping on the cold tunnel floor.

Now, buried deep in the mountain with only two batteries left and no food or water, he struggled with the uselessness of even trying. He knew people could live for days without food, but they needed water, and he'd drank the last of his water days ago. Now his lips were swollen and cracked. His tongue stuck to his teeth and the roof of his mouth, and he couldn't even produce enough spit to swallow.

He'd read somewhere that Indians used to place pebbles in their mouths when they crossed the desert. It supposedly activated the saliva glands and eased thirst, so Jonathon had tried it. He placed two cold pebbles in his mouth and sucked on them. They tasted awful—like dirt and stone—but it worked for awhile . . . until he got tired of the taste of raw earth and spat the stones out into the darkness of the cave. Now his parched throat and mouth wore a coat of dirty dryness.

In the light, he stared at his PSP. It seemed useless to conserve the batteries anymore. He hadn't found a way out, was too far into the tunnel now to go back, and without food and water it didn't matter. He wouldn't last much longer. No, the only reason to save his last two batteries would be so he wouldn't have to die in the dark.

At the thought, Jonathon covered his eyes with his good hand. Silence engulfed him—the tomb-like silence of being buried alive. An anguished sob escaped his throat, but no tears left his eyes. Dehydrated and completely defeated, Jonathon had nothing left to give, not even tears.

"I can't do this anymore." His voice cracked with painful dryness. He rested the side of his head against the tunnel wall. "I'm finished," he whispered. "I'm through." Shutting off his PSP, he let the darkness come, then Jonathon slipped into the world of dreams where he laughed with his family and enjoyed being home.

◆　　　◆　　　◆

David Bradford dropped the newspaper to the tabletop. His head tipped back in fatigue and frustration. It had been six days since his son vanished, and there had been no news, no sightings. In fact, it had been so silent it was as if his son stepped off the face of the earth.

From the hotel room behind him he heard the hiss of the shower. His wife, Rosa, had joined him on the third day of the search. She hadn't slept much since arriving, she'd eaten even less, and he knew she stood in the shower each night and sobbed. He knew because he too let the shower wash his tear-drenched face each night. His heart ached day and night, and it seemed the pain would never go away.

He looked again at the headlines. All around him people were being murdered, their throats crudely slashed, and yet no one had seen a missing American teenager.

The sound of the shower stopped, and a few moments later Rosa emerged. A robe enveloped her body, and a towel covered her wet hair. Seeing the sadness on her face, David rose and embraced her. "I am so sorry," he whispered.

For several minutes they stood still. "Why can't we find him?" Rosa questioned. "We keep searching, but there are no answers."

"I don't know. I keep feeling like he's out there, like he's still alive. Maybe that feeling is an answer, but I don't understand it." David shook his head. "I keep feeling like he's trapped somewhere but can't get home. Over and over the feeling comes to me that he's trying, that he truly wants to be back home—not just because it's safe, but because it's *home*."

The words surprised David, and as his mind realized what his mouth had just said, he was filled with a new, strong emotion . . . of hope. Still holding his wife, David's soul grabbed onto the words, clinging to them. He now understood one powerful truth: his son truly wanted to come back *home*.

◆   ◆   ◆

Jonathon awoke from dreams of his family to the black nightmare of his reality. His eyes felt crusted. Had he wept in his dream? Jonathon tried to swallow but his throat and mouth, hardened by dryness, encircled a parched tongue too painful to move. Stiffness and cold claimed his body and, in the darkness, he didn't know how many hours had passed. He only knew his dreams had renewed his resolved. He *wanted* to get home, even if it meant following the tunnel in darkness all the way to Lima. He would not let his determination die before he did! But that meant he would have to travel as far and as fast as he could while there was still light.

In the grip of subterranean blindness, Jonathon felt for his PSP. Once it was in his hands, it took several fumbling attempts before his sluggish fingers found the switch on its side and turned on the game. The tunnel filled with light. Forcing his weakened body to work, he climbed to his feet and staggered forward.

His entire body throbbed and his stomach rolled with nausea—an odd sensation because he had no food in his system. His face and hands were cut and swollen from collisions with stone walls, and he was covered with the stings and bites of unseen creatures. Shaking from fever or poison—he didn't know which—he found it harder and harder to walk. His gait became an increasingly clumsy shuffle. He stumbled more and more often. As he moved forward, time ceased to exist. He didn't know how long he had been trapped in this world of stone and cold, and he didn't care anymore. Onward he pushed, his will driving his body far beyond its limits.

Alternating between fever and chills, Jonathon found himself unable to stay warm. He shivered continually now. Waves of increasing dizziness caused the carved tunnel to swirl and spin in front of him, playing with his vision. Twice he vomited in the blackness. Once he thought about eating it but couldn't. Dry heaves constantly twisted his stomach.

Jonathon's mind kept slipping between reality and delusion.

Delirium walked beside him, and he thought he heard noises . . . people moaning, whispers behind him, often he thought he heard footsteps. Once he heard his father call for him in the darkness. Yelling an excited response, Jonathon ran through the tunnel but his body, weak from starvation, tripped over itself, and he collided with the mountain, smashing against stone and dropping his PSP. Instantly the corridor disappeared in darkness. On the floor, Jonathon groped in blindness, feeling around for his PSP. He swept his hands over the dirt and stone, desperation filling him. He couldn't lose the PSP! Not now!

Increasing his search area, he found himself pleading out loud for help. A darkness he could not banish filled him. He couldn't die here, alone, in the dark! He wanted to go home! There were things he still wanted to do. "Please," he whispered out loud, "I don't want to die here! I need to find my PSP!"

He shut his eyes in desperation, his mind filled with yearnings— not for his PSP but for his family! Deep inside, he felt a desire to be with them again, just *be* with them. Movies and money and friends didn't matter as much as watching his little brother try to swing a baseball bat or seeing his sister smile at a silly joke. He wanted to talk to his mom in Spanish or English and listen to his father telling stories again at the dinner table.

That's what made a family strong, he realized, the little things they experienced together every day!

Lifting his head with new insight, Jonathon opened his eyes to the darkness and in that brief moment thought he saw the vague shape of his PSP lying ahead of him and slightly to the left. He blinked. Blackness enveloped him again, yet the brief image of his PSP remained clear in his mind. Trusting that impression, Jonathon crawled forward.

There, right where he thought it had been, Jonathon reached out through the darkness. His hand settled directly on top of his game as if he could see it. Holding still in the sightless world, Jonathon felt emotion wash over him. For several moments, he did not move.

Later, probing fingers told him the fall had expelled the PSP's dimming batteries. No longer irritated, he sat against the stone wall and retrieved the last two batteries from his pack. Calmness worked through his hands as he inserted the batteries, feeling how to place them into the game's hold. Activating the switch, light again filled the tunnel.

He saw the missing batteries and the protective cover but didn't move to retrieve them. The urgency to push forward had left him. Sitting in the bowels of the mountain with no food, no water, and no way home, Jonathon felt peace. His thoughts turned from the dark mountain bowels to home. Reliving moments with his family, he felt calm. If the end came he would die with his family close to his heart. Turning off the light, he closed his eyes and drifted away.

Hours passed. From the world of his dreams, Jonathon heard it—the soft, incessant sound of dripping.

Rain. He must be dreaming about rain.

Drip. Drip. Drip.

Jonathon stirred and blinked his eyes. The movement of his eyelids told him he wasn't dreaming. He was awake.

Drip. Drip.

The sound continued.

He lifted his head and listened.

Drip. Drip.

It sounded like rain; but it couldn't be—not thousands of feet beneath the Andes mountains. Turning toward the sound, Jonathon fumbled with his good hand for the PSP. When his thumb found the tiny switch, he activated the light. The tunnel was empty

Drip. Drip.

It had to be water. Jonathon struggled to clear his mind, to discover the sound's location. His parched throat ached for relief.

Drip. Drip. Drip.

It seemed to be coming from further ahead in the tunnel.

Staggering to his feet, Jonathon stumbled forward but his movements masked the soft sound. He forced himself to move slower, more quietly. Using his light, he searched the walls for moisture.

Drip.

It had to be nearby.

Moving up the tunnel, he inspected every surface. His mouth ached for moisture. Even a small amount of water would ease his thirst and give him strength.

He saw a natural fissure just ahead of him. Stopping in front of the narrow opening, he listened.

Drip. Drip.

The sound was louder. The water, or whatever it was, dripped from somewhere inside the crack.

Jonathon hesitated, unsure about leaving the larger tunnel. He had not encountered any tomb traps in its sealed embrace. He might not be so lucky in the smaller passageway. What if the Incas had intentionally booby trapped the crack with dripping water to lure a victim inside?

Drip. Drip.

Pressing his fevered lips together, Jonathon took a cautious step toward the fissure. He waved his light over the walls. They were dry, yet his ears distinctly heard dripping from within.

"It's not a trap," he told himself. "Caves are formed by water."

A wicked feeling pierced his mind. **But this isn't a cave, stupid. It's a man-made tunnel.**

Jonathon pressed his hands to his temples. He didn't want to let his fears and doubts defeat him, not now. Yes, he might die if he entered the tunnel, but he would definitely die if he didn't get something to drink. Ducking his head, he entered the smaller passage.

Drip. Drip. Drip.

The dripping grew noticeably louder. Hunched beneath the low ceiling, a smile cracked his parched lips and worked the muscles of his battered face. Somewhere close, water dripped.

Advancing through the darkness, the crack grew narrower, until the walls brushed against him on both sides. He tried not to think of what might be climbing over the walls as he passed through. He only focused on moving forward.

The light from his PSP cast eerie, elongated shadows onto his path as the opening twisted and descended, leading him into cooler air. He shivered. For several yards, Jonathon struggled down the tunnel until the tight fit of the passageway closed completely and left nothing—only a solid, dry stone wall in front of him.

Confused, Jonathon turned his weakened body around, to see if he'd missed anything, but in the silent world only rocks and shadows surrounded him.

He stood there, stunned, PSP lowered to his side. Had he been wrong?

Drip. Drip.

The sound came again, from above.

I wouldn't look up if I were you. **What if it's blood from a decaying corpse dripping down on you?**

Jonathon tried to ignore his delirium and force his gaze to peer into the shadowed recesses of the ceiling. The effort caused his head to spin in dizzy circles, and he staggered, close to collapse. Leaning against the stone walls, Jonathon tried to stop the frantic pitch of his world and regain his strength. When he steadied himself, he lifted his PSP upward and again tried to see above. This time, he noticed a dark streak moistening the stones several feet up.

Relief and despair filled his mind. He didn't know if it was water but he knew he didn't have much strength or control left. In his weakened state, he wasn't sure he could climb high enough to reach the unknown liquid.

Exhaling his despair, he looked around and saw a small ledge just above the ground. He could step there. Holding his PSP in his teeth, Jonathon climbed onto the ledge and balanced himself with his hands. From there he found another ledge and then a third. His injured hand made it difficult to climb. At times shooting pain moved through his hand and up his entire arm. Other times his pack caught on stone protrusions, forcing him to exert more effort to pull free. Often he could only hoist his weakening body up to the next level by bracing his legs against the opposite wall and pushing his back against the opposite wall, working his way higher. Always, though, he found the strength to keep climbing.

Finally arriving at the stain, Jonathon noticed it came from a long, horizontal crack in the cave wall. The crack only measured about a foot and a half high. Liquid seeped from its interior and flowed over the side. He touched the liquid with his finger and felt cold wetness. Bringing his finger to his nose, Jonathon smelled for acrid odors. There were none, only the scent of wet rock. He tested it. The taste of wet dirt spread across his tongue. It seemed to be water.

Pressing his face against the stain he licked moisture into his mouth. Tiny particles of dirt and grit spread across his tongue with cold, precious water. Closing his eyes he tried to suck more liquid into his mouth. It came but still was not enough to swallow, only tease him with the desire for more.

He studied the crack that ran sideways across the rock face. Water came from inside the fissure. Extending his hand into the darkness he felt more moisture but still not a flowing source. The deeper he reached inside, the more convinced he became that he would have to enter the crevice—and he really didn't want to go in there.

There might be spiders in there, the dark voice hissed, *or dead people.*

Jonathon peered as deep into the crack as his light would allow. "There won't be dead people in there," he answered quietly.

Maybe the Incas threw all their dead workers into this crack.

Jonathon didn't like the thoughts plaguing his mind. His legs, tired from holding him in position several feet above the ground, began to tremble. He knew he had to make a decision soon to crawl into the crack or head back down. He looked below him. On the ground there was no water, and no hope. At least the fissure's moisture offered a tiny trickle of hope.

Making his decision, Jonathon shrugged out of his backpack. The narrow crack would not allow him to wear his pack as he crawled through. He would have to drag it behind him and hope neither he nor the pack caught on anything.

Free of his nylon companion, Jonathon slung his leg up onto the ledge and rolled his body inside. Instantly he felt moisture dampen the front of his clothes. Realizing the water was enough to soak through his clothes brought him increased confidence and excitement. Lying on his stomach he shoved the PSP into the crack ahead of him. Light played over the recesses and protrusions, casting eerie shadows before him but, to his relief, he didn't see any creatures scurrying for darkness. "And no dead bodies," he breathed, "at least not yet."

Sliding cautiously forward, he pushed his PSP ahead of him with his bruised hand. His good hand dragged the pack behind him as he worked his body cautiously through the narrow crevice, following the light into the unknown. His legs scooted him through the passage, and his ribs hurt with this new motion to his body. He soon grew cold with the dampness starting to soak against him.

Jonathon hoped he wouldn't have to slide too far. He tried to ignore the rock ceiling, only inches above his head, and the scrape of rocks on his shoulders and butt. He only thought of following the water until he found enough to drink and, maybe, a way out on the other side. "All water has to come from the surface," he mused.

For several feet, he moved sideways through the crevasse. Then the rock opened up in front of him, and a black cavern met his gaze. He stopped, uncertain. Extending his game into the opening, he tried to scan its size and depth, but his weakening light only illuminated a few feet. It was enough, though, to show him there was a floor or ledge just a few feet below him, with more water glistening on the rock surface. He didn't know what he was climbing into, but he did know if he found himself on a ledge he could just climb back up and try something else.

Turning around, he slid backward into the grotto then he eased himself over the side, feeling for support below. When his feet found footing, Jonathon carefully lowered himself from the crack into the opening, dragging his pack after him. Hefting it onto his shoulder, he turned around, letting his PSP light the unknown world around him.

As light and shadows revealed the new world, a terrible roar erupted in his ears. Filling the cavern, it echoed off the walls. The black eyes of dozens of brown-skinned mummies stared at him, their hideous faces surrounding him in the dim light.

His exploration had plunged him into the midst of horror!

Jonathon cried out again as he scrambled back for the opening. He needed to escape the disfigured evil around him, but his foot slipped on the wet rock. He stumbled, stepping from the small ledge onto a basket of some type. The ancient container tipped beneath his weight, then broke, spilling gold coins onto the floor in a shower of sound. He teetered frantically for balance, his arms waving. His damaged hand lost hold of the PSP. In horror, he watched the only light he possessed drop to the stone floor. With the sound of shattering plastic, the game broke apart, and darkness swallowed the light.

Screaming in protest, Jonathon tried to jump for the opening but his hand closed around a dried arm. The mummy turned toward him and Jonathon felt its horrid face smash into his. He felt the stiff hair, the skin-tight flesh. Its teeth raked across his cheek.

Knocking away the mummy, Jonathon staggered backward . . . into another body . . . and then another. They were all around him in the darkness. He cried out, struggling for freedom from contorted hands and bodies. Turning, spinning, he tried to escape the dead—but they seemed to be all around him. His lungs gagged on the strange, smoky odor. A mummified limb tripped him, and he stumbled past his final point of balance. As he tumbled to the ground, he felt mummies fall on him, felt their weight, their hideous forms, and smelled their death. Cries filled his ears . . . his cries. They were burying him beneath them. In this horrid chamber of the living dead they would make him one of them!

Then Jonathon's mind went as black as the cavern, and he smashed into the ground.

◆　　◆　　◆

Through tomb-like silence, it came. The darkness paled then gave way to a warm, white glow.

The flashlight beam made a last turn in the passageway and pierced the cavern—falling on a room of carnage, scattered gold . . . and ancient mummies. Filled with terror at the sight, the girl turned and fled.

ELEVEN

SEVERINO rolled his eyes. "It is not the work of the devil."

"*¡Sí, es!*" Delia stood before her brother, her face flushed. "Yes, it is. I *saw* them!"

He scowled, pushing a chicken away with his foot. It squawked a protest and fluttered to the other side of the dirt yard. "You probably saw the effects of an earthquake, *un terremoto.*"

"We haven't had an earthquake here for weeks, and you know it. We would have felt an earthquake."

Exasperated, Severino turned to his sister. "The mountain could have had an earthquake deep inside, and we did not feel it."

"Severino, please."

Walking across the dirty courtyard, Severino kicked at a stick. "I cannot help you."

"Why not?"

He turned. "Because I have other responsibilities right now."

"Your family *is* your responsibility!" she demanded.

Her comment brought Severino to an abrupt stop. He turned back to her, his voice low. "Yes, my family is my responsibility and because of those mummies every night I risk my life for you! I am trying to keep you alive. You just don't seem to remember that!"

At his words, Delia halted her angry protest. Tears began to glisten in front of her brown eyes. "I remember, Severino, but you do not seem to help your family during the day. I am important when the sun is out too."

Seeing the tears and realizing he had hurt his sister's feelings, Severino rolled his head in disgust and turned away. "*Aye*. Do not start that . . . not now."

Delia sniffed and brushed her hand across cold, brown cheeks. Severino cursed in frustration and reached for a rifle leaning against the thick mud wall of their tiny home. "All right. I will go inside the mountain and look." Shouldering the rifle, Severino turned around, catching a glimpse of his sister. In her eyes he saw her hurt, her pain, and it became his. Reaching for her with his free arm, he pulled her into an embrace. "Delia, you are a good girl, but you need to stop fearing." He smiled. "I have told you, the mummies will never leave the mountain. It is my promise, and I will die keeping it."

She wiped away a tear. "I know you promise but I do not want you to die, Severino. I just want everything to be safe—the way it was."

His voice tired, he spoke. "It can never be that way again, Delia. Not now, not with *Papá* dead. All we can do is make sure the mummies stay inside the mountain. We've made a promise to guard and protect them. Come, we'll go clean up the mess together."

◆　　　◆　　　◆

As his flashlight split the darkness in the chamber, Severino whistled. "You weren't kidding about a mess, were you? It is *sucio* down here."

"Was it caused by an earthquake?"

"I don't know." Severino studied the ceiling but saw no damage to the rocks. "When was the last time you came to the chamber?"

"Three days ago." Nervous, Delia fanned her light across the shambled room. Light and shadows rippled across mummified corpses and toppled baskets. "Do you think robbers did this?"

Severino pushed aside a disturbed basket of coins. "No. If they had, the mummies and all the gold would be gone, but it doesn't look like anything has been taken." He pulled a lighter from his pocket and sparked it into a flame.

"Then what do you think caused this?"

"I have no idea." Through the dancing glow, he smiled at his sister. "But I do know we have a mess to clean up." Reaching toward an oil lamp set in a stone crevice, Severino touched the flame to the wick and a warm glow filled the room. Stepping over a fallen mummy toward another lantern, he ignited its wick and added more light to the dark cavern. As he puzzled over what had caused the destruction, he shook his head. Something didn't seem right.

Just then he heard Delia cry out in fear. Spinning toward her, he gave a frantic call. "What is it? What's wrong?"

She lifted her frightened eyes from the tangle of mummified bodies and met her brother's gaze. "A person."

Severino raised his rifle defensively. "Here? Where?"

Her body trembled as she pointed. "There, on the floor."

Stepping over several mummies in the hand-hewn chamber, Severino approached the area his sister indicated. There he saw the body lying face down on the cold, hard floor, buried under a mound of corpses. It wasn't moving.

"*Aye*, this is not good."

"Is he a robber?"

"I don't know." Severino poked at a leg.

"Careful."

The form didn't move. Severino kicked the bottom of the shoe with his foot.

"Severino, don't!"

"What do you want me to do? Just leave him here?" Severino motioned for her to hold the gun for him. "Here, take this. I need to move him. If he's still alive and starts anything, use it on him. You know how."

Ready to defend her brother, Delia took the rifle and pointed it at the stranger. "Is he dead?"

Severino shook his head as he began lifting mummified corpses from the stranger. "I don't know, but it would be better for us if he was. Obviously he's seen the mummies."

She blinked through new tears and watched her brother. "Will he tell others about the mummies and gold?"

"Most likely."

Sorrow filled the cavern as Severino worked to move the mummies in silence. Finished, he squatted near the form. "I do not know how he could have found this place. I sealed the main entrance! Did anyone ever see you go through the other opening?"

"No!"

"Are you sure!"

"*Yes!*"

Taking a deep breath, Severino reached out and slowly rolled the figure onto its back. As the battered features rolled into sight, he and his sister gasped in unison.

"He is *joven!*" Delia stepped closer. "He's our age." The unconscious youth groaned softly and tried to move his head. "He's still alive!" Quickly she retreated, the rifle once again pointed at the filthy, dark-haired stranger. "What if he's a terrorist?"

In front of her Severino shook his head. "He's not a terrorist."

"How can you be sure?"

"I just know, okay?"

On the cold floor, the battered youth moved again. At the sight, concern filled Severino—not for the stranger but for the mummies. "He's waking up. We need to get him out of here, and fast."

"But where are we going to take him?"

Slipping his arms beneath the youth, Severino lifted him into his hold and stood. "Away from here. I don't want him to see this place again. Let's go."

✦   ✦   ✦

In Jonathon's mind, things began to swirl from darkness to light. The mummies were moving, removing their hideous limbs and hardened teeth from his body. They were also talking.

He felt his body roll. Through a flickering of strained eyelids, Jonathon thought he saw light. He winced at its brightness and heard a girl's voice. She moved in front of him but didn't look like a mummy. More things moved. He heard sounds—a male voice—and he thought he saw a gun.

Beneath him the world shifted. Jonathon sensed movement between the tunnels and a home, between stone and softness. But, in his mind, the mummies followed. They surrounded his dreams and captured him, burying him beneath their hardened bodies. Over and over he tried to escape, but always they found him. He could feel the mummies everywhere . . . their rough skin, stiff hair, the lumpiness of a mattress beneath him, and the warm embrace of blankets above him.

A mattress? Blankets?

His eyes tried to open but soft light pierced his senses, and Jonathon closed them again. Even through his shut lids, the light hurt. Jonathon moaned and reached to cover his eyes. Was he still in the tunnels?

A girl's voice spoke. "*Ssshh, cuidado.* Be careful. You are still very weak."

He understood her Spanish, but his words came in English. "Where am I?"

Her response sounded worried. "*Lo siento. No entiendo,*" she apologized.

She didn't understand his English. Slowly Jonathon licked his lips and shifted his mind to the other language of his upbringing. "*¿Donde estoy?*" He spoke again, his voice weak. "Where am I?"

This time she understood and responded in Spanish. "You are here, in my home."

The answer satisfied his tired mind, and he turned away, resting. He was in someone's home; he was out of the tunnels. For now he didn't need to know anything more, and Jonathon returned to the world of sleep.

For several more hours, he slept until movement came. Something touched his face, checking his fever. The touch moved from his face to his body, tucking blankets around him. The contact, soft and gentle, did not feel like the harsh grip of the mummies.

Where was he? Again he asked in English, and again silence came as the answer. Only when he spoke in Spanish did the voice seem to understand.

"You are in my home," the gentle voice said.

He'd heard the answer and the voice before, but he couldn't identify either. "How did I get here?"

"My brother brought you."

With his eyes still closed to the light he could feel someone watching him. "Did you see them?"

"See who?"

"The mummies. They were in the tunnels."

A damp cloth touched his forehead and bathed his fevered body. "You are very sick with fever and rambling about strange things. Lay still. Do not talk."

Though he didn't understand her denial, the cooling strokes felt good, and Jonathon turned to them, seeking more. "Who are you?" his voice came slowly; his eyes were still closed, tired. "What's your name?"

"My name is Delia Milagro Cipriani Velarde."

Another long name. Jonathon sighed and lifted a weak hand to rub his forehead. "Yeah." He didn't want to deal with confusing things. "So, where is your home?"

She seemed confused by the question. "In Peru."

It wasn't an answer he could work with. "I already know that. Where in Peru?"

"Near Yunka Wa-yuna." Her voice flowed out of her like a song, the beautiful melody of the mountain people.

Jonathon let his hand fall to the bedside. Yunka Wa-yuna sounded familiar, but she still had not answered his question clearly. "Where is that?"

"In the mountains, between Cusco and Ayacucho."

Cusco. Well, he knew where that was . . . sort of.

"What is your name?" Delia asked.

"Jonathon."

"You speak another language besides Spanish. Where are you from?"

"The United States." In the uneven bed, he tried to moisten the inside of his mouth.

Delia saw his efforts and passed him a small cup. "Here, drink this. It is *muña* tea. It will help you feel better."

With her help, Jonathon sat forward in bed. She lifted the warm mug to his mouth, and he took a weak sip of the liquid. The sweet tea tasted good and slid easily down his throat. Two more sips and he could drink no more. Jonathon laid his head back on the pillow and, for the first time, opened his eyes. A blink allowed him to focus his gaze on a girl about his age, sitting on the edge of the bed beside him. "You must be Delia."

"*Sí.*"

"Where's my dad?"

Delia hesitated. She glanced over her shoulder, searching her mind and house for the answer before turning to Jonathon. "I do not know. You were alone when we found you. Was he with you?"

"No, he wasn't with me. He's studying the ruins at Machu Picchu."

"Then he is probably still at Machu Picchu."

Frustration grew inside Jonathon. Didn't she understand the situation? "I know he's probably still there, but I got lost in the tunnels and he's probably searching for me. Didn't you tell him where I was? Didn't anyone try to contact him so he could come and get me?"

"No," A male voice interrupted. It did not hold the musical quality that Jonathon heard in Delia's voice. The new voice sounded hard and direct.

Startled, Jonathon turned his gaze. A Peruvian teen, only a year or two older than Jonathon, sat quietly at a small table, watching.

"Who are you?" Jonathon asked.

"Severino."

This time Jonathon found himself exasperated by the shortness of the name. "Severino who?"

Stony silence came in response.

Jonathon didn't retreat. "You don't say much, do you?"

Severino watched the American from across the room, and didn't speak. His expression was hard.

Irritated, Jonathon rolled his eyes. "Why didn't you call my dad?"

Now Severino spoke, his voice as harsh as Jonathon's. "How could we? You've never told us his name." Severino rose from the chair and moved across the room, stopping in front of a stove built from mud and stones.

Realizing his folly, Jonathon's words softened. They didn't call because they didn't know who to call. It had been an honest obstacle. His anger melted into an apology. "*Lo siento.* I'm sorry. I'm not thinking clearly yet. David. My father's name is David Bradford. He's staying at the Hotel Samay in Cusco." Jonathon felt tired. "Will you please call him?"

This time Severino shook his head. "No."

"Why not?"

Staring at the American, Severino's face held the smile of victory. "We don't have a phone."

"Everyone has a phone!"

At the outburst, Severino lifted a rifle from its berth against the wall and inspected a handful of ammunition. Jonathon felt a wave of fear pass through him. Severino glared at him. "Maybe in America everyone has a phone, but this is Peru." With smoothness, he pocketed the bullets and shouldered his gun. "Here we have rifles instead."

Without waiting for a response, Severino turned and moved for the door. He stopped at the crude wooden barrier and turned back to Jonathon. His icy words matched his countenance. "In case you have forgotten some simple Spanish, the word is *gracias*. It means thank you. 'Thank you for saving my life.' Maybe you ought to try saying that first, before you start making demands." Then Severino opened the door and disappeared into the night, letting the door bang shut behind him.

Weak and unable to move from the bed, Jonathon felt his body reel while his mind struggled with what had just happened. He didn't know where he was, his dad didn't know where he was, and Severino had just refused to contact his father. Maybe they didn't have a phone but they could have offered to go find one, or send a telegram, or a letter—anything.

Yet they had offered none of that. It seemed as if they didn't want to contact his father. *Why?*

Then Jonathon's thoughts turned to the gun. It bothered him, not just its existence but Severino's whole attitude with it. The Peruvian seemed too confident with the rifle, with his ability to use it. Why did a teenager possess such a deadly weapon and where did he go with it tonight? He obviously wasn't out hunting sparrows in the dark.

No, Severino carried the rifle for some reason other than birds.

Then realization began to pierce through the fog of his mind and Jonathon remembered a rifle in the tunnels—a rifle that had been pointed at him!

Stunned, he looked over at Delia but her dark eyes avoided his gaze. Nervous, she rose from the edge of the bed and reached for his mug. As she did, Jonathon saw her hand tremble. In the tiny mud-brick home, he felt fear return. Only this time it wasn't a fear of the dark. He felt the cold, icy dread that comes only when fearing another human being.

◆　　◆　　◆

Late that night, the wooden door opened, and Severino returned. Cold mountain air swirled inside with him, driving away the warmth inside the bare, single-room home. Delia rose to meet her brother.

"What are you still doing up?" Severino's voice came in a whisper. He shut and secured the door.

"I could not sleep. I was worried about you."

"I am fine." Crossing to the other side of the room, Severino laid his rifle against the wall then turned to the earthen stove for its heat.

Delia did not find his answer satisfying. "You are not fine. You go out at night, when it is dangerous!"

"Ssshh." Severino glanced over at the form of the American, but Jonathon didn't move. He appeared to be sleeping. Severino rubbed his hands in the warm air above the stove. "I go out with my friends."

Delia refused to be silenced. She stepped closer to her brother, lowering her voice more. "They are not your friends. What kind of friends make you carry a gun? I have heard rumors, Severino. Your *amigos* are members of the Shining Path!"

"Ssshh!" Severino tried to cut her off. "You will wake the American."

Delia continued. "The Shining Path is dangerous. They use rifles to get what they want, not brains. You are smarter than that. *Papá* said you had a good brain, but you are not using it. You need to stay away from the Shining Path."

"You sound like *Mamá*."

"Good. I am sure if *Mamá* were here, she would tell you the same things—only you would listen to her."

"Well, you aren't *Mamá,* so I don't need to listen to you."

"I am only worried about you, Severino."

With a curse, Severino waved his arm toward the sleeping American, his voice a low growl in the quiet house. "If you are worried about me, as you claim, you should stop talking. You do not want the American to hear any of this." His final words worked, and the house fell silent except for the sounds of Severino and Delia going to bed.

But Jonathon could not sleep. He had heard all of it. Awake in bed, his face pressed against the dark shadows of the wall, Jonathon's heart beat in horror. Severino was a member of The Shining Path! They were the terrorist group responsible for so many murders throughout Peru!

They also kidnapped foreigners and used them for their own purposes. That was why Severino refused to call his father. Jonathon was now his hostage!

Too frightened to sleep, Jonathon's weakened body lay prisoner to his fear until morning light arrived, piercing the door cracks and squeezing through shuttered windows.

Still unmoving in the bed, he heard Delia awaken behind him. She rose and dressed quickly, added wood to the bowels of the earthen stove, stirred up the hot embers, and then left the house. Outside, chickens clucked in excitement as grains of feed rained down around them. Moments later, Jonathon heard the splash of water in a container. He closed his eyes and tried, again, to swallow his fear. He had to get out of here, but how?

Returning from her chores outside, Delia carried a bucket of icy water into the humble home. She poured some of the liquid into an old kettle and placed it on the stove to boil. Drops of water fell to the fire beneath. They sizzled and boiled away into mist.

Delia moved to her pantry next, a collection of plastic containers stacked on one corner of the tiny table and the dirt floor beneath the table. From this collection, she retrieved a bowl and began to add various contents to its basin. Behind her, the kettle started hissing, steam escaping into the one-room house.

A movement came from the floor on the far side of the room. With Jonathon sleeping in his bed, Severino bunked on the earth. Wrapped in a blanket, his rifle close, his head pillowed from the cold earth by a jacket, Severino rolled away from the movements of his sister and pulled the blanket further up onto his shoulder. He chose to continue sleeping.

Delia placed an iron skillet over the flame and poured oil across the bottom. While this heated, she retrieved the steaming kettle and carried it to the table to pour hot water into the bowl's dry ingredients. Combining the mixture with her bare fingers, she molded it with skill as the oil began to sizzle in the skillet.

When ready, Delia pinched off a piece of dough. Brown fingers stretched it into a round, flat tortilla which she placed in the hot oil. It sizzled as the dough cooked, puffing and growing like a scone. Soon the smell of fry bread filled the tiny room. While it cooked to a golden brown, Delia reached above her to a tied bunch of foliage hanging from the ceiling. She broke off a sprig and dropped it into a cup. Over this she poured boiling water and left the tea to steep.

Turning to the skillet, Delia used a fork to turn the Peruvian pancake once, frying the other side. Each of her movements in the tiny kitchen was exact and experienced.

When the second side browned, she removed the golden scone

from the oil and placed it on a plate to cool. Immediately a second flat cake of dough entered the hot oil.

When both had cooked, Delia retrieved the cup of tea, lifted the plate of hot fry bread and carried them to Jonathon. "Here," she said gently, not worried about whether she woke him. "You should eat."

"I am not hungry."

"My brother, Severino, says when a person has been without food for a long time, he has a hard time eating or drinking. His stomach is small."

"Then your brother is right."

"But you must eat to gain your strength."

Her words struck him with power. Jonathon knew if he wanted to grow strong enough to escape this new threat, he would have to eat. It was the only way to regain his strength. Rolling onto his back, he managed a weak nod, avoiding her gaze. "You're right. I should eat something."

Delia smiled and returned to the stove where she proceeded to cook the rest of the dough and make two more cups of herbal tea. A small stack of fried pancakes grew on a second plate.

From his prison of blankets, Jonathon tried to sit up but could not. His body still defied him. It ached from pain and a growing fever. Reaching for a piece of warm fry bread, he brought it to his mouth and took a small bite. It did not settle well.

Compassion filled Delia's face. "Maybe you should just drink for now. It will be easier, until your stomach is ready to accept food." She moved back to the bed, slipping her hand behind his back and helping him sit forward. She then lifted the cup of tea from a small dresser nearby. Steam swirled above the yellow liquid.

He removed the mug from her hand and took a timid swallow. Delia had been right. The fresh tea went down easier than the bread. Blowing cautiously on the beverage, he took a second swallow. Delia smiled at him. She rolled up a blanket and slid it behind his back to support him. The pain in his ribs caused him to wince at the movement.

"I'm sorry," she apologized.

"It isn't you. It's my ribs."

"They are swollen and very bruised."

From his bed on the floor, Severino couldn't ignore the noise and smells any longer. He rolled to a seated position and ran his hands through his thick black hair. "Why does morning come so early in the mountains?"

"It does not come early to those who go to bed early," Delia responded. She gave Jonathon's shoulder a kind pat before standing and returning to her breakfast preparations.

Severino grumbled a reply and climbed to his feet. "I'm going to wash up." He dropped the blanket over a chair, grabbed a hot pancake on his way out the door, and ignored Jonathon, closing the door behind him.

Silence swallowed the house. Jonathon took another weak sip of tea, watching Delia as she fried more bread. She seemed more approachable than her brother. Lowering his mug, he took a deep breath, testing her willingness to respond to him. "How did you know I was lost in the tunnels?"

At his words, Delia fumbled with her fork trying to turn over a pancake. "I do not know what you mean."

"The tunnels, you found me in some tunnels. How did you know I was there?" He rubbed his eyes, trying to wipe away the fever building there.

"I . . . I am sorry." Her voice stammered. "I do not understand your Spanish."

Delia's reaction, so abrupt and noticeable, gave Jonathon hesitancy. "You understand my Spanish perfectly. I've spoken it since I was a child." He proceeded with caution this time. "How did you find me in the tunnels?"

She pulled at a new piece of dough, forming another pancake, her hands trembling. "You are very sick and must be remembering things from your fever. You are here, in our house, and have been for three days."

If her words were meant to distract him from the tunnels, they did. The time he'd spent in their home shocked him. "Three days?"

"*Sí*. This is the third day. You slept all the first day and most of yesterday."

Jonathon shook his head, refusing to believe her words. "What day is it today?"

"Tuesday."

"No—I mean the date. What's the date?"

"I . . . I do not know."

"You've gotta know the date!"

Delia caught her lower lip between her teeth, unsure about her answer. "Here in the mountains, we do not have many calendars."

"Take a guess!"

"Ah . . . it would have to be about the nineteenth."

The date horrified him. "No!" Jonathon tried to get out of bed. "That means I fell into the tunnels almost two weeks ago." He cast the blankets from his form. "I have to find my father. He must think I'm dead."

Delia saw his movements and went to his side, gently holding his scraped and bruised shoulders, trying to keep him from getting out of bed. "Careful," she admonished. "You must rest."

"I can't. I have to find him."

"But you cannot leave this house."

"Why not?" His voice hardened as he lifted his gaze to hers.

Her dark eyes filled with nervousness, and she blinked quickly. "It is dangerous."

"I can take care of myself."

"Please," she pleaded. "You do not understand."

"What I don't understand is why you won't call my father and let him know where I am. You know who he is now. Why have you kept me here for three days? I'll pay for the call, if that's what you need."

"It is not the money."

He tried to stand. "Then let me call him."

Her eyes showed concern. "I am sorry, but you can't."

"Why not?" Anger and desperation filled Jonathon. "Why do you want to keep me here? I am *not* your hostage!"

A brilliant shaft of light pierced the interior of the home, interrupting Jonathon and Delia. In fevered horror, Jonathon sank back to the bed.

Severino stood in the doorway, his wet hair dripping water onto the blue of his sweater. His brown face showed the rawness of a recent washing, and his piercing eyes reflected fresh anger. "Hostage or not, you are not leaving this house!" Severino's voice came with deadly control. "You are staying."

Then Jonathon noticed Severino's wet hands. They were holding the rifle, its muzzle pointed toward Jonathon's chest.

TWELVE

R EALITY and dreams swirled through Jonathon's fevered mind. He couldn't think clearly; he didn't know where he was. Trapped in a dream that seemed too real, he saw the mummies' chamber deep in the bowels of the mountain. A gnarled head and shoulder twisted, shrugging off six hundred years of inertia. Across the dark space another contorted arm extended. The fingers on its hand splayed outward then retracted, feeling its power. From throughout the chamber came shuffling sounds—slow, rasping. Dried bodies straightened their folded limbs and, one by one, the mummies rose to stand. In the darkness, balanced on withered feet they turned toward the opening. They did not have to see it. They knew it was there. Lurching, shifting for balance, they scraped hardened bodies over stone floors and moved toward freedom. They had waited for this night for six centuries.

Wrapped in delirium and fever, Jonathon hoped he would find help before the mummies or Severino discovered his escape. He tried to force his weakened body to move down the dark street.

Nothing moved—no cars drove by, no dogs barked. All the doors and windows were closed and boarded against the night.

Approaching a streetlight, Jonathon watched his shadow contort then lengthen and flee into the darkness ahead of him. His shadow didn't want to be here either, on this empty street.

Casting his gaze around in the darkness, Jonathon's fear grew. Where was a police station? Where were the people? Moving through the vacant town, Jonathon searched desperately for a pay phone. He needed to make contact—soon! He didn't have much energy left. He had to get away.

A crash echoed through the street, and Jonathon jumped, his heart pounding. He glanced behind him but saw nothing. In the entire world he seemed to be the only living creature.

Another sound came, this one closer. Jonathon's insides felt wired, his blood pounding wildly through each vein. He searched the darkness, wondering what moved behind him in the night. Could it be Severino? Why couldn't he see anything? His eyes scanned the midnight black as the sound continued to approach, relentless and steady. Then came the odor—faint at first but growing. The smell of wood smoke. He recognized the smell. In the tunnels . . . in the mummies' chamber!

Horror caused Jonathon to turn and flee, but he failed to escape. In front of him a creature stood in the night, its thin brown lips drawn into a mocking half smile—a muted scream. Stained teeth snarled at him from within a dry and pinched face. Black hair framed its skeletal head in a dusty mane, and bony, brown limbs—grotesquely twisted— reached out for Jonathon.

Shocked, Jonathon stumbled backward, away from the monster. He only had time to release one long, terrified scream. Then the circle of hideous faces and shriveled corpses closed around him, and Jonathon felt them once again.

◆   ◆   ◆

Delia heard Jonathon cry out in his sleep. She moved to his bedside to calm him. Touching his fevered brow, she pushed away his matted hair and spoke softly to him through his dream.

At the touch, Jonathon recoiled, his fevered mind still telling him mummies surrounded him. Wrapped in blankets, he fought to escape their horror.

Delia spoke again, touching his shoulder. This time her caress penetrated his mind and Jonathon's eyes flew open. For a moment he lay on his side, gasping for breath, fighting to recall his surroundings. He wasn't on a street being captured by mummies. He had escaped his nightmare, but he didn't remember where that put him.

From behind him came Delia's quiet words, her gentle touch.

"*Calmeté*, Jonathon. You are fine. It was only another nightmare. You are safe here."

Safe here? Her words opened the floodgate of his memories, and Jonathon shut his eyes tight. He was not safe here. A terrorist held him hostage. Swallowing, he shifted onto his back then dared to open his eyes. From his bed, he saw a single lantern glowing on the table. There Severino worked, unconcerned about nightmares or contacting help.

Jonathon turned his gaze to Delia, sitting on the bed beside him. "Please," he whispered so Severino would not hear. "You have to help me."

"I am helping you."

"No. You have to contact my dad. Call him, send a letter, I don't care which—just tell him where I am. He'll come get me, no questions asked."

Her eyes filled with sorrow. "Jonathon, I cannot let him come."

"Why not?"

Rather than answer him, Delia stood and retreated from his bed, but he caught her hand. "Delia, don't go. Help me, please."

His words stopped her. She hesitated then turned to him, her voice quiet. "There are things you do not understand."

"Then tell me so I can understand. Tell me why you're keeping me here."

She glanced down at his hand holding hers. When she lifted her gaze to him, her brown eyes glistened. "There is danger here, in this valley. I cannot get you out, nor can I bring your father here. If I could, I would."

The honesty of her words hurt. "Then let me face the danger alone," he pleaded. "Let me go so I can at least try to get home."

She withdrew her hand from his and backed away, shaking her head. "*Lo siento*," she breathed. "I'm sorry, but we can't. You do not understand what you risk."

As she moved away, he raised his voice in frustration and anger, not caring if Severino heard. "Then tell me what it is I risk. Why are you keeping me a prisoner here?"

His words filled the small home with electricity. Delia looked at her brother, and a powerful silence followed. Sitting at the table, Severino lifted the kettle and poured himself a cup of boiling water. To this he added a stream of canned milk. Steam escaped into the air as he stirred the two ingredients into a new liquid.

Despite his casual movements, Jonathon sensed anger. He watched as Severino tapped the spoon off on the side of the mug.

"You are not a prisoner. You may leave if you want." Finished, Severino laid the spoon down on a saucer and met Jonathon's gaze. "But if you try, you won't get very far before you are found."

Were his words a threat or a warning? Jonathon didn't know. Cautiously he questioned Severino, his eyes searching the Peruvian's face for signals. "Found by whom?"

In the silent house, the two stared at each other until Severino broke the standoff. "You don't want to know, but if they find you, you won't live long." His words hung ominously in the air.

◆　　◆　　◆

Later that night, Delia prepared a meal of potatoes fried with onions and tomatoes and served it to Jonathon with rice. Jonathon struggled to eat. His mind churned. He had to get away from here. Severino was hiding something, and Delia seemed to be frightened by it.

Delia watched him push the food around on his plate. "Don't you like it?"

"It's fine," he said. "I still can't eat much since the tunnels."

Severino cleaned the barrel of his rifle with a cloth. "There are no tunnels."

His comment brought Jonathon's gaze up in surprise. "Yes, there are! You found me there."

"We found you in the mountains."

Stunned, Jonathon sat forward. "No you didn't. You found me in the tunnels!"

"You have no proof of that." Severino worked his rifle bolt with a quick movement, closing the action.

"I *am* proof! I remember them!"

"You remember your nightmares." Severino lifted the rifle to his shoulder. Pointing it at the door, he looked down the barrel through open sights. "You should not speak of tunnels. The people will say you are crazy, or worse, they may kill you."

The words chilled Jonathon. "Kill me, why?"

Severino pulled the trigger back on an empty chamber, dry-firing the rifle. The heavy, ominous sound filled the small house. That finished, he lowered the weapon and turned hardened eyes to the American. "You talk too much. You should shut up."

"And you don't talk enough! Why won't you admit it? The tunnels and mummies are real!"

Severino did not answer, silently counting out bullets. Slowly understanding began to flow into Jonathon's mind. His words came in quiet shock. "You know the tunnels are there. You already know about the mummies and lost Inca gold! That's why you're keeping me here. You're holding me hostage because you don't want anyone else to find them first. You want to take all the gold and artifacts out of there first!"

"*You stupid American!*"

Severino's words blew through the room with the power of a rifle blast. He came to his feet, his entire frame shaking in anger. "You have no idea what you are saying! Do you really think I am looking for lost Inca gold?"

"I know you are!"

"You know nothing! Evil walks this valley, more terrifying and real than anything your naive imagination could create. I keep you here because if you walk out that door, that evil will hunt you down and find you. If you think you can face it and win, you'll pay for that mistake with your life." Grabbing more bullets from the table, Severino cursed the American and then disappeared out the door into the night.

As the wooden door bounced shut against the portal, Delia turned to Jonathon. Her face showed fear. "Please Jonathon, don't talk about such things anymore."

"This evil scares you too?"

She blinked and turned away so he wouldn't see her tears. "It terrifies me, Jonathon."

◆　　　◆　　　◆

Jonathon made his decision. Even though he still felt weak, he would take his chances. With Severino gone, he would wait until Delia fell asleep and then sneak out. He'd find a house or police station and there he would get help. Whatever 'evil' they talked about, he'd rather take his chances with strangers he approached than stay here and risk his fate at the hands of a teenage terrorist.

When night came Jonathon pretended to sleep. With eyes closed, he purposely slowed his breathing yet paid careful attention to what went on around him. Severino was still gone, and he hoped the teenager would stay gone.

Behind him, Delia moved around the small home, cleaning and preparing for the night. Jonathon listened to her movements, his heart pounding as she blew out candles and lanterns. *Go to sleep*, his mind pleaded, *before Severino returns*.

Finally, to his relief, he heard her settle down in her bed on the opposite wall of the one-room home. When she extinguished the last light, darkness pressed over the house.

He lay still, listening to the sounds of his heart and her breathing until he knew she had drifted into the world of sleep. Waiting a quarter of an hour more to make sure, he quietly pushed back the blankets and sat up. Delia did not stir.

Jonathon knew his shoes were on the floor beside the bed. He couldn't find his backpack, but he didn't care. He would leave it there. His clothes, washed and clean, were draped over the foot of the bed. Carefully Jonathon retrieved them, the metal springs of the bed creaking in protest. Jonathon cringed. He didn't want to wake Delia. Not that he feared her; he felt she was more friend than enemy, yet he didn't want to alert her to his escape. In the far bed, Delia did not stir.

He slid into his jeans and quietly stood up to fasten his pants and do up the zipper. His heart pounded in his chest with the fear of discovery. The longer he stayed here, the greater his chance of awaking her. Silently gathering the rest of his clothes, he decided to finish dressing outside.

Moving on bare feet, Jonathon crossed the dirt floor to the door. As he reached its wooden barrier, he paused, his ears straining for any sound from the other side that would indicate Severino's return. There were none.

With a slow, steady lift of the handle, Jonathon unlatched the door, pushed it open, and stepped out into the night. Quietly he drew the door closed after him and returned the latch to its place. From inside the tiny house, Delia slept on.

Almost free!

Jonathon turned his eyes to the darkness around him. After the darkness of the tunnels the moonlight made the night easy to view. A small courtyard surrounded him. Several chickens roosted in the night, and a tiny flock of sheep watched his movements from their bedding area in a sheltered corner.

On the far side of the yard, a tiny gate led outward. He crossed to the gate, hoping to find a road nearby. A chicken cackled at the disturbance, and Jonathon froze. Glancing back at the house, he waited for Delia to come through the door, searching for him. If she did, he would run. He did not want to be caught again.

No movements of discovery came, and Jonathon exhaled in relief, continuing his trek to the gate. Finding the latch in the darkness, he released the last barrier to his freedom and slipped into the mountain night.

Delia and Severino did not live in a town. A small foot trail wound its way from their home down a hillside. Worried he might run into Severino on the path, Jonathon moved up the hill and followed a stone wall that twisted toward the valley.

Still carrying his clothes and shoes, he put as much distance between him and the house as he could. The frosted ground bit at his feet until they ached and then went numb. Still weak from his time spent in the tunnels, he stumbled often. His side ached. In his physical state, Jonathon knew it would be difficult for him to travel far. His eyes scanned the dark night for signs of a town or village but he could only see a few tiny homes dotting the valley. Disappointment filled him. He could not plead for help here. The homes probably sheltered friends of Severino and Delia. He would have to travel further.

Forty-five minutes later, Jonathon relaxed enough to take a rest. Sitting on the ground against some rocks, he pulled on his socks and shoes. His feet were frozen, but he hadn't felt safe enough until now to stop and put them on. His body shivered violently, the strain taking its toll on his ribs. He shrugged his arms through the sleeves of his shirt and pulled on his jacket. His chest and arms shook from the cold, rattling his body and tiring muscles. Inside his shoes, his feet throbbed. For several minutes he huddled in the night, until the shivering lessened and he could feel the numbness leave his feet. Then he stood and began a careful descent to the open valley floor.

He knew that if he couldn't find a road leading to a nearby town before it got light he would have to find a place to hide. Severino, or some of his terrorist friends, could be tracking him even now, and Jonathon didn't have the strength to outrun any pursuers. He would wait until it grew dark again. He also decided to trust only those he approached, not those who approached him.

Reaching the valley floor, he found a dirt road. Staying off the open road, he followed it through the night by staying hidden among the foliage and rocks. He quit counting the times he stumbled and fell. Gathering dew chilled the sparse grass, and his shoes grew wet. Despite his clothing, he again began to shiver in the night air. Often he had to stop and rest, his body barely able to carry him over the rocky terrain. Each time he climbed to his feet took a great deal of exertion.

Hours added together. He searched the horizon for signs of approaching daylight. Finally the sky began to shift from black to gray.

In the approaching dawn, Jonathon spotted a small cluster of buildings hugging the road ahead. Near the buildings he saw the tall, straight forms of poles with dark lines crossing between them. Telephone poles! Relief washed through him. At least one of those buildings had a telephone.

It took him twenty minutes to approach the hamlet. There he saw a cement structure boasting the sign: *Tienda*. A store. Phone lines ran from a nearby pole into the building. It also had a phone. Forcing his wet feet to move forward, Jonathon felt the weakness in his legs. He couldn't collapse now, not this close to help.

Staggering toward the dirt road, his heart pounded within him. He wasn't worried about being hit—he worried about being spotted. At the dirt byway he checked for approaching vehicles but in the rural, mountain community nothing came. The town still slept in the predawn.

Jonathon looked across the road at the store and hesitated. It was still early, an hour or more until light. Maybe he shouldn't try and wake anyone just yet but he knew that if he waited an hour it would put Severino an hour closer. His decision finalized, Jonathon crossed the dirt road and moved toward the tightly secured store.

A gate of iron bars had been pulled down in front of the store to shield the windows and door during the night. Jonathon approached the store's door. He knew most Peruvian shopkeepers lived behind their store or in the rooms above it. They would hear him knocking.

Balling his hand into a fist, Jonathon ignored a growing fear and reached through the iron bars, banging rapidly on the metal door. In the morning silence the sound reverberated across the tiny town. He glanced around, nervous that others had heard. The town stayed quiet. Why did he feel that danger was close?

Banging again, Jonathon didn't worry about the sound this time. He now worried about being caught before someone came to his aid. Again no response came. A feeling of desperation filled him and he began a third series of loud knocking.

This time, from deep inside the darkened store came a muffled sound and an irritated voice. "*Ya vengo.* I'm coming."

At the words, Jonathon stepped closer to the metal bars, willing the man to come quickly. His dread increased with each heartbeat. He wanted to get off the street before someone discovered him. "Hurry," he whispered under his breath. "Please hurry."

From the inside the store movement stopped on the other side of the door. "*¿Quién es?* Who is it?"

He answered in Spanish. "My name is Jonathon. Please, I need help."

Momentary silence greeted his plea, but then he heard the sound of several locks being released. Relief swelled within Jonathon. From behind the iron bars, a small door flung open and a darkened face peered out into the gray light.

"*¿Americano?*" The man asked.

Moving close to the bars, Jonathon nodded, speaking quietly through the final iron barrier. "*Sí.* I need to use the telephone. Do you have one?"

"*Sí.*" The man turned away.

Fear filled Jonathon. "No," he pleaded, "don't go. Wait."

"I am unlocking the gate," came the response. "You must come inside if you want to use the phone."

The rattling of chains split the morning quiet, and the barred gate lifted a few feet off the ground then stopped. Jonathon didn't wait. He ducked underneath and stepped inside the tiny store.

The man lowered the bars and again shut the shop. "Follow me," he said.

A dim light trickled into the store front through an open door leading to a room near the back. Jonathon followed the man around a counter and toward the lighted room. As he passed through the darkened store the pounding of his heart increased, his blood racing through his veins. Why did he feel so nervous inside?

"Do you need to know who I am or who I want to call?" Jonathon asked.

"Come this way." The man moved down a narrow hall.

Puzzled that the shopkeeper didn't seem concerned about the call, Jonathon hesitated. The strange sense of fear surged inside him as he moved down the hallway. Why should he be getting more nervous? He was almost there.

Stepping to the side, the shopkeeper motioned Jonathon ahead of him, into the lighted room. Through the open door, Jonathon saw an old, black phone with a rotary dial sitting on a table.

"There it is," the man said. "Try to make your call."

Still feeling uncertain, Jonathon gave the man a nervous smile and stepped past him and toward the phone. "*Gracias.*"

He stepped into the room before he noticed their presence. Evil filled the room. Lined along the walls were men . . . and rifles. Jonathon stopped in surprise, feeling the hardened expressions of almost a dozen brown faces as they watched him with wicked countenances. A commotion came from behind, and the door swung shut. The solid *bang* of its closure caused Jonathon to jump. He spun around and watched the lock snap into place—trapping him inside the room.

Removing his hand from the metal dead bolt, the guard turned around, a rifle resting in his arms. Smirking at the American's fear, he nodded a greeting.

"*Buenas dias*, Jonathon."

Severino stood in front of the door.

THIRTEEN

SEVERINO! Jonathon's mouth went dry. "I . . . I just came to use the phone, to call my dad."

The man who led him into the room motioned toward the phone. "There it is. Try and make your call." His words sounded like a challenge. Jonathon didn't know what would happen if he tried.

A man close to the phone leaned over and picked up the receiver. "To call America you must first dial the operator."

Still Jonathon hesitated. "I . . . I don't want to call America. I just want to call my dad. He's staying in Cusco, at the Hotel Samay. He's looking for me."

Passing the phone to Jonathon, the man gave a taunting smile. "To call the Hotel Samay you must still dial the operator."

Cautiously Jonathon took the receiver and eased toward the phone. Around him hard faces watched. The men's features had been leathered by a hard life of thin diets and cold climate. Their clothes were old and stained. Many wore thick, homemade sweaters. All had a rifle close at hand. Glancing toward the door, Jonathon saw Severino staring at him, his arms folded across his chest, his own rifle nestled in the fold of his arms.

With a swallow, Jonathon reached for the phone's dial. His voice and fingers began to shake. "How do I dial the operator?"

The shopkeeper stepped forward and took the phone from him. "Allow me." With the receiver in one hand, he abruptly sliced through the cord with a giant knife. Laughing, he handed the useless phone and its severed cord back to Jonathon. "Now you don't need to worry about calling the operator, *gringo*."

Jonathon's stomach grew sick, and his legs weakened. He was in big trouble.

◆   ◆   ◆

Sitting on a burlap bag filled with dry beans, Jonathon wrapped his arms around his knees. Ropes cut into his wrists and bound his ankles together. From beyond the storeroom door, he could hear men laughing and talking. Sometimes he heard his name being said, other times he heard "*Americano*." He knew they were talking about him, and he wondered what they were planning to do. He also wondered if he would ever see his family again.

The door to the storage room opened, and Severino entered, followed by another man. Though Severino had traded his rifle for a mug, the man with him carried an automatic rifle. Severino moved across the room while the other man stopped to stand guard just inside the doorway.

The Peruvian teen stopped in front of Jonathon. Gray steam curled and floated up from the mug in Severino's hands, swirling in front of his face. "I brought you something to drink." Severino took a deep swallow of the steaming liquid before passing the mug to Jonathon's tied hands. His actions were deliberate—the drink had not been poisoned.

Despite the ropes binding his wrists, Jonathon managed to cup his hands around the heated mug. The warmth of its sides felt good. In the chilled storeroom, his entire body shook with cold. Peering down at the thick drink, he felt the warm steam encircle his face. The scent of chocolate and oatmeal drifted up into his senses, and Jonathon's stomach growled.

Severino heard it. He squatted by Jonathon, checking the ropes on his ankles. "You better drink while it is still warm."

Jonathon lifted the mug to his lips. He blew across the surface, letting more heat escape to warm him, before tasting the mixture with a slow sip. The creamy chocolate drink filled him with sweet warmth. As he swallowed, he felt it slide down his throat and into his stomach. He took a second swallow.

A hard jerk on the ropes ensnaring his feet caused Jonathon to spill some of his drink, scalding his damaged hand. "What was that for?"

Severino watched him with annoyance. "No reason."

Jonathon sucked the thick, hot liquid off his hand but a burn mark remained. Looking at Severino, Jonathon's anger and annoyance welled but he knew he needed to control his response. "So what are you going to do with me?"

Straightening, Severino shrugged. "That is a group decision."

Still fighting for control and not liking the answer, Jonathon's eyes narrowed into a frown. "And what is the *group* planning to do with me?"

Severino gave a taunting smile. "We haven't decided yet but when we do, you will definitely find out."

Jonathon drew back to throw the liquid at Severino, but the Peruvian reacted quickly, reaching out his hand to cover the mug and stop his motion. "Don't," he warned. "That is your only food. There will be no more. I suggest you drink it and not waste it on me."

Scars and calluses crisscrossed Severino's brown hand. Dozens of wounds, in various stages of healing, marked the brown flesh. Jonathon's anger melted into shock as he saw a lifetime of damage. No American hands he knew looked like that. He lifted his gaze to Severino's face. For a moment, the two stared at each other, as if peering into each other's thoughts.

Severino withdrew his hand, breaking away. "You have seen our faces and where we meet. That makes you very dangerous to us."

"I won't tell anyone, I promise."

A sour laugh escaped Severino. "That type of promise is only kept when people are scared." His expression hardened and he leaned closer. "Are you scared, *gringo*?"

Jonathon looked at Severino but could not answer. He was scared, terrified.

Severino's voice remained low, ominous. "Because you have seen us and know our faces, some want to kill you. They say that would be best. What do you think? Do you think it would be best for us to kill you and let the authorities or the wild animals find your body?"

"No." Jonathon's response was a swallow of fear.

"Still others want to use you to make us rich. They want to collect a huge ransom."

Jonathon grasped at that option. "Tell them to call my dad. He'll pay." Fear fed his rapid words.

"Can he pay five million dollars?"

Jonathon's hope dissipated. "Five million dollars?" His voice managed only a whisper. "But he doesn't have five million dollars."

"You mean you are not a wealthy American? I thought all Americans were rich." Sarcasm filled Severino's voice.

"No. Only a few Americans are rich. Most of us are poor."

Now Severino laughed out his disdain. "Poor? You don't know what poor is. Even a poor American is wealthy to a Peruvian. To you, being poor means you can't eat at McDonald's for lunch. Here, being poor means you eat from the garbage dump for lunch, and there are a *lot* of poor people in Peru! You *mocoso!*"

Jonathon lifted his head in anger. "I am not a brat."

"That is right. You are a *spoiled* brat, *mocoso engreído*. In fact, you are so spoiled, you are rotten!"

Now Severino lowered his voice to a whisper, anger hissing through his quiet words. "I told you to stay in bed, but you didn't listen. You didn't think I was worth listening to. You thought I was an ignorant, uneducated Peruvian."

The comment surprised Jonathon, and he sensed there was something more. In silence he mouthed back his own rage. "You never told me why!" Near the door, the guard did not hear them.

"I told you 'Evil' would find you, and it did."

"You never told me the 'Evil' meant terrorists."

"What did you think the 'Evil' was, mummies from your tunnels? At least those mummies are dead. These terrorists will make you dead whether you dad pays five million dollars or not. Because you did not listen to me, you just walked into your own funeral, you *imbecíl*."

Stunned, Jonathon could not answer.

Straightening, Severino moved away from the prisoner and toward the door. As he drew alongside the guard he turned back and laughed out loud, raising his voice. "You got yourself stuck right in the middle of the Shining Path. You walked right up and knocked on their front door, and they let you in; but they won't be letting you back out."

◆　　◆　　◆

David Bradford watched the night lights of Lima fall away behind the increasing speed of the taxiing plane. His wife curled against him, fighting her tears, while rain pattered against the plane windows.

David felt darkness inside. Two weeks of searching uncovered no sign of their son; now they had to return to the States. They had other children who needed them, but David agonized over leaving. He knew Jonathon was still out there, somewhere.

They had made appeals for help on national television. All the major papers carried their story on the front page, but no solid leads resulted. The unusual silence convinced David, even more, that his son was still alive. He believed, with everything he possessed, that someone knew about his son but was keeping quiet. That thought cut through David's heart like a knife blade. Why? What were they doing to his son?

He tried not to think about the answer. The possibilities of what they might be doing to his son shredded his very soul. At times it seemed impossible to hold himself together, but he needed to . . . for Rosa and for Jonathon.

Deep inside, David forced himself away from those thoughts, forced himself to find the connection that wouldn't die—a connection he felt with his son. He knew Jonathon was alive. He could *feel* it!

But David also knew his son desperately needed help. He could feel that truth as well. Often his heart began racing for unexplained reasons, and when it did, David knew it was because his son's heart was racing at that same moment. Jonathon was part of him, and when David felt his nerves explode in dread, he knew Jonathon was experiencing fear.

And right now, David's heart and nerves were pounding in sheer terror.

Beneath him, David felt the plane lift as it left the ground. Rosa choked on a sob at the sensation, and he closed his eyes, tightening his hold on his wife. They were leaving Peru, despite the thought that screamed through David's mind that Jonathon desperately needed him . . . *now*!

Pressing his face against Rosa's hair, David fought his tears and murmured words he needed to hear. "He's strong, Rosa. If anyone can make it home, Jonathon can."

◆　　◆　　◆

The door flung open with a metallic bang, and Jonathon jerked awake, his heart pounding wildly. Before his mind and memory focused, several hands grabbed him, yanking him to his feet. Unseen hands jerked a cloth bag over his head while a knife cut the rope tying his ankles. Terror filled him as he felt a rope tie the bag around his neck, encasing him in darkness. He fought the men and the bag. "What are you doing? Let me go!"

A fist to the side of his head came in answer. The blow staggered him and left his mind thick. Dragged through a narrow passage, Jonathon struggled to stay on his feet, his fear sharpening. "Where are you taking me?"

Another blow knocked him sideways. "Shut up, *gringo!*"

More voices filled the air. "*Apurate!* Hurry. The truck is waiting."

After he'd been dragged out into the cold night, hands lifted Jonathon off the ground and tossed him through the air. His body collided against hard metal and sharp boxes. He yelped in pain at the impact. Through the bag came the pungent smell of diesel fuel. More hands grabbed Jonathon, pulling him deeper inside a truck bed. He heard the sound of a sturdy engine rumbling into gear. Then, with a lurch, the truck shifted forward, its tires rolling over the rough road and into the night.

Blinded by the bag, Jonathon curled on his side, trying to protect himself. As the truck shook and rocked in its rapid path, Jonathon became aware of three, possibly four men, sitting on benches around him. Occasionally a foot kicked at his back in the dark, followed by laughter, or a boot stepped purposely on his battered fingers, reminding him they were still there. Jonathon wanted to curse with pain and cry with fear, but instead he gritted his teeth, forcing himself to draw on his inner determination.

Over the noise of the engine, Jonathon could hear a few words from them but never enough to determine what they were saying. Once he thought he heard Severino's voice, but again, he couldn't be sure. He didn't know where they were taking him or what they were planning to do once they got there, but he knew it wouldn't be good.

After half an hour, the truck pulled off the road. Still lying in the bed of the truck, Jonathon felt his heart begin to pound wildly, and he felt his stomach turn with fear. They were stopping. Then the engine shut off and silence settled over the Andes Mountains.

Footsteps approached the rear of the truck, and a voice issued commands. "Raul, Pablo, *bajen* and come with me." Near Jonathon two men scrambled to their feet and climbed from the truck. "Luis," the voice spoke to a third man, "take your rifle and check the bridge ahead. Go quietly. Do not be seen." A third man complied. The commanding voice spoke again. "Severino, stay here with the American. We will return as soon as we are sure the road is clear. If he needs to *mear*, let him, but leave the hood on."

Voices silenced and footsteps vanished into the night. Only the sounds of night birds filled the mountain jungle. For a moment the world held still then a foot shoved him in the shoulder. "You heard the boss, get out of the truck and go to the bathroom, but leave the hood on."

"I can't see to climb out."

"Feel your way, genius."

Angered at the taunt, Jonathon controlled his words. "My hands are tied."

Severino cursed and rose from the bench. A hand reached out and caught Jonathon under the arm. "Stand up. I'll help."

Awkwardly, Jonathon climbed to his feet. Forced to follow Severino through the packed and crowded truck bed, he stumbled several times, tripping over unidentified piles. Each time, Severino caught and steadied him. When they got to the tailgate, Severino helped Jonathon climb to the earth then dropped down beside him.

Taking him by the arm again, Severino led him away from the truck. Jonathon felt the earth rising beneath his feet and knew they were moving uphill. He thought about reaching up to pull the hood off with his hands but didn't know if it would easily free itself from the rope wrapped around his neck.

"This is fine," Severino concluded, halting the American's advance. "Now hurry up."

Waiting until Jonathon finished, Severino turned him down the hill and they descended the incline together. In the quiet of the night, Jonathon questioned his guide. "Where are they taking me?"

"You don't want to know."

"Yes, I do."

Severino chuckled. "Are you always this prying?"

"When it's my life, yes. Are you always this evasive?"

"When it's mine."

They reached the truck. Turning to the night, Severino spoke. "You don't have to climb inside right now." His voice gentled. "Stay out for a moment and stretch your legs."

Startled by the kind gesture, Jonathon's responded quietly. "Thank you," he whispered.

"It's nothing."

In the darkness of the night, Jonathon heard the sounds of insects and other animals. Needing to find calming thoughts, he forced his mind to focus on them. Unbidden, his memories turned to a camping trip he'd enjoyed in the mountains with his father. While everyone else slept, they'd left the tent together to listen to night sounds, but mostly they just listened to each other. They spent hours that night, visiting quietly. Jonathon wondered if they would ever be able to spend time together again. The memory brought emotion welling to the surface.

"I miss my father." Jonathon said softly. He didn't know why he said it, but he didn't regret the truth.

For a moment Severino stood silent, then, "I miss mine too."

The response surprised Jonathon. He turned his hooded face toward Severino's voice. "Where is he?"

"Dead."

Jonathon's voice came, quiet in the night. "I know you probably don't believe the spoiled American brat, but I'm sorry he died."

"You're right," Severino took Jonathon's arm, guiding him to the truck. "You are spoiled." Just then something caused Severino to come to an abrupt halt. He stopped Jonathon. "Ssshh."

"What is it?"

"I hear something. Be quiet."

Jonathon could tell Severino's face had turned away. With his heart pounding in his chest, eyes still covered by the bag, Jonathon strained to listen. Only night sounds disturbed the darkness. "I don't hear—"

"Quiet! Something's out there." Releasing his arm, Severino stepped away from Jonathon, toward the mountain jungle. "Don't move. I'll be right back."

Jonathon listened to Severino's footsteps fade into the night. Silence settled over the mountain road. Left alone in the night, he wondered what Severino had heard. What would frighten a terrorist?

As Jonathon stood in the dark beside the truck, a new thought crept into his mind. He was alone, completely unguarded.

Action happened faster than thought. Reaching up with tied hands, Jonathon pulled at the rope, undoing it. Free, he jerked the hood off his head. A moonless night enveloped the mountains, but millions of stars dotted the sky, giving dim light to the terrain. He cast a rapid glance around him. The truck sat perched on the shoulder of a gravel road, nestled at the base of a steep slope. On the other side of the road, trees hugged the edge—dark and frightening. He didn't know what Severino had heard or where he was, but Jonathon knew those trees were his only chance of escape.

His decision made before the thought was finished, Jonathon sprinted across the road and ducked into the waiting trees. The jungle accepted him without complaint, and he raced deeper into its thick embrace. If the terrorists wanted the stupid, spoiled American brat they were going to have to find him in the jungle at night!

Moving through the mountain foliage, his hands tied in front of him, Jonathon found it difficult to keep his balance. Branches lashed at his face, and several times he fell, but he was too afraid to stop running. He had to get as far away as possible. Pushing through the trees he continued onward, stumbling through the mountain jungle. Finally he stopped against a decaying tree trunk while he fought to quiet his breathing and bring it under control. If only he could get his wrists untied! He could move faster and easier.

Glancing around in the night he tried to find some way to cut the heavy ropes but saw nothing. In frustration, he lifted his bound hands to his mouth. He would bite his way through the ropes, gnawing at them like a rat if he had to.

Just then a scarred hand clamped firmly over his mouth, muffling his startled cry. "Don't move, or you'll die."

Jonathon felt frustration swell within him. Severino had found him. He sagged with discouragement.

Severino tightened his grip on him. "I said don't move." Severino's voice came, a mere breath of air. "They're out there. Don't even breathe or they'll hear you."

His unusual words shifted Jonathon's fears. Who was out there?

From the jungle came the screech of a night bird, then the shuffling of movement through the trees. Severino eased Jonathon away from the log and into the thickening jungle. In the dark night movement came closer, passing through the clearing where he had rested only seconds before. From behind them came more sounds, more movement passing through the jungle foliage. Then it passed on up the valley and into the dark.

When the jungle returned to its normal sounds several minutes later, Jonathon felt Severino relax. The Peruvian teen exhaled slowly but did not release his hold on Jonathon. Then he felt Severino shift and reach over Jonathon's shoulder. A massive knife blade flashed in the light and Jonathon recoiled. Without a word, Severino inserted the blade between the ropes and cut Jonathon's wrists free. The bands of hemp fell to the earth with a soft double *thwap*. Moving around to the front, Severino held a finger to his lips then slowly released Jonathon's mouth.

Understanding the sign, Jonathon honored it, despite his confusion. Rubbing his wrists, he studied the dark-haired youth before him. "What are you doing?" His question emerged as movement, not sound.

The Peruvian sheathed his knife then retrieved his rifle from the jungle foliage. "You'll be able to travel faster that way; but don't be stupid and try to escape. I can't save you from them twice." He turned away in the night. "Come."

Jonathon's hopes fell. He wasn't being set free. He was being commanded to follow a terrorist. "What if I don't want to go with you?"

Severino turned, his eyes furious. "Then they will find you, and you will die right here, on this mountain—tonight. Now get moving and don't say another word!" Severino's expression and the rifle he held left no room for debate. Dutifully, Jonathon followed . . . this time down the steep slope and *away* from the truck!

"Stay close," Severino whispered. "We've only got a few minutes. If Delia got the word passed along, there should be a friend waiting for us down by the river. Let's move."

"A friend?" The words staggered Jonathon. "What are you talking about?"

"There will be answers after you get safely across the river. We're running out of time. They may be following even now."

"Who?"

But Severino did not answer. He moved quickly through the thick growth, forcing Jonathon to follow or be left behind. Jonathon struggled to keep up with Severino as they moved rapidly but quietly down the tree-choked slope. Then the foliage abruptly gave way to a water-swollen creek. Without hesitating, Severino turned and moved along its bank. Once he stopped at the water's edge and whistled then paused to listen. Over the rush of the water, Jonathon heard nothing, but Severino did. He nodded in the night.

"He's here. Come on."

"I didn't hear anything."

"You weren't supposed to."

A few yards more and a dark figure stepped from the shadows. Jonathon jumped, but Severino's face showed relief to see his friend from the restaurant by the bus stop. "Carlos, it's good to see you."

"Is this the American?"

"*Sí*. Can you get him out for me?"

"*No problema*. Do you want us to take him all the way to Lima?"

"Yes, if you can."

"We're getting the runners in place now. It shouldn't be a problem. And what about you?"

The question caused Severino's face to twist with concern. He glanced up the slope. "I guess I'll know in a couple of minutes." Turning back to Jonathon, Severino placed a hand on his shoulder, the grip firm. "Go with Carlos. He's a friend. You can trust him. He's going to get you to your father." Then, nodding at Carlos, Severino disappeared into the trees, leaving Jonathon stunned, standing beside a stranger and a river in the dark.

FOURTEEN

CARLOS DIDN'T WAIT for formalities. He turned and over his shoulder addressed Jonathon's hesitation. "The best way to help Severino is to get out of sight—fast." With his announcement, Carlos stepped off the bank and into the icy water.

Still on the bank, Jonathon paused, staring up the slope. "Now!" The command was whispered but unmistakable. Jonathon cast a final glance up the slope then stepped down into the swift flowing river.

When the freezing water poured through his shoes and plastered his jeans to his legs, Jonathon's mouth opened in shock. Ahead of him Carlos waded further out, the water rising to his waist.

Sucking in a deep lungful of air, Jonathon pressed forward, hating the icy pain assaulting his body. The rocks on the bottom of the river were slick and rounded. His feet slipped. One large boulder rolled beneath his foot and plunged Jonathon under the frigid surface. The rushing water caught him and spun him around, shooting him downstream. Suddenly a hand grabbed him and held him firm. Sputtering for air, Jonathon emerged and fought for his footing in the fast current.

"Sshh." Carlos had a hold of him.

Choking on swallows of air and water, Jonathon tried to control the noise. This time the Peruvian spoke quietly. "Are you okay?"

Giving a nod, Jonathon spat water from his mouth and nose even as a massive tremor of cold convulsed his body.

"Good. In a few more feet we will be out of the water."

Releasing Jonathon, Carlos returned to his task. Moving down river, the man came to a rock overhang covered by debris swept there by the swift water. Trees and branches formed a massive wall in front of the overhang. Here Carlos stopped and turned to the American. He spoke only loud enough to be heard over the rush of water. "Stay close and follow me exactly. Step only where I step and do only what I do. We're almost there. *Vamanos* . . . let's go."

Almost where? Jonathon stared at the steep canyon sides rising above him, but he didn't look for long. Carlos had already begun weaving his way *into* the tangled mass. Stunned, Jonathon followed the man, trying to replicate every move.

After a minute of twisting and maneuvering through river debris, Carlos ducked under a final log then rose up inside a narrow crack in the rock. He turned sideways and edged deeper into the crevice. Amazed, Jonathon followed.

The river on this side of the log jam was calm. As they moved through the crack, the water level subsided, dropping from Jonathon's chest to his hips, then to his knees and ankles, finally disappearing completely. They continued to move in the dark, up the stone fissure and away from the river.

At one point the crack narrowed so abruptly Jonathon didn't think they could go further, but then Carlos, using the opposite wall as a brace, shimmied ten feet up the fissure. Above him in the night, Carlos reached backward into a hole and vanished altogether. For a moment Jonathon froze, unsure of what he had just seen and uncertain he wanted to follow.

Carlos's head emerged from the opening above him. "Come," he said. "I will talk you through."

Replicating Carlos's movements, Jonathon found it easier to shimmy up the wall than he imagined. Soon the opening loomed behind him. From inside the dark space, Carlos spoke.

"Reach up into the hole behind you. There is a wooden beam. Grab it with both hands and pull your body inside the opening. The floor will be a few feet below you. Just drop down."

Swallowing, Jonathon reached up into the darkness. With surprise, he felt the smooth, cool surface of a thick, wooden beam. Pulling on it with one hand, it held firm. His confidence increasing, Jonathon grabbed it with both hands and pulled his body backward into the tiny opening.

Once his feet cleared the rim they fell into darkness below him. A hand reached out and touched his lower leg. "Let go of the beam. I am standing on the ground."

Jonathon did as he was told and dropped to the earth. He grimaced at the pain in his side. Clutching his ribs, he tried to speak. "How . . . how did you know the beam was there?"

"It has been there for centuries."

"Where are we?"

"Inside the Andes Mountains."

The words terrified Jonathon. In the darkness, with cave walls pressing all around him, he felt his chest tighten. Sucking hard for control, Jonathon tried to fight the growing terror he felt. Horrifying images flashed through his mind of sightless days, spiders, and mummies. He didn't want to be here, and his mind raced in the darkness, ahead of his control.

Carlos heard his labored breathing and reached over to give Jonathon a firm squeeze on the shoulder. "It will only be dark for a little ways, trust me. Just hold on to my shirt. You will be fine. I promise."

Numbly he nodded and grabbed a handful of shirt, closing his eyes so he wouldn't have to see that he couldn't see. Jonathon shivered violently but didn't know the cause: his wet, icy clothes or his fear.

Following blind orders, Jonathon ducked when he was told, turned sideways or got down on his knees and crawled. Finally the walls seemed to fall away in the darkness, and Carlos stood upright. "You can stop now. We are through the worst part."

Jonathon released his guide's shirt and slowly straightened, trying to catch his breath. Next to him he heard a *snicking* sound, then a spark of light burst into a flame and illuminated the cave. Holding a cigarette lighter, Carlos smiled at him. "You made it. Good job."

Jonathon could not respond. His eyes avoided glancing around him.

Walking to a stone shelf, Carlos lit a candle resting there, then extracted a burlap bag and carried it to Jonathon. "Inside is a change of clothing for each of us and several flashlights. As soon as you are dressed in dry clothes, we will leave."

"Where are we going?"

Carlos stripped off his wet shirt. "To Lima—through the tunnels."

Jonathon's body reeled beneath the power of Carlos's words. The bag hung in his hands, forgotten. "Through the tunnels?"

"Sí."

Jonathon started to shake his head, backing away from the situation. Color drained from his face. "I can't. I can't go back inside those tunnels."

"You can do more than you know. Besides, if you go out there the Shining Path will find you, and they will kill you." Carlos removed his wet pants.

"You are not a member of the Shining Path?"

Soft laughter came from Carlos. "No." He took the bag of clothes from Jonathon and pulled out a dry shirt and trousers for himself. "You could say I am part of the Hidden Path—through the mountains. Now get dressed."

Still unsure, Jonathon questioned him more. "You're not a terrorist?"

"Would a terrorist help you return to your father?" Carlos pulled the pants up over his hips and zipped them closed.

"I . . . I don't know. What about Severino? He's a terrorist."

"I am glad he has you convinced of that. Hopefully he will continue to convince the others as well."

In the mountain cave, Jonathon hesitated. "But he meets with them! He has a gun!"

"Does owning a gun make you a terrorist?"

"No, but he kept me at his house and wouldn't contact my father!"

Carlos stopped getting dressed and looked at Jonathon. "Severino is no more a terrorist than I am President of your United States." He motioned for Jonathon to remove his wet clothes. "He had to do what he did to protect you."

"Protect me?" Still unsure of what he was hearing, Jonathon pulled off his wet jacket and shirt, his chest tight and shivering.

"Terrorists are everywhere, and the only phone in the area—as you found out—is owned by a terrorist. If Severino had called your father or let you place the call yourself, the terrorists would have found out about you and taken you hostage, maybe even your father hostage, before we could figure a way to get you safely home."

The words stopped Jonathon. "Severino *wanted* to help get me home?"

"*Sí*. He does not want anyone to suffer at the hands of the Shining Path."

Jonathon felt confusion. "But he meets with them and he went back to them just now. Why?"

Carlos smiled. "To help them look for you."

The words jolted Jonathon, and he spun around, looking down the dark path they had just followed. "He's going to tell them where we are!"

"No. He will lead them away from here if he can." Then Carlos's face grew serious. "And hopefully they will not learn Severino helped you escape."

Realization began to open Jonathon's mind. A knot took hold of his stomach, and his mouth went dry. "He was assigned to guard me."

"*Sí*"

"And he helped me escape. He brought me here, and you were waiting. He had this all planned."

Carlos nodded. "He decided if you survived that long in the tunnels, dying was not in your plans, so he gave you a chance to escape and let you take it."

"But won't the terrorists be upset I escaped while he was supposed to be watching me?"

"Yes, and Severino already knows that. He will be punished severely for letting you escape."

Jonathon felt his insides tremble. "How?"

"He will be beaten."

"And what if the terrorists actually saw what happened? What if they find out he *helped* me escape?"

Carlos's gaze did not move from Jonathon's. "They will kill him, and this I know—they will make him want to die long before they let him. Terrorists are not kind when one of their own turns against them."

Jonathon's stomach rolled. Deep inside, he fought sickness. "I was wrong about him. I misjudged him terribly—I'm sorry."

Carlos motioned to Jonathon to continue dressing. "I hope you can tell him that one day, but until then we must honor his wish and his risk by getting you to Lima."

Jonathon slowly pulled a dry shirt over his head and pushed his arms through the worn sleeves. "But if he's not a terrorist, why does he meet with them?"

This time Carlos hesitated, struggling with the answer. For several moments he fought his response before coming to a decision. "Three years ago terrorists killed his father." Jonathon glanced up. The Peruvian continued. "Severino pretends to be one of them, in the hopes of finding out who was responsible for his father's death."

"But that's dangerous!"

"Very." The sound of water cascading to the stone floor filled the cave as Carlos wrung all the extra water from his shirt and jacket. "But so is living among terrorists and not doing anything to stop them."

Jonathon studied the man in front of him. "Can I ask why they killed his father?"

Carlos handed Jonathon a pair of pants. "Severino's father was in the wrong place at the wrong time, so they tied both of his hands behind his back, forced him to kneel, and then shot him in the face."

The words stung Jonathon. He let their full impact sink in before sharing his next cautious words. "Where was the wrong place?"

"The town's post office. Like Delia and Severino, their father was a weaver. He made and sold tapestries to the tourists of Cusco. He went there to mail some tapestries to a buyer when terrorists ambushed the police officer assigned to guard the mail. The police officer could not be bribed, so they put him on their hit list. They executed the officer and four others who just happened to be at the post office, including a woman and her baby."

"They killed a woman and her baby?"

Carlos stared at Jonathon, his expression and gaze unwavering. "Do not be so surprised. Terrorists get their name because they cause terror. They *earn* that name. Yes, they executed a woman and her baby."

Inside Jonathon sorrow filled him. He removed his shoes, socks, and blue jeans in silence.

Carlos retrieved Jonathon's discarded clothes and wrung the water from them. "Severino was fourteen when it happened. He decided that day if you have to live in danger, you might as well live trying to stop it. He is determined to stop the killing, even if it means he will die."

Jonathon eased a worn pair of brown pants over his hips. "He's had to live a very different life than I have, hasn't he?"

"*Sí.*" Carlos's words gentled. "Life is different here, but never forget *we* are not different. We may look different. We may live differently but we laugh over the same things and cry over the same things.

Severino misses his father deeply and has cried many tears for him. Maybe that is why he felt it so important that you be able to return to your father."

A slow understanding nod came from Jonathon. "I think I understand some of Severino's pain. Maybe, in some ways, he and I are not all that different after all"

"No, you are not. Not now anyway." Carlos smiled. "Those are his clothes you are wearing."

The trousers buttoned easily around Jonathon's waist, and he smiled, grateful for an opportunity at lighter conversation. "I guess this means I've lost some weight."

With shoes laced into place over mended socks and a hand-knit sweater pulled over the outfit to keep him warm, Jonathon stood. "How do I look?"

Carlos smiled warmly. "Like one of us."

The words brightened Jonathon's expression. "Good."

Stuffing the damp clothing into the bag, Carlos slung it over his shoulder and handed Jonathon a flashlight. "Ready?"

"I hope so."

With a nod, Carlos turned and headed deeper into the labyrinth.

Jonathon watched Carlos move into the tunnel system and he hesitated. Fear entered his veins. He didn't know if he could go back inside them.

The light from Carlos's flashlight faded as the man moved around a bend and out of sight. As the light disappeared, the thought of staying behind frightened Jonathon even more. Scrambling over the dirt floor, he rushed to catch his Peruvian guide.

Through the twisting, turning caverns, Jonathon followed Carlos, his mind struggling with every step. He cast the beam from his flashlight around, frightened of every shadow and crack. The tunnels had almost killed him once. Gripping the flashlight with intensity, his fingers started to tingle.

Each sight, each memory constricted his chest, bringing his breath in shorter and shorter inhalations. He fought for breath, fought for control but he felt himself losing both. His mind began to dim, and his vision faded in and out. The walls started closing around him. He couldn't go on. "Carlos—"

Ahead of him the man turned and saw Jonathon's expression in the beam of his flashlight. Instantly he returned to the boy. "What is it? What is wrong?"

His face muscles slack, Jonathon shook his head. "I can't do this, Carlos. I thought I could, but I can't."

"We have good light."

"I know but—" Jonathon turned around, shining the beam from his flashlight on the ceiling, the walls, the floor. Images and feelings returned, layering themselves over his mind, as suffocating and thick as the blackness beyond his beam. As he turned, his eyes wide with panic, a low sound emerged from him, growing louder until a guttural roar sent his emotions through the endless labyrinth.

"*I hate this place!*" Jonathon closed his eyes as the sound reverberated off the stone and echoed down the passageways.

Pain claimed every feature on his face, and Jonathon doubled over in defeat, balancing his hands on his knees for support, pressing his eyes tightly shut, trying to keep the tears inside. His voice came quieter this time. "I hate this place, Carlos. It almost killed me. Worse, the tunnels made me want to die." He lifted his gaze to Carlos, his light brown eyes glistening. "Can you understand that? I wanted to die but not down here in these tunnels. Now you're asking me to face this all over again."

Carlos rubbed Jonathon's back, comforting him. "You are not going to die. Not here, not in these tunnels."

"But the tunnels have killed others. I saw it. They are supposed to kill." He groaned out loud. "The floor caved in. It tipped beneath me and fell away. And there were spiders—hundreds of spiders. They'd been trapped in a basket that fell down on top of me. And the mummies—" The wave of memories weakened him more. "Carlos, there were mummies everywhere."

"Jonathon, as long as you are with me those things will not hurt you."

"But they are here in these tunnels!"

"Yes, they are here. Yes, you saw things that were designed to kill—things no one is *supposed* to be able to survive." The truth buckled Jonathon's knees. Groaning in agony, his body sagged. Carlos caught him, bracing him up. "Listen to me, Jonathon. You lived through those things. Somehow you survived them because you are *not* supposed to die down here. You are supposed to return to your father, and I am going to get you there, but you are going to have to trust me. Can you do that?"

Jonathon closed his eyes tight, fighting for courage.

Carlos spoke again, his words firm. "Trust me, Jonathon, please. We are here together. Every step we travel I will go first. If there is danger I will face it first, I promise you that. These tunnels did not conquer you the first time. Do not let them conquer you this time. Let me help get you home to your father."

Swallowing the sour bile filling his throat, Jonathon fought for control of his mind and his body. He had to get home to his father, he *wanted* to. Reaching deep, he managed a nod. "Okay," he whispered. "Okay." He straightened slowly, trying to calm his trembling body. "I'll try."

Carlos smiled. "Good. By agreeing to try, you have just conquered half the battle. Now let's do this together."

◆　　　◆　　　◆

Moving through the underground world, Jonathon fought his emotions. He worried about what the darkness hid and what it might reveal. Sensing his unease, Carlos set a slow pace through the tunnels, letting Jonathon stop often to catch his breath and reclaim his nerves, but as the teenager began to trust himself again, Carlos increased their speed.

Soon the tunnel they traveled widened and, as they moved along its path, Jonathon saw several smaller openings, other tunnels branching off theirs. He felt insecure passing their dark holds, worried by what they held. "So what are these tunnels?"

"Those are called minor tunnels; you want to stay out of them. As you discovered, they are filled with deadly traps."

Jonathon hurried his step to stay closer to Carlos. He didn't want to encounter another trap, or mummy or spider.

On the pair moved, Carlos always knowing where to go. He never turned back or corrected a misstep, and Jonathon became aware that the man in front of him actually knew the tunnel system.

As they moved forward, Jonathon began to marvel at the passageway they followed. It was different than the tunnels he had wandered through before. Fresh wind whistled through this shaft, and at times the carved tunnel was wide enough to drive a truck through.

Other times their twisting journey took them past clear water flowing through hand-carved aqueducts or gathering in stone cisterns.

After a couple of hours they entered a mighty chamber, surrounded by several tunnel openings. Against the walls, Jonathon saw a tremendous collection of ancient baskets and clay pots. Apprehensive, Jonathon stepped toward his guide and motioned to a basket "What's in those? I found dead spiders in mine."

Laughter came from Carlos. "Relax. There are no spiders in those. They contain food."

"Food?"

"Mostly dried corn and potatoes."

"Really? How come I never found any food when I was stumbling around starving?"

The man's voice lightened. "You were in the wrong tunnels. Food and water are only found in the major tunnels. This is a major tunnel."

"That's not fair. Tourists in the minor tunnels need to eat too."

Smiling, Carlos glanced over at Jonathon, glad the youth's sense of humor was returning. That meant his courage was also returning. "You would not want to eat that food. The Incas stored it here centuries ago. It is probably stale."

"You mean that stuff is five hundred years old?"

"At least."

Jonathon whistled. "Old or not, I think I would have tried it. Even my school's overcooked spinach sounded good to me then."

Carlos grimaced. "You would have eaten *espinaca? Aye* . . . you were hungry."

As they passed, Jonathon looked at the baskets to assure him there were no spiders crawling out. "Why did they store all this food down here? Did it keep better or something?"

"They stored it to help in their escape from the Spaniards."

The words stunned Jonathon. "You're kidding. The Incas really used these tunnels to escape?"

"They really did."

The revelation astounded Jonathon. Swinging his flashlight around, his mind pictured thousands of Incas passing through the chamber with their children, their flocks and their possessions. "They were here?"

"Yes. They were here."

At the pronouncement a new feeling flowed through Jonathon, one of discovery. He was standing in the middle of a piece of history that had been hidden from the rest of the world! "I can't believe this, Carlos. I wonder what my dad's going to say when I tell him about this place."

The abrupt halt in Carlos's movement caused Jonathon to collide with him. Carlos turned around, his face tense. "You cannot tell your dad."

Startled, Jonathon questioned him. "Why? He's an archaeologist. He'd love to see this stuff. Besides, what am I supposed to tell him when I show up? *'Hi, sorry I'm late for dinner'*?"

"I do not care if you tell him you were late for dinner or even if you stopped to play cards before breakfast. Just do not tell him about these tunnels."

"Why not? I don't understand. Obviously they exist. Why don't you want me to tell anyone? These tunnels are filled with so much history."

Carlos's dark eyes held his conviction. "History is what you flaunt before the world. Heritage is what you guard. These tunnels are filled with heritage."

"But Carlos, the world needs to learn about all this."

"A world that spends its time learning video games does not need to learn about these tunnels."

"Don't you want the world to know what happened to the Incas?"

Carlos's steady gaze never wavered from Jonathon. "We have kept these tunnels sacred by keeping them secret. For centuries the world has stepped all over the Incas. We do not want them doing it again. We will not let them step into these tunnels, *comprende*?"

The tone of his voice and firm expression on Carlos's face left no room for arguing. "Okay, I'm sorry. I didn't know."

For a moment Carlos stared at him, studying his sincerity, and then he nodded. "Come, we need to continue." Walking across the chamber he turned and entered a minor tunnel.

Jonathon stared at the smaller, dark opening, suddenly bothered by Carlos's departure from the main tunnel. "Hey, that's a minor tunnel!"

"*Sí.*"

Jonathon hesitated. "But you said to stay out of the minor tunnels, that they were filled with deadly traps."

"*Sí.*" The light form Carlos's flashlight continued to fade.

Fear over Carlos's motive began to fill Jonathon's mind. Was Carlos upset over Jonathon wanting to tell others about the tunnels? "So why did you go there?" He sent uncertain words after his disappearing guide. "Do you *want* to get me lost or killed?"

"You do not need to worry as long as I read the directions."

Shaking his head, Jonathon stepped away from the minor tunnel. "I'm sorry but I don't remember seeing you read any directions or maps down here and I haven't seen a single road sign."

From inside the smaller tunnel, Carlos laughed. It sounded genuine, not veiled in anger. "That is because you do not know where to look."

The Peruvian returned to where Jonathon stood. As he stepped back into Jonathon's flashlight beam, Carlos's expression told Jonathon he was already aware of his concern. "It is not a trap, Jonathon. You can trust me. I have given you my word. I will not lead you any place that will hurt you." Shining the beam of light to the wall just above his head, he pointed toward the ceiling. "See those?"

Shifting his gaze away from Carlos, Jonathon peered into the glow. There he saw a faint carving in the rock. Puzzled, he stepped toward the marking and reached up, letting his fingers explore the carving. "What is that?"

"A road sign. If you know what you're searching for they mark the path. Some tunnels lead to Machu Picchu others lead to Lima, some north to Iquitos and some to other locations. This marking tells me the tunnel leads to Lima. It connects with another major tunnel about half a mile from here."

"Wow," Jonathon's eyes studied the marks. "Do all the tunnels have markings?"

"You tell me." He motioned toward the other tunnels fanning the chamber.

Curiosity moved Jonathon toward an opening. Shining his light upward in the cavern, he found faint markings near the top. "This is cool! Where does this tunnel go?"

"To Pisco, out in the desert by the coast."

"So all these tunnels lead you someplace?"

Carlos nodded his beam at the tunnels. "*Sí*, but unless you understand the markings, you may not like the destination. The Incas considered the entire tunnel system as a symbol for life. They believed that there were correct paths and incorrect paths. To help them find the correct path through life, the gods gave the Incas instructions, but you had to look for those instructions and study what they said. These markings replicate that same principle. Only one of these tunnels will take you where you want to go, but it is up to the traveler to look for the right marks and study what they say. If we choose not to lift our eyes high enough, or if we choose not to study the instructions left for us by those who know the way, we may make a wrong choice."

"And if you choose wrong, you may not survive." Jonathon's words came quietly.

Carlos looked at the youth and nodded. "You understand."

"I think I'm beginning to."

Looking around at the various tunnels, Carlos continued. "While the Incas believed each person was free to choose any tunnel or path in life they wanted, they were not free to erase the consequences of their choice. If they entered a path they must face every trial along that path. That is one reason the Incas also believed you needed to know where you wanted to go before you started your journey. Knowing where you wanted to go would help you make the right choice."

Shining his light on the different tunnels, Jonathon mused over their various contents. "That makes sense—like a goal. It's that way in life, too."

"*Ama Qella, Ama Suwa, Ama Llulla, Ama Hap'a.*"

"Ama what?" The unfamiliar words turned Jonathon around.

His guide smiled. "Quecha instructions. *Ama Qella*—no matter how small or menial your task, *work hard*. Give everything your very best effort. Work to make all of your life important. *Ama Suwa—stay honest*. Always speak the truth and do not let anything tempt you into relaxing your integrity. *Ama Llulla—be true* to yourself. Never soothe yourself with a lie or a rationalization. Your soul will feel the difference. *Ama Hap'a—be full of faith and stay loyal*. Hold to the belief that life is good and everyone really does try to do their best. Be loyal to your word and your intentions. Honor your family, your friends, and your acquaintances. Even give honor to a stranger for you may discover he is your best friend, your closest family, or even your very salvation.

Ama Qella, Ama Suwa, Ama Llulla, Ama Hap'a: work hard, stay honest, be true, be full of faith, and stay loyal."

With his mind tumbling around the words, Jonathon stored them in his thoughts. Carefully he nodded. "I like that." Reflecting on the words, Jonathon moved to another tunnel free of engravings. He let his beam cut an arc over the stone. "These tunnels are not marked. Where do they lead?"

Carlos looked at the teen, his words quiet. "*Un muerte eterno*, an eternal death." Stunned, Jonathon looked back at him. "I am surprised you survived in them. People who go into the unmarked tunnels die there. They are not meant to survive."

Backing toward Carlos, Jonathon moved away from the gaping hole. "I don't like those tunnels."

"I do not blame you."

In the faint light, Jonathon caught a faint symbol carved into the rock above another opening. This mark seemed to call to him; it did not look like any of the characters above the other tunnels. With awe, he approached the tunnel, reaching up to touch the strange marking. "What about this tunnel, Carlos? What's in here?"

Instantly Carlos caught his wrist before he made contact with the symbol. "*Stop!*"

"Why? What's in that tunnel?"

"You do not need to know so leave them alone."

"*Them?*" Jonathon swung his light into the passage as Carlos pulled him back to the other tunnel. "Leave who alone? Who's in that tunnel?"

"I told you—you do not need to know."

"Hey, if I'm going to be bringing up the rear here, I do too need to know! I'm not sure I want any of *thems* following me."

Carlos held silent and the two stared at each other, time passing slowly. Finally Jonathon nodded his head in understanding. "Mummies are down that tunnel, aren't they?"

"We need to keep moving."

"Answer my question, Carlos! Are there mummies in that tunnel? I want to know!"

This time Carlos stepped close to Jonathon, his voice low. "In life and in death there are some questions better left unanswered, some things better left unknown, and some things should *never* be disturbed!

You know nothing about the powers in that tunnel. Stay away from them and do not ask about them."

His warning worked. With a final glance at the strangely marked tunnel, Jonathon eased away and followed Carlos into the smaller tunnel, but his mind could not release Carlos's warning, nor free him from the memories of his encounter with the mummies.

Jonathon didn't know if the mummies actually moved that day in the tunnels or if he had only imagined it, but he could still feel their hardened limbs and teeth on him and smell their nearness. The cut on his cheek, where ancient teeth had raked away his flesh, pulled as a tight reminder against his skin.

In the sanity of his waking mind, Jonathon couldn't believe that mummies really came to life. He wanted to believe the corpses had merely tumbled on top of him, but fear roiled, unsettled, deep inside. Carlos's warning convinced him the Peruvian was keeping something from him, something that involved mummies.

Moving through the dark and twisting tunnels, Jonathon often cast his flashlight's beam behind him afraid of seeing something there, but more afraid of not looking. Each time he turned, the tunnel only revealed darkness. Carlos noticed Jonathon's fear, but did not say a thing. If Carlos was frightened of the mountain maze or the legends about mummies, he didn't show it even when the mountain sounds rumbled through the tunnels or rocks tumbled in the darkened passages. Carlos never looked behind him. Jonathon, however, cringed at every sound and hated the blackness all around him. He hated wondering what the tunnels hid.

FIFTEEN

HOURS later they entered a tiny opening, and Carlos stopped their journey. He opened the bag he carried and removed the wet clothing, laying it on the cave floor to dry as Jonathon lowered himself to the cold earth. Jonathon's entire body ached, and his mind pounded with a headache. He had lost much of his strength and endurance in the last two weeks, and their trek had been difficult. Laying his head against the stone wall, the teen swallowed. "Thank you."

"*De nada*, you're welcome." Reaching deeper into his bag, Carlos withdrew a candle. Trimming the wick, he lighted it with a cigarette lighter. "You can turn off your flashlight now. We need to save the batteries."

A bit reluctant to lessen his light, Jonathon looked around the tiny chamber before shutting off the flashlight. When Carlos did the same thing, only the flickering light of the candle danced on the tunnel walls.

Undisturbed by the dim light, Carlos extracted two rolls from the bag and tossed them to the American. "Eat and then we will sleep for a few hours."

Grateful for food and a distraction from the encroaching darkness, Jonathon caught his sparse meal. "I am hungry." He tore a bite from his roll, enjoying the soft inside and chewy crust. He stretched out his tired legs. "How far do you think we traveled today?"

"Just over eleven kilometers."

The distance surprised Jonathon. "That's about seven miles. No wonder I'm tired."

"For your first day that is good but Lima is a long way from here. As you regain your strength we will be able to go faster and farther." Carlos settled onto the earth across the chamber from Jonathon and took a bite of his roll.

"I sure hope you really do know where we're going and we're not really lost." Swallowing the first bite, Jonathon hungrily took another one.

"We are not. Trust me."

"I'll try, but I still don't like this place."

Carlos smiled. "I understand. For what you have survived, you are doing very well."

"I never did get used to it down here; I hated the darkness, always wondering what was out there. Worse, I hated waking up and feeling things crawling on my face or my hair."

"Ah, the *bichos*."

"Yeah, well I hated the bugs."

"Did you ever see them?"

"I didn't want to."

Carlos laughed and quickly blew out the candle.

"Hey," Jonathon burst. "What are doing?"

He clicked on his flashlight but Carlos reached for his wrist. "Turn it off. I want to show you the bugs." Jonathon hesitated. "Trust me," Carlos said.

Jonathon felt the man's quiet calmness and turned off the light. The cave fell into darkness. "Now just wait, hold still," Carlos instructed. "The bugs will come."

He groaned. "I know they will, and I really don't want them to, Carlos."

"You will be fine. Trust me."

After a few minutes Jonathon felt the all too familiar return of bugs, crawling on his arms and neck. He swiped at them, but Carlos stopped him. "You can't see them if you squish them. Just wait a minute more."

Jonathon closed his eyes and gritted his teeth, trying to ignore the sensation of movement. He could hear a hint of laughter in Carlos's voice. "Okay, now. Turn on your flashlight."

He didn't have to ask twice. Jonathon clicked on his beam and roared in horror. Jumping from the floor, he swatted the insects from his body then stopped. As they fell to the stone floor he peered closer at them. The bright light of his flashlight revealed a world of cave crickets and beetles. Insects with bodies of earthy brown or rich orange lived alongside pale yellow creatures. White millipedes scurried across the floor and away from the light. Long-legged spiders slowly worked their way across the cave walls and thin, transparent webs glistened high against the stone ceiling. It wasn't desolate in the underground world, it was thriving.

"Are they poisonous?" he breathed

"Some yes, but most no more than any other insect."

"I had no idea there was a world like this underground." He turned to Carlos and smiled. "I still don't like it, but it is amazing."

"We will leave a candle burning tonight while we sleep, if you would like. That will help keep the *bichos* away."

Looking around him at the rough tunnel walls, Jonathon nodded. "I would like that. I don't want bugs climbing on me." Glancing down the darkened tunnel he quietly hoped the light would keep other things away too.

Relighting the candle, they finished their rolls then Carlos waited until Jonathon fell into an exhausted sleep. Closing his own eyes, the Peruvian lay down and slipped quickly into the world of dreams. He would keep his word to Jonathon and allow the candle to burn while they slept.

The candle flame flickered and danced on its wick. Its light created a small, fluttering circle of vision. The tiny flame slowly descended the wick, melting the candle's wax until the weak light sputtered and danced just above the tunnel floor, trying to stay alive. When the last bit of wick could not longer feed the hungry fire, the candle went out, and the cave returned to its world of darkness.

For a long time only the insects moved in the sightless world. Then, from deeper in the tunnels, something else moved. Something large.

A sound passed through the labyrinth, a shuffle, moving along the subterranean passageway. The soft noise registered in Jonathon's unconsciousness. He frowned in his sleep.

A bug moved across Jonathon's face, and his hand brushed it away. From the tunnel depths, the sound of movement drew nearer, passing through the underground corridor. On the cold earth, Jonathon's mind began to return to the conscious world. Something didn't seem right. He shifted on the ground just as the sounds of advancement registered in his brain. Instantly his body surged awake, his heart pounding. Something large was approaching through the tunnels.

The candle, long dead and cold, left the chamber cloaked in blackness. Jonathon blinked his eyes, trying to remember where he was, what was happening. Beside him came the rhythmic sound of Carlos's deep breathing then, from the tunnel depths, Jonathon heard the distinct passage of footsteps. Someone was moving through the tunnels toward them!

Reaching through the darkness, Jonathon found Carlos's arm. "Carlos, wake up." The man moved but did not wake. The noise in the tunnel drew closer. Jonathon shook Carlos harder. "Carlos!" he hissed, "Wake up. Someone's coming!"

He heard Carlos give a soft moan and return to wakefulness. Before the man could speak, Jonathon ordered him to silence. "Ssh. Listen," he whispered.

Carlos did then pushed himself up into a sitting position.

"What is that?" the teenager asked under his breath.

"I do not know."

"These are your tunnels, and you don't know!" In the dark, Jonathon also moved into a sitting position as the movement continued to approach, steady and unerring.

Carlos turned his head toward the sound. "It's coming from a minor tunnel," he whispered. "No one is supposed to be in there."

"So who is?"

"I do not know! Where is the flashlight?" Carlos felt in the darkness for the flashlight then the chamber filled with light. He pointed the beam down the minor tunnel. "Who's there?" he called.

Jonathon groaned. "Oh, that's great! Just call out and announce we're here."

"¡Hola! ¿Qué tal?" From the recesses of the minor tunnel came a voice and a light, growing brighter until a man stepped into the chamber, holding a flashlight.

Carlos exhaled and lowered his beam. "Pedro, it's you. What are you doing in that tunnel?"

The man's face was somber. "I was being watched. It is the only way I could reach you."

Stunned, Jonathon looked between the two men. "You know him?" he asked Carlos.

"*Sí.*" Carlos leaned his back against the wall, obviously relieved. He shook his head at the new man. "Were you followed?"

Pedro looked behind him. "I hope not."

"Me, too. That would mean a lot of trouble."

Worried, Jonathon looked at his friend. "Followed? By who? What kind of trouble?"

Carlos cleared his throat. "You do not need to know. All you need to understand is that this is Pedro. He's here to help us. He's a runner, just like me."

Nervous, Jonathon looked back at the new man while he questioned Carlos. "What's a runner?"

Sighing, Carlos explained. "Anciently, whenever the Inca emperor needed to send a message, he used trained Inca Runners over the Inca Highway."

"I know that. They were situated at every mile."

"*Sí.* Because they only had to run for a mile, they were able to go at top speed. If the king wanted seafood for dinner he just sent out a message through the runners and fresh fish from the coast would be delivered to him in Machu Picchu in just a couple of days."

"That's some pretty fast running."

"It worked because each runner was assigned his own section of path. He knew it well—where to slow up and where he could run the fastest."

Jonathon motioned to Pedro. "But this is not the Inca Highway, and I didn't order fish for dinner. What does that have to do with him?"

"*Bastante*—plenty. What the world doesn't know is that the Inca kings also used the same idea *underground* with tunnel runners. Inca runners carried fish but tunnel runners carried confidential messages and secret military or political communications. They even helped guide soldiers through these tunnels into position against an enemy. In fact, these tunnels and trained tunnel runners were used for two centuries before the Spaniards even arrived. When the Incas needed to flee and not be found, the tunnels were their answer."

In the semi-light, Carlos smiled. "My father was an Inca tunnel runner down here like his father. Now the honor falls to me. It is a heritage passed down from father to son. Even now my own son is learning the tunnels in our part of the mountains."

More surprised flowed into Jonathon's mind. "You're Inca? But I thought the entire Inca Empire was lost."

The smile on Carlos' face grew. "We are not lost, just hidden." He motioned toward Pedro. "He is also full-blooded Inca. We are both tunnel runners and take pride in our calling. Although I know my area well, even with the special markings, I could not easily take you to Lima without help. That is why other tunnel runners will help us. They know their portions well. Each will guide us through their section and to the next runner."

The complexity of the tunnel system amazed Jonathon. "So why didn't I see or hear any runners down in the tunnels when I was lost?"

"Because we were not in the tunnels. We do not go into them unless we have a reason. Until there is a purpose, the tunnels stay silent. The fewer trips we make down here, the safer it is for everyone." He nodded. "But now we have a reason—to take you to Lima."

Carlos motioned to the walls around him. "These tunnels were hand-carved by the Incas centuries ago, and it is the job of all remaining Incas to protect what their forefathers labored so hard to create." With pride obvious in his face, Carlos spoke in ancient Quechua then translated his words for Jonathon. "I am descended from Ixtalpal. He ran these very tunnels for the Emperor Atahualpa."

"Isn't that the king the Spaniards killed?"

"Sí. After his death, The Spaniards appointed Atahualpa's younger brother to be king. They thought they could control Tupac but he was smarter than they thought. Even though Tupac contracted smallpox from the Spaniards and died shortly after he was crowned, he had already sent a secret message to all the tunnel runners to lead the people to safety away from the Spaniards."

Sorrow crossed Carlos's face. "A few of the Incas did not choose to leave. They thought they could trust the Spaniards, but my forefather honored Tupac's call to lead the Inca people through his section. He brought his wife and children, the king's family, and all the other refugees safely through his portion of the tunnels. They gave up everything they had to be free. They left their homes, their possessions, and only took with them their beloved mum—" Carlos stopped abruptly.

Jonathon sat forward, finishing the statement for Carlos, "Their beloved mummies. That's what you were going to say, isn't it? They only carried their beloved mummies into these tunnels."

"I have said too much."

"No you haven't. That's the problem. No one wants to talk about them, but I know the mummies are still down here. I found them! I found a room full of mummies and gold. And you know they're down here, too. That's what that marking was above the tunnel. You know it's the tunnel that leads to the mummies and all that gold."

Carlos and the other runner exchanged looks. Turning back to the teenager, Carlos frowned. "Maybe it is *you* who talks too much."

"Tell me about the mummies, Carlos. Why are they down here? Why are they with all that gold?"

Carlos climbed to his feet. "You ask too many questions."

Not hesitating, Jonathon also rose to his feet. "And you don't answer enough. Every time I mention mummies, someone tries to change the subject. It's like you're afraid of them." Carlos did not respond. With his heart pounding inside him, Jonathon stepped in front of him and looked at the runner. "You *are* afraid of them."

A curse erupted from Carlos, and he faced Jonathon, his eyes flashing. "*Do not suppose you know what I fear! You do not understand. Do not disturb what has slept for six hundred years! If you do, people will die!*"

The power of his comment rocked Jonathon, and for a long moment he could only stare at Carlos. In the eerie glow of the flashlights, no one spoke.

✦   ✦   ✦

Aided by their new guide, Jonathon and Carlos continued their journey through the tunnels. Every two or three days the runners would change. As one finished his section, he would leave, and a new runner would mysteriously appear through the dark to lead them through the next part. Each runner knew exactly where to go and what to do next. Always there were fresh batteries, candles, and food waiting for them along the way, and Jonathon grew to suspect they had transported many things through the tunnels before—just not an American.

While the runners varied in age, Jonathon guessed most of them to be near Carlos's age, in their mid-twenties. A few appeared older. They were all athletic, thin, and hard like greyhounds. None appeared rich, and he wondered about their lives outside the tunnels. Many wore old sweaters and stained trousers with worn shoes and lined faces. Yet they did not seem to complain about life.

Though Jonathon could tell the runners spoke Spanish, they preferred to speak to Carlos in Quechua. Often he caught them watching him as if he were an intruder in their home, and he suspected they were honoring a request to help, nothing more. Jonathon got the impression that they did not want him in their tunnels; worse, that they did not trust him.

After more than a week of traveling in the hidden world, a new runner entered the tunnel, drained and fatigued, dirt streaking his face and clothes. Carlos climbed to his feet, concern filling his voice. "What happened?"

The runner didn't answer, he just peered at Jonathon. "Is this the American?" Unsure of what he saw in the new man's expression, Jonathon nodded. The runner stared at him for a moment, then he turned to Carlos and made his announcement. "The tunnel is blocked by a landslide. We cannot get through. We will have to go on top."

Stunned, Jonathon stood. "Why didn't we just do that before?"

The runner returned his gaze to Jonathon, his face expressionless. "Terrorists are searching for you. They want to kill you." He turned to Carlos. "They believe he is trying to get to Lima and have people watching the roads."

Carlos groaned and rubbed his hand through his hair in frustration. "*Aye*—this is not good. Can we get through the tunnel some other way, take a minor tunnel?"

"At this point, no. The landslide is too large."

"Can we dig through?"

"If you want to take a month or more."

With a sigh of defeat, Carlos looked at Jonathon. Nervousness surged inside Jonathon. His heart pounded, and he shook his head. Suddenly he didn't want to go up on top. This black, horrifying maze now felt like his cocoon of safety. If he was on top, the terrorists would find him, but he also wasn't sure the new runner was telling the truth. He paced the tunnel in frustration, his mind churning every possibility. Finally he turned back to his friend. "Carlos, can I talk to you?"

Nodding, Carlos retrieved a flashlight and the pair entered the privacy of one of the marked tunnels. Traveling it for a distance, Carlos stopped and then turned back. "I know you're worried, and you should be. If the terrorists find you again, you will not get away."

Jonathon spoke in low whispers. "What if this is a setup? What if he is taking me on top to hand me over to the terrorists?"

"You can trust him."

"I don't even know him."

"You don't have to know him. All you need to know is that he is an Inca tunnel runner. That is enough."

"Maybe for you!"

"If he is an Inca tunnel runner he is trustworthy."

"You can't say that! None of the runners want me down here, and you know that."

Standing in the quiet tunnel Carlos took a deep breath. "Jonathon, regardless, we are not going to let the terrorists find you."

"Why should I believe you? They could be paying him to set me up."

For a long time Carlos stared at the floor. His features showed the inner battle that played through his mind. Finally he lifted his gaze back to Jonathon. "He won't turn you over to the terrorists precisely because you are down here. You've seen too much."

Stunned, Jonathon fought for a response, his voice quiet. "And you don't want the terrorists to find out about them."

Carlos did not respond.

"You aren't trying to help me stay away from the terrorists to protect me," Jonathon hissed. "All this time you've been hiding me to protect your stupid tunnels from the terrorists."

Carlos looked down the passage toward the other runner. "Jonathon, we will protect you from the terrorists and we will return you to your father. That is our promise, but do not question our motives. Right now there are things in this tunnel you do not understand and things more terrifying than what's waiting up on top. So I guess you need to decide whether to stay here and try to get to Lima on your own or trust us."

"I don't have much of a choice, do I?"

Carlos's eyes stayed calm. "You are wrong, Jonathon. Men always have a choice, even if they do not like them."

◆   ◆   ◆

Hiding under the dark and oily floorboard of a forty-year-old truck, Jonathon fought the sickness brought on by engine heat, fumes, rutted roads, and not being able to see where he was going.

A sudden pounding from above rapped the boards as Carlos stomped the floor of the truck with his foot. "There are armed men standing in the road." Carlos called over the growl of the truck. "They are probably terrorists. Stay still. Do not make a sound. They have blocked the road, and we will have to stop."

Slowly the ancient truck rumbled to a halt. In the hidden floor compartment behind the torn seat, Jonathon closed his eyes and held his breath. Right now he didn't fear the secrets he felt sure Carlos was keeping from him. He feared being discovered by the terrorists.

The driver unrolled his window. From beneath the floor boards, Jonathon could hear angry words being spoken outside. They were searching for an American boy who robbed a family store, stabbed the son, and attacked the wife.

In the passenger seat, Carlos whistled at the charges. "That is a serious story. Are the police looking for him?"

"The police are afraid to get involved with the Americans but we are not. We want that boy and believe he is trying to get to Lima." The voice was harsh. "What are you carrying in the back of your truck?"

"Squash, for market."

"He may have climbed up and be hiding among the squash. I think we will search."

"Go right ahead."

Jonathon heard a truck door open, and Carlos climbed out into the cold mountain night. "In fact, I will help. I do not want a criminal hiding in my squash."

The other door opened and Jonathon heard a man roughly order the driver out of the truck. "Get out while I search the cab."

The truck rocked. From under the floorboards, Jonathon heard the sound of squash being tossed and moved around in the truck bed. A sharper sound, closer to him, caused Jonathon to jump. The truck's bench seat had been released from its latch and pushed forward. It *thumped* against the dashboard and the man began to search through the blankets, ponchos, and discarded trash that filled the space covering the hidden compartment. Curled up in the tiny compartment,

Jonathon prayed the man would not notice the false floor.

A loud *crack* reverberated above Jonathon's head, followed by another one. The garbage now removed, the man slammed the butt of his rifle onto the floorboards, testing it for hidden places. Each crashing blow of the rifle butt shook the cab, and Jonathon worried the rotted boards would shatter.

"No one's in the cab," the man announced. He didn't return the seat, merely withdrew from the cab.

Convinced no one hid inside the truck or among the squash, the men left to search another vehicle. With a lurch and grinding of gears the truck moved back onto the rutted road, its American cargo still hidden in a floor compartment.

Half an hour later, the truck pulled over. This time Carlos flipped the seat forward and released the lock on the hidden compartment. Opening it up, he peered down at Jonathon, concern showing on his face. "Are you okay?"

Jonathon coughed on a lung full of diesel fumes and dust. "Yes. That was close." Shaking his head in protest, Jonathon spoke to Carlos and the driver, wanting them to know the truth. "I didn't do what they said. It's a lie."

"I know." Carlos offered his hand, helping Jonathon climb out of the tiny holding box.

"So why are they still looking for me?"

Carlos and the runner exchanged private glances. With a frown, Carlos looked at Jonathon. "You are money in the bank if they find you and a liability if they do not. You have seen their faces and their meeting place, so they search." He handed Jonathon a peeled chirimoya fruit. "Eat this. It will clean the fumes from your throat."

Jonathon took a large bite of the soft, white fruit. Its juicy tang soothed the rawness left by the diesel fumes. Grateful, he took another bite.

"Now we need to get you back into the tunnels."

The *chirimoya* lodged in Jonathon's throat. Didn't Carlos say there was something more terrifying inside the tunnels than up on top? "Why do we have to go back inside the tunnels? Why can't we just go straight through to Lima in this truck?"

"Because the terrorists will find you on top, Jonathon."

"I can hide again."

A deep sigh escaped Carlos. "You are naïve if you think those were the only terrorists. The mountains have many eyes, Jonathon. More than you realize. We were lucky they did not find you this time. If they do find you, your luck will end and so will your life. We must keep you hidden in the tunnels as long as we can."

SIXTEEN

ENFOLDED DEEP in the mountain tunnels, Jonathon found himself enjoying the journey—and his companion. Traveling through the hidden corridors, Carlos would often stop him and the other runner to show the American some of the treasures of his carved world. He pointed out aqueducts that channeled fresh, cold water. He showed tiny ventilation holes drilled through solid rock that allowed the air to circulate below the surface. He also told Jonathon of the history ensconced in the tunnels, sharing with him stories of the lost Inca nation and teaching him much of the language. Subterranean miles melted away, and Jonathon grew fond of the restaurant owner. Traveling the corridors with Carlos's quick laugh and friendship became the easy part.

Jonathon didn't like waiting. He grew tense when they had to stop inside the labyrinth and wait for a new runner to arrive. He always felt unsure of what lay ahead or behind, unsure of the new runner or if their guide would even appear. It could take hours, even a day or more, for a new runner—a new *pusaq*—to arrive, and Jonathon didn't like those waits. He didn't like wondering if he would find himself trapped under the Andes and die down here.

"Don't these tunnels ever scare you?" Jonathon asked.

"*De vez en cuando.* Sometimes." Resting across the tunnel, his back propped against the cold stone sides, Carlos looked at him. A candle shimmered close beside him. "Do they scare you?"

"I almost died down here; I found someone who did. What do you think?"

Carlos nodded. "I think you are very brave to return to the place that almost killed you. Not many could."

Jonathon picked at a rock, contemplating. "Have you ever found a dead body down here?"

Carlos shifted against the wall, moving into a more comfortable position and closed his eyes. "No."

"Has anyone else?"

"My father did years ago, when he was just a young runner."

"Where?"

"In a minor tunnel."

"What did he do?"

"He left him there. To remove the body from the tunnels would risk being discovered. Maybe you found the same body he did."

"Or another one." For a silent moment, Jonathon pushed small stones into designs on the floor. "Are you ever worried you will find a dead body?"

This time Carlos chuckled. "I was right when we first met—you do ask a lot of questions! *Sí*, all tunnel runners know they could find a dead body, but that does not frighten us."

"Why not?"

"A dead body cannot hurt you."

"Do you think there are many down here?"

Opening his eyes, Carlos smiled. "Obviously you want to talk, not rest." He agreed to visit. "I do not know if there are other dead bodies down here. There are rumors of people falling into the tunnels and disappearing, but that does not happen very often."

Jonathon played with a broken pebble, drawing courage for his next words. "But what about the mummies, don't they frighten you?"

For a long time Carlos held his silence. He looked at Jonathon. "Jonathon, why do you keep asking about the mummies?"

"Because I've seen them. I know they are here, but you and Severino and Delia won't talk about them. It's like you're afraid of them, or something."

Leveling his gaze at Jonathon, Carlos spoke quietly. "I am more afraid of other things down here."

The comment lifted Jonathon's gaze. "Like what?"

"Like you."

"Me?" The words shocked Jonathon.

Carlos inhaled deeply and sat forward, resting his forearms on his knees. He shook his head, clearing his mind and emotions for what he needed to say. "Jonathon, I am going to be honest with you and I hope you will respect that honesty. Yes, the mummies do exist. They are down here, but they do not have a curse on them. They are my ancestors, and we do not fear them. Instead, we fear *for* them. That is why the other runners worry about you. You are what frightens us the most. We are worried *you* may become the mummies' curse."

"How can I curse the mummies?"

Carlos closed his eyes, struggling within himself. He pressed his hands against his temples. "For six hundred years we have guarded the remains of our ancestors. We have protected and cared for them here, in these tunnels. And during all those centuries we have kept them hidden from looters and those who want to profit from them. We have protected them from archaeologists and scientists who would parade them before the world or examine them in back rooms. And we have protected them from the terrorists who would sell them to fund their terror. But now we feel we have to protect them from you even as we keep our promise to protect you."

"I don't understand."

"You have discovered the mummies, and that knowledge jeopardizes our ancestors and the sanctity of their final resting place." Carlos paused, deep in thought. "When Severino and Delia found you, you were in a sacred chamber filled with the mummies and the Inca treasure of their ancestors. They knew the room was there because it is Delia's job to care for those mummies. Like tunnel runners, the call to care for the mummies is passed down from mother to chosen daughter. Delia has been called and trained to care for the ancestors of her family."

Jonathon grew quiet, listening to the words Carlos spoke. The Peruvian stared at his calloused hands. "Delia and Severino risked a great deal to save your life. They knew what you had seen and they knew the risk your knowledge carried. They could have dragged you off into a minor tunnel somewhere and left you to die—no one would have ever known, and you would never have been found. You should be grateful they chose to let you live." His words sunk deep into Jonathon's mind. Jonathon had not thought of that.

Sadness touched Carlos's voice as he continued. "It is because of *ama hap'a* that they honored the life of a stranger—your life. I only hope, as you hear what I am about to say, you will return that honor. Severino risked his life and his ancestors to take you home and then keep you out of sight of the terrorists."

"And I walked right into the middle of them."

"Yes, you did. But Severino again risked his life to free you from them. He knew what the terrorists were planning to do with you. They were taking you to a guarded location that night where they were going to torture you and video tape it, to frighten your parents and pain the world into meeting their demands."

Jonathon's stomach heaved. Carlos rubbed his eyes, fatigued. "Severino didn't want that to happen. But he also knew there was more at stake that night than your life, Jonathon. There still is."

"What do you mean?"

"If during your hours of torture you had said anything about the gold or these mummies for any reason . . . in your fear or pain or in an attempt to buy your freedom . . . they would have forgotten a ransom from your family. They would have brutally extracted all the information they could from you, slit your throat by dawn, and ravaged these tunnels by noon. They have done it before, and they will do it again."

Jonathon ran both his hands down his face, churning Carlos's words through his mind again and again. "You are trying to protect the mummies."

Carlos met Jonathon's gaze. "We are trying to protect the people. The terrorists want what these tunnels hold. They have heard the legends, and they are searching for them. Why do you think they stay in these mountains? If they find these tunnels, the mummies will be sold on the black market, and the gold will be used to buy more weapons. The terrorists will be able to finance their reign of death and terror for decades to come, and people all across Peru, even the world, will die. Can you understand why we cannot let you be found by the terrorists? Why the knowledge you carry frightens us?"

Jonathon did not respond; he didn't know how.

Carlos continued to speak. "But it is not just the terrorists who could destroy and take everything from these tunnels. We worry how you will use the knowledge you now possess once you are safely in Lima, away from the terrorists. You have too much knowledge for us not to feel the risk."

"I wouldn't take anything, Carlos."

"No, but your knowledge could allow others to do just that."

Jonathon fingered the stones on the earth. "Carlos, what am I supposed to tell people?"

"I suppose you need to decide if knowledge is only valuable when shared with others."

"No—personal knowledge that is kept personal is also valuable, but why can't this knowledge be shared and used to *help* people?"

"What do you mean?"

"Think about it, Carlos. You could use some of the gold for your children, to pay for their education and give them a better life. People like Delia and Severino could have a home with a real floor and running water, a toilet, a telephone . . . ."

At his words, Carlos lowered his head, shaking it with disagreement. Desperate for approval, Jonathon sat forward. "Carlos, I've seen the lives your people live. You and the other tunnel runners don't possess much; Delia and Severino live in poverty. Why don't you just use some of the riches here to help? Your ancestors are dead. They don't need it, and you do. You can't possibly believe they would actually want you living like this. They would *give* you the gold if they knew."

The soft chuckle that shook Carlos's shoulders surprised Jonathon. He spoke through his laughter. "Your ideas are sincere, but you do not understand the Inca way."

"What is the Inca way?"

"We believe each person must earn his own way in life, not have it given to him. To take something that does not belong to you is stealing. To be given gold you have not earned is welfare. I know that belief is difficult for many in this world to accept. Many these days are not concerned with gaining a heritage, they only want to be given an inheritance. Yet there are many things far more important than gold. Honor is one of them. Remember, *ama qella*—work hard."

Frustration fueled Jonathon's words. "Oh, come on! Don't tell me you're living on dirt floors because of honor or because you are working hard to earn your own possessions in life!"

He cocked an eyebrow at Jonathon. "Maybe we are."

"That's stupid!"

"Is it? Then tell me, Jonathon—if we decided to go with your plan, where could we spend the lost Inca gold, at the local bakery? Do you think they have change for ancient coins?"

The question eased a smile from Jonathon. "No, I guess not. I hadn't thought of that, but you could take it to a bank or gold dealer."

"My question was serious, Jonathon. No matter where you take it, once that gold hits the streets *anywhere* it will start a barrage of questions. People will want to know where we got it. The gold coins will be snatched up by museums and collectors and locked away in vaults. Only a few trinkets would ever be seen by the public, and none of it will be used by those who need help the most. Even if we decided to melt down the gold, there would be many questions about where it came from. That gold—no matter how we used it—would put the mummies at risk, the last link to our forefathers would be threatened, and none of our people would be helped."

The truth of his information sobered Jonathon. "So, that means you're stuck being poor."

A gentle smile grew across Carlos's face. "No. We are rich. That is what you need to understand. We do not *want* the gold. We may not have many things, but we have our heritage and our honor. *Ama llulla.* We are being true to ourselves. We are descended from the greatest empire in the world, and we are proud of that! We will honor our family by keeping *our* honor and guarding theirs."

For a moment Carlos fell silent, his mind deep in thought. When he spoke again, Jonathon saw deep emotion on his face. "Jonathon, I am going to talk to you from the heart of an Inca and I hope you will listen with your heart. There is more in these tunnels than mummies and gold. There is also *Ayaq.* It means soul or spirit. These tunnels posses the soul and spirit of our heritage. The room where Delia and Severino found you belongs to their ancestors. There Delia cares for their remains and their *ayaq.* But Jonathon, the room you found is not the only one. There are other rooms just like that throughout these mountains, guarded by other Inca families. My family has such a room, and there are countless more. These rooms are important to us. We can go there when we have a problem or a concern. We can pray for guidance. There, among the ancestors we still love, their *ayaq* can fill us with peace and help us better live the Inca ways. That is what we are protecting in these tunnels. It is more than gold or mummies. It is a peace the world does not understand. It is the peace of family."

"So you are saying *ayaq*, the soul of your family, is the most important thing down here?"

"Exactly."

For a long time, Jonathon studied his friend then he gave a soft answer, his voice carrying his awe. "Most people think gold and money is what their families need most, but your people don't believe that. The famed Inca gold is not lost. You know where every piece is. You just value something more."

A full smile settled on Carlos's features, and he nodded with approval. "Now you understand the wealth of the Inca. Family is our most priceless possession." Holding Jonathon's gaze, Carlos nodded. "But I think you already know about *ayaq*. I think you already know family is worth every sacrifice."

Carlos rose to his feet and left Jonathon to think about all he had learned. Turning, the Peruvian walked a short ways into the darkness and there closed his eyes in agony. In over six-hundred years no one had ever been allowed to walk from these tunnels with the secrets of the Incas. Despite Jonathon's understanding, he still knew too much.

Pain filled Carlos. The plan had already been activated. Even now the runners were moving a message along *outside* the mountains. A stranger was passing through their tunnels and every runner, including Carlos, knew what needed to be done in the canyon above Lima. Jonathon couldn't leave the mountain with this much information. His knowledge had to stay lost with the mummies.

❖   ❖   ❖

As Carlos and Jonathon descended through the hard granite cliffs, the carved shafts carried warm, damper air. In some places, water lay in stagnant puddles on the passage floor and moss grew on some of the rocks. The tunnels paralleled a river that ran through the outer canyon and emptied into the Pacific. They were approaching the canyon above Lima. Because of the rugged river, which carved a deep channel through the canyon, they would need to make one last trip outside.

❖   ❖   ❖

Dressed in a heavy sweater, knitted cap, and long scarf, Jonathon fought the sinking feeling in his stomach. This time he knew leaving the tunnels wasn't good. He felt danger. Jonathon shifted his gaze to

Carlos, silently pleading with the man to change their plan. They were to meet a driver at a crowded marketplace, who would shuttle them through the canyon to the next portion of the tunnels.

Carlos avoided his gaze and led Jonathon into the open-air market.

Even at night, the market remained noisy and crowded. Most of the produce and animal vendors had gone home. Now a new group of vendors appeared to sell their wares in the brisk night air. They stacked sweaters and folded blankets on the ground. Carts with propane burners sent the smell of cooking food into the night. Loud music blared, alcohol poured free, and people pressed everywhere.

With his face hidden beneath the scarf and his hair covered by the woven cap, Jonathon reluctantly followed Carlos into the crowd. Though much of his mother's heritage showed in his features, he had inherited his father's eyes. Somewhere, in this throng of people, were terrorists searching for an American teenager with *ojos tostados*—light brown eyes.

The pair passed through food vendors, moving to the place where drivers cried out the destination of their vehicles. "Lima! Lima! Two passengers! Two passengers needed for Lima."

"La Oroya, three! Three people for La Oroya."

"San Pedro de Cajas! San Pedro de Cajas!"

The calls of drivers filled the night air. They waved their hands at Jonathon and Carlos, holding up fingers to designate how many riders they could take. One driver stepped directly in front of Jonathon, "Tarma," he called, holding up two fingers. Looking down, Jonathon saw the man's feet just in time to avoid a collision. Startled, he glanced up and his gaze locked with the man.

The driver hesitated then returned to his pitch. "Two for Tarma." Jonathon waved him away, and relief filled him as the driver stepped away and continued his call, seeking other passengers. "Tarma, Tarma, Tarma! Two for Tarma!" Pulling the scarf tighter around his face, Jonathon moved after Carlos. He didn't see the Tarma driver turn to watch, his eyes tracing Jonathon's path. Then the driver left his car and disappeared into the crowd.

They crossed through the marketplace to where men were loading trucks with the day's purchases. Carlos sent a smile toward a giant man. "Ruiz, *cómo estas*? How are you?"

Turning from a massive truck, the man laughed out loud. "Carlos, *mi amigo*! It is good to see you!" The man's large arms enfolded the smaller man, and he lifted Carlos off the ground in an enthusiastic hug. Setting him down, Ruiz wrapped his arm all the way around Carlos's shoulder and gave him a rattling squeeze from the side. "My friend, I believe you get smaller every time we meet."

"And you get bigger."

Ruiz gave a hearty laugh and patted his stomach. "It is my wife. I keep telling you she is the best cook in the area."

"And that is a very large area you are getting there, my friend."

Throwing back his head, Ruiz laughed into the night sky. "Oh, it is good to see you." When he finished his laughter, and with eyes still twinkling, Ruiz examined the quiet youth swathed in concealing clothes. "I see Carlos brought help. That is good. I'm Ruiz. I need to get this load of potatoes onto the back of my truck and down the canyon." He jerked his head toward the covered vehicle. "Grab a bag and start loading."

Carlos gave Jonathon a nod of approval. Still uncertain, Jonathon picked up a sack of potatoes and hefted the forty-pound weight to his shoulder. Carlos nodded for him to follow Ruiz. Taking a breath, Jonathon followed the giant man up a ramp and into the back of the vehicle.

Ruiz pointed across the bed of the truck. "Just set the bags right there. We have lots to load, so keep moving."

Jonathon knotted his scarf tight against his face to keep his features from showing then did as he was told, going down the ramp to retrieve a second bag. He heard the large man walk down the wooden ramp behind him.

From the pile of bagged potatoes, Ruiz lifted two sacks onto his shoulders and followed Jonathon into the truck. This time his voice came quieter, "When we tell you to, crawl under that tarp over there." Ruiz nodded to a tarp at the front of the truck bed. "We will keep loading potatoes and set them in front of you. With these many bags to load, the people will eventually lose track of who is going in and out. They will not notice when you have disappeared."

By this time Carlos carried a bag into the canvas-enclosed truck. "We will tell you when it is safe to get under the tarp." His smile grew. "Until then, keep stacking the potatoes." He dumped his bag on top of some others and headed down the ramp for more.

Jonathon's stomach churned with nervousness. He didn't want to go under the tarp or out into the marketplace for more potatoes. Everything told him danger lurked close. He wondered about the

Tarma driver. Exhaling for control, he looked at Ruiz, then followed Carlos back to the potatoes.

Up and down the ramp the three of them moved, lifting bags and carrying them into the truck. It seemed the loading would never end. Finally Carlos nodded at Jonathon. It was time.

Hoisting a sack onto his shoulders, Jonathon walked up the truck dropped the potatoes with the others. For a moment he stood with eyes closed for courage. He didn't like anything about this night. He breathed a silent prayer and then opened his eyes and forced himself to crawl under the tarp.

A few seconds later, Carlos entered the back of the truck with his sack. This he placed in front of the tarp and disappeared down the ramp. Continuing the routine, Ruiz and Carlos carried more potatoes into the bed. For fifteen minutes the rhythm of their footfalls and the sound of potatoes being stacked in front of the tarp filled the truck with a sense of routine, yet Jonathon's fears never calmed.

Carlos entered the truck and stacked more potatoes. He spoke softly to Jonathon. "I am going to get us some food."

Jonathon's heart began to hammer. It was wrong for Carlos to leave. "No," he quietly protested. "I'm not hungry."

"It is for later. With all the terrorists watching, it may be a while before the new runner can meet us in the tunnels."

"Carlos—"

"I will be right back. Ruiz is still here, loading." Carlos turned and disappeared down the ramp.

The loading continued as only Ruiz carried bags of potatoes into the truck. The truck rocked with his movements. Beneath the tarp, Jonathon's heart pounded wildly. They weren't supposed to be here! This place held danger. Something was wrong. He tried to ignore Ruiz's movements but he couldn't. Everything inside him shouted a warning, but he didn't understand any of it . . . the where, when, or who. He just knew something was not right.

A few minutes later the truck grew silent.

Stillness.

Behind the tarp and potatoes, Jonathon turned his head and listened. Nothing moved inside the truck. As the quiet continued, his fear increased. He didn't know if he should climb out from beneath the tarp.

Suddenly the entire truck shook as Ruiz climbed the ramp, his angry voice arguing with someone. Jonathon froze in fear. The new man wasn't Carlos.

"I tell you, I do not know who was helping me load! I never asked his name. He just showed up, needed a little money, so I let him help. He disappeared after a couple of bags. I didn't even pay him, which is fine with me! Do you see him anywhere?"

A harsh new voice answered. "No, but the driver to Tarma said he was here, he said he saw a kid with light brown eyes. The American has light brown eyes."

Ruiz dropped two bags of potatoes, shaking the entire truck with his action. "Well, I did not look at his eyes, and I did not see which way he walked."

"You should pay more attention to your help. You are lucky he did not rob you. The American youth is dangerous. He stabbed a shop-keeper in the mountains and attacked his wife."

Ruiz snorted. "Then get the authorities to help you find him and leave me alone."

"The police will do nothing. We want that boy and believe he is trying to get to Lima."

Raising his voice in anger, Ruiz challenged the man. "Then you'd better head to Lima and move out of my way unless you want to help. I have potatoes to load."

The man swore and left the bed of the truck, followed closely by Ruiz's heavy steps. A minute later, Ruiz returned, alone, carrying more potatoes. To everyone watching, he appeared as a man intent on loading his truck. "We have trouble." Ruiz's voice came soft as he set down the potatoes. "Some men have Carlos and now they search for you. They are terrorists." Ruiz turned and started to move for the ramp.

From behind the tarp, Jonathon's mind exploded. Now he knew why he felt fear—not for himself but for his friend. Scrambling for freedom, his quiet voice called after Ruiz. "Wait!" The large man turned as Jonathon climbed from his hiding place. "They have Carlos? Where?"

"Right now they have him at a table at the *cantina*—the bar. I think they are waiting for someone else to come." Ruiz's voice low-ered. "You get behind there. I told you, they are looking for you! We will get you to Lima, but you *must* stay hidden."

"We can't leave Carlos!"

Troubled emotion filled Ruiz's eyes. "For now Carlos is safe. He is at an outdoor restaurant. They will not harm him there. But if they find you, they will take both of you away from here and neither one of you will survive. You must stay hidden."

"What if they don't find me? Will they let Carlos go?"

Ruiz closed his eyes as he struggled. He shook his head. "No. They know he was traveling with you. They will not let him go. Carlos is a dead man."

The words horrified Jonathon. "We can't leave him! Not like this." He climbed through the potato bags, balancing on the uneven terrain until he dropped to the bed of the truck. He came to stand by Ruiz in the dark hold, his scarf hanging down over his shoulders, his face exposed. "Where is he? Where's the bar? Can you see him?"

A nod directed Jonathon's gaze over the nighttime crowd to an outdoor cafe. "He is there, at the table under the tree. Three men intercepted him when he went to get some food. Two stayed with Carlos at the table, and the third one was just here, searching for you, but I sent him away."

"I know. I heard. Thanks."

In the truck, the two stood side by side, staring across the night. They could see Carlos at the distant table, his hands in front of him, waiting.

Swallowing the lump of agony that filled him, Jonathon shook his head. He couldn't leave Carlos to this fate. He had to help. Carlos had guided him through so many miles of tunnel and risked so much for him already! He watched Carlos and the two guards. One man lifted an Inca Kola to his mouth and took a swallow. As he did, Jonathon's mind erupted with light. An idea poured through his brain as a story his father shared on a Cusco train ignited everything inside of him.

"Ruiz, I heard you tell that man you never paid me." A smile began to grow on Jonathon's face. "Do you have some of that money you owe me?"

The large man glanced at him with surprise. "Why?"

Jonathon's smile increased. "I need you to buy some cooking oil, and a bottle of Inca Kola.

Returning with the two items, Ruiz handed them to Jonathon and stared in shock as the teen poured the carbonated drink onto the floorboards of the truck bed and refilled the bottle with golden cooking oil. "What are you doing?"

Jonathon's eyes twinkled. "Preparing to go get Carlos back and ruin someone's shirt in the process."

"You cannot go out there!" Ruiz's face filled with worry. "They are searching for you. Whatever you are planning, tell me, and I will do it."

Shaking his head, Jonathon refused the offer. "You can't. It is *because* they are looking for me that I have to do this." Taking a deep breath, Jonathon peered across the night toward his friend. Carlos sat at the table, head down. The posture of his entire body spoke of defeat.

Continuing to plan, Jonathon spoke to the large man next to him. "Besides, I need your help with something else. As soon as I leave, I need you to get this truck turned around. Take it up on the road, head up the canyon about a mile or so and wait for us there. Leave it running with the lights on so we can see you. When we get there, we won't have much time. The terrorists will probably be right behind. Can you do that?"

"I will be there. Is there anything else you need?"

"Your prayers."

"You already have them."

Standing up, Jonathon pulled the woven cap back over his hair and wrapped the scarf around the lower half of his face. He didn't know exactly how he would accomplish the next steps, but he knew from Carlos that half the battle was won just by trying. Nodding to Ruiz, Jonathon picked up the oil-filled bottle of Inca Kola and moved down the ramp.

Pressing through the people, Jonathon worked his way toward the outdoor tables. Though the crowd hampered his journey, nothing interfered with his mind. Carlos needed help, and he would give it to him. Whether he failed or not, he would at least try. Carlos had done more than that for him.

A few yards from the tables, Jonathon slowed, pulled the scarf down slightly, and pretended to take a sip from his oil-filled bottle. So far no one had stopped him nor seemed to notice. As Jonathon lifted the bottle to his lips, he glanced toward the marketplace he'd just left. From his vantage point he could see the running lights on Ruiz's truck as it turned around slowly in the congested area. A few seconds later it headed toward the road.

Edging closer to the bushes, Jonathon cast his gaze toward Carlos's table, but he wasn't looking for Carlos. Instead, he needed to see the Inca Kola bottle sitting there. His eyes found it and he noted it was half full.

Making sure no one watched Jonathon wiped his mouth and stepped toward the bushes. Reaching through the foliage he poured out some of his bottle's contents, lowering the level of oil by half. Withdrawing the container from the bushes, he again glanced around before wiping the lip of the bottle clean with the edge of his sweater.

"Well, Dad," he whispered in the night. "I hope this works as well now as it did twenty years ago. If it doesn't, you and I are going to have a little talk."

Behind him, the lights of Ruiz's truck left the market and turned onto the dirt road. Picking up speed, it headed for the main highway where it would turn and then move up the canyon.

Time to go to work, thought Jonathon.

With resolve he straightened and moved in a rapid walk straight for Carlos. "Carlos!" he called.

It took a moment for a reaction to enter the minds at the table. Jonathon used that time to close the distance between them. "Carlos, where were you?"

When Carlos saw Jonathon coming toward them his eyes widened, horrified. Quickly he shook his head, trying to warn the youth away. Jonathon ignored the warning and kept coming, the Inca Kola bottle held in his hand. He spoke his Spanish with a distinct American accent, wanting to make sure the terrorists sitting at the table knew he was the person they sought.

Motioning behind him toward the market, Jonathon raised his voice. "I didn't know where you were, Carlos, and now the potato guy's gone. We missed him. He took off and didn't even pay us!" Stopping at the table, Jonathon continued to question his friend. "What are we going to do? How are we going to get the money we need?"

As the men realized this was the American they sought, both terrorists came to their feet. The closest man caught Jonathon's arm, determined not to let him get away. He growled out a quiet command. "Sit down, *gringo*."

Jonathon startled. "Let go of me. Who are you? Carlos, who are these guys?"

The man holding Jonathon's arm tightened his grip, wrenching the youth into control. "I am your new friend. Now sit down."

Jonathon nodded in agreement and cautiously sat in a chair. "Okay—" As he did, he placed his Inca Kola bottle on the table next to the other one. "Uh . . . Carlos, do you want to introduce me to this 'new friend' of mine? I don't remember making any new friends lately."

From across the table, Carlos exhaled and closed his eyes.

Lowering himself into the chair next to Jonathon, the man who owned the Inca Kola pulled the scarf away from Jonathon's face and jerked the cap from Jonathon's head. A wicked smile grew as the sight confirmed their capture. "We've been looking for you, *Americano.* Seems you left halfway through your ride last week."

Feigned recognition came to Jonathon's face and his forehead furrowed. "Oh, that's right. Seems someone trusted me to *mear.*"

The man's expression hardened, and he moved to strike Jonathon, but a quick scowl of disapproval from the other man stayed his cocked fist. "Not here," the other man commanded. "There will be time for that later. Go tell everyone we have him."

Controlling his anger, the first man nodded and left, but not before passing a quiet warning to Jonathon. "I will enjoy *later.*" Jonathon watched him go, truly hoping that there would not be a 'later.'

Around the boisterous *cantina*, noise and laughter bounced through air. Giving his friend a slight nod, Jonathon pressed his lips together and glanced around him. He finger-combed his hair into place and whistled, acting naïve to the danger around him. Looking bored he stared at the trees, the outdoor lights, the other tables. The terrorist scowled and looked away.

Jonathon leaned forward and reached for an Inca Kola, but instead of picking up the oil-filled bottle he brought, he cupped his hands around the real Inca Kola. No one noticed. Tipping the true beverage back and forth, Jonathon watched the bubbles of carbonation rise and fizzle in the golden liquid. Glancing at the oil-filled bottle, he noticed the oil also held tiny bubbles in suspension. The trick just might work.

Blowing air out through anxious lips, Jonathon glanced at the other customers. They were drinking and laughing, oblivious to him. Jonathon tapped the bottle on the table. Glancing over at Carlos, he raised his eyebrows and shrugged, as if unsure of what to do next. Finally, Jonathon lifted the real Inca Kola to his lips and took a deep swallow. It worked. The transfer of ownership hadn't been noticed.

"Wanna sip?" Jonathon offered the real drink to Carlos, but the older man shook his head. Jonathon pressed him again. "It's good, and I know you're probably thirsty after loading all those potatoes." Again Carlos refused, giving Jonathon a puzzled look.

Jonathon took another swallow of the real beverage and turned to his new friend. "Hey, how long are we going to have to sit here before the other guys show up?" He smiled innocently, waving the real bottle of Inca Kola in gesture. "I may have to *mear.*"

"Shut up!"

Jonathon gave another shrug and lifted the real drink to his mouth. His actions worked. Feeling thirsty, the terrorist reached for the oil-filled bottle.

SEVENTEEN

A S THE MAN lifted the oil-filled bottle from the table, Jonathon caught Carlos's gaze across the table and rolled his eyes slightly in the direction of the man. Carlos saw the look and understood the gesture. Something was going to happen, but he didn't know what. Cautiously he straightened, watching and ready.

The terrorist tipped the bottle to his mouth and swallowed. When the oily liquid registered in the man's senses, Jonathon braced for his reaction. The counterfeit drink erupted from the man's throat, spraying through the air in gagging rejection. The terrorist staggered back from his chair, coughing and choking. As he did, Jonathon grabbed the table and threw it at the man. Chaos erupted in the outdoor eatery.

"Go, go, go!" Jonathon roared the instructions to Carlos, who bolted to his feet.

The hurled table collided with the choking man as he fell back onto another table. It collapsed beneath the sudden weight, and furniture, dishes, and people crashed to the ground. Jonathon and Carlos sprinted into the scattering crowd, purposely throwing chairs and knocking tables to the ground, cluttering the trail behind them. All around people yelled in shock, bottles shattered, and dogs barked. Curses rose into the air.

Racing toward freedom, the two entered the crowded market. Confused people blocked their escape, unsure of the noise from the *cantina*. Jonathon bumped into someone, knocking him to the ground. Scrambling over the trash-strewn earth for several awkward steps,

Carlos tripped and fell, his hands splaying out in front of him. Jonathon grabbed for his friend, pulling him upright, and they rushed on. Vendors cursed their passing, but they didn't stop.

Suddenly the retort of gunshots barked through the air. Women screamed, and people dove to the side, leaving openings for their escape. Jonathon and Carlos sprinted forward, intent on reaching the dark, rocky canyon.

Breaking free from the pressing hoards, their speed increased as they fled across a small field. More shots rang out. A tree branch shattered above them. They came to the edge of the ravine and clambered down its steep sides. The crashing river roared in power beneath them and deafened the sounds behind them. Neither Jonathon nor Carlos knew how close the terrorists were, and the river offered no bank or shore for their escape.

Jonathon shouted to his friend over the river's tumult. "We have to head up the canyon! Which way is it?"

Sucking in a lungful of air, Carlos pointed ahead, over the boulder-strewn ravine which dropped right into the water. The only way up the canyon was to climb back on top or head forward, over a mile of rugged boulders.

Swallowing hard, Jonathon picked their path. He nodded toward the rocks, and the two raced on, scrambling over the stone-covered earth.

A boulder exploded in front of them. Flying pieces of stone ripped into Jonathon's face, stinging him with their cuts. Their pursuers were still behind them, and now there were more. Ducking low, Jonathon and Carlos clambered faster over the uneven terrain. Together they careened over rock beds, up steep embankments, and down pitched fissures. The boulders and sharp stones tore at their bodies. The rocky ground wrenched their legs and ankles. Numerous times they fell but always the other stayed to help, lifting the other to his feet. They moved on together. They still heard the sharp sound of bullets hitting rock, but each one seemed to be further behind. Carrying rifles, their pursuers could not keep up.

The canyon turned to the left, and they raced around the bend. Exhaustion pulled at their bodies, and their limbs throbbed. Ahead lay the road. Jonathon hoped Ruiz would be there.

Seeking an exit up the steep ravine, they climbed the sides and broke over the top. Frantic, Jonathon's eyes searched the dark road for running lights. He found them several hundred yards down the road. "There," he pointed. "Let's go."

Stumbling down the blacktop, the two continued their race for protection, desperate to reach the truck before they were seen or shot in the open. From the cab the heavy-set man saw them. He placed the truck in gear and it lurched forward through the night, driving to meet the two staggering on the road, exhausted but still running.

Leaning across the seat and swinging open the passenger door, Ruiz's eyes twinkled in delight. He called to them from the cab. "Wanna ride?"

Catching the door, Carlos climbed up into moving truck. Reaching back, he groped for Jonathon's arm, pulling him into the cab with him. With the truck already increasing speed, they tumbled in and shut the door behind them.

Inside the ancient *camión*, Jonathon leaned over his stomach, gasping hard. Everything hurt—his hands, his knees, his lungs. His trousers were cut; blood stained his clothes and flesh. Next to him Carlos coughed for air, his own clothes and body equally torn. The rapid escape through rough country had taken its toll on both of them.

Ruiz didn't worry about their injuries. He pounded the steering wheel with delight. "You did it! You made it!" The man whooped in the cab, his voice and personality filling the air. "Jonathon, I do not know what you did, but it worked!"

Coughing for breath, Carlos questioned Jonathon. "What did you put in the bottle?"

Jonathon swallowed and tried to suck in a lungful of air. "Cooking oil."

"Cooking oil, *verdad*—really?" Carlos tried to laugh but his inability to breathe hampered it. "Where in the world did you come up with that idea?"

Still doubled over in pain and gasping hard, Jonathon glanced over at his friend. "My father."

Getting more air in him, Carlos laughed easier. He wiped his mouth with the back of his hand and sat back against the seat. "When you see him again, thank him for me, will you?"

Smiling, Jonathon gave a nod. "I will."

Carlos put his arm around Jonathon's shoulder and shook him with appreciation. "I can't believe it worked, but I'm glad it did. You saved my life. Thank you."

"You may not want to thank me when you see your sweater." Looking over at the driver, Jonathon smiled. "See, Ruiz? I told you I was going to ruin a shirt."

Carlos glanced down at his oil-splattered garment and laughed out loud. "What a trick. I will have to use it myself one day."

"If you do," Jonathon advised, looking at the oil stains, "remember not to stand too close!"

◆　　　◆　　　◆

Angered, the man lowered his rifle and swore as the ancient truck disappeared from sight around the mountain curve. The American had escaped—again! That wasn't good.

In the darkness he fought to draw breath into his burning lungs and control his rage, but it did no good. Furious and frustrated he cursed louder this time and ran his hand through his hair. The American could identify their meeting place but worse, he could identify *them*! And the man with the gun did not want to be identified.

Two others doubled over beside him, coughing and out of breath. "*¿Que hacemos ahora?* What do we do now?" one asked.

Tipping the rifle muzzle toward the earth, the man ejected his remaining shells and put them in his pocket. "We kill him in Lima."

"Where in Lima? It's a city of eight million people!"

Turning, the man shoved someone with his rifle butt. Bent over in pain, his hands resting on his knees, a teenager lifted a battered face to the commander. The commander snarled at him. "Where in Lima would the American go?"

Severino shook his head grimly. He did not want to answer the man. Secretly he was glad Carlos and Jonathon had escaped and amazed by the American's resourcefulness. But Severino also knew that too much silence could be deadly—for all of them. He shrugged. "I do not know. They stayed at a hotel in Lima before they came to Cusco."

"What hotel?"

Again Severino shook his head. Enraged, the man slammed the rifle butt against Severino's shoulder and knocked the bruised teenager to the ground. Swearing against the pain, Severino rolled onto his knees and stayed there for a moment before climbing slowly to his feet.

Though healing, his body still hurt from the beating he'd taken almost two weeks ago.

Gritting his teeth in hatred he looked at the leader. Luckily the man with the gun mistook his clenched jaw for pain. "I don't remember which hotel," Severino hissed. "They're Americans. Find out where the rich Americans stay."

Turning to the other men with them, the leader nodded. "I want as many ears and eyes watching the Lima streets as possible—the hotels, the American embassy, the airport. That *gringo* will not live to identify us."

❖   ❖   ❖

A noise from the tunnels woke Jonathon and Carlos. For Jonathon there was no fear, no worry of what approached. He felt comfortable in the tunnels now; he understood their value. Turning on the flashlight, he waited as a new runner emerged from the darkness.

Entering the chamber, the runner glanced at the American then moved toward Carlos. Squatting by the Peruvian, the runner spoke quietly in Quechua, his words causing Carlos's face to grow somber. When the runner finished, Carlos turned to Jonathon, an odd expression on his face. "He says he is your last runner. There are only ten more miles to go. You are almost at the end."

At the news, Jonathon jumped to his feet and shouted his joy to the tunnels. It echoed brightly through the dark maze. He was only a few hours away from seeing his family—his father! As he celebrated the news, Jonathon didn't notice the runner hand Carlos a small package. His heart heavy, Carlos slipped the packet into his pocket.

Excitement kept Jonathon from eating the roll the runner brought for a meal; he wanted to get started. But as he began his final day in the tunnels, Jonathon felt surprise that his heart filled with a mixture of emotions. Elated by the news that he would soon be in Lima, he also began to feel a strange sadness at leaving the underground passages for good. He had grown to appreciate, even love, this unknown world and he knew the final exit would be hard to make. Each beautiful sheet of flow stone that draped over a rock, or each group of hollow soda straw stalactites that dripped and grew on the moist ceiling filled him with renewed awe. If only others could see this place.

Traveling through the steep, downhill passage to Lima, Jonathon slipped often on the wet surfaces. Moisture filled the caves, making the trek more treacherous. Once he fell, striking his head against a boulder and cutting open his knee and hand at the same time. The wounds dripped blood to the tunnel floor.

Inspecting the injuries, Carlos shook his head. "I am sorry, but I will not help you." When he saw the surprised look on Jonathon, he smiled. "You have been lost for a month. If you were to show up in Lima wearing a fresh bandage, it would not look right."

Trying to wipe the blood that flowed down his forehead, Jonathon frowned. "Great. I survive terrorists and tomb traps and now I'm going to bleed to death this close to home."

Laughing, Carlos playfully shoved him. "You will not bleed to death. The cut on your head will only help you look like you have been lost for over a month."

The runner pointed to his knee. "So will your leg and hand."

Carlos's smile brightened. "And your cut chin."

"And your bruised cheek."

"Do not forget the smell," Carlos teased. "You smell like you have been lost for a month."

Despite the throb of his injuries, Jonathon smiled. "Hey, you're getting personal now. I get the picture." Pressing to his feet, he favored his cut leg, balancing as much as he could on his good limb. Sticking his bleeding hand under his arm, he held it tight to his side and tried to stop the flow. The blood stained his clothes and added to his disheveled appearance. "Let's get going. I'll hop all the way to Lima if I have to. I just want to see my family."

Watching Jonathon, Carlos felt the weight of the packet and the truth of what lay ahead. He did not want this trek to end like this. If only there was some other way.

Jonathon's injuries slowed their journey. Twelve hours later the tired threesome entered a large chamber. There the runner turned to speak quietly with Carlos in Quechua. The man nodded grimly. Turning, he watched Jonathon ease his battered body to the ground, his injured leg extended in front of him. "He says we are here."

"In Lima?" Jonathon could not hide his excitement.

"Just above Lima."

Jonathon pushed back to his feet, eager to continue. "Well, let's go!"

Carlos's voice revealed his mental fatigue. "Jonathon, the terrorists are waiting for you in Lima." Stopping, Jonathon balanced on his injured leg and looked at Carlos. "They have offered a reward to anyone who helps them find you. They want you dead."

Jonathon groaned and tipped his head toward the ceiling. "I'm just a kid," he protested.

"You are a kid who can destroy them with what you know. You have seen their faces, many faces even the authorities have not seen."

"I could never identify them on the streets in a million years!"

"But you could identify them from a handful of police photographs." The restaurant owner shook his head. "Their leaders have never been clearly identified. That is why they have never been arrested. They do not want that to change."

An exhale escaped Jonathon. "Carlos, all I wanted was to use a phone, not lose my life."

His heart heavy with a private burden, Carlos retrieved a bag of rolls and some bottles of soda already placed on a shelf in the stone tunnel. "We will see what we can do. Until then, you should eat something while we wait until it is safe to leave." He passed the rolls to the Jonathon.

"I'm not really hungry," Jonathon announced.

"Then at least drink something. You will need the energy." Using his teeth, Carlos pried the caps off each bottle. He passed the first bottle to the runner. The runner stepped between Jonathon and Carlos to retrieve it. His move had been intentional. With Jonathon's view blocked, the runner nodded softly to Carlos. Feeling his soul heave, Carlos extracted the small package from his pocket. Tearing off a corner, he poured a fine, white powder into one of the bottles.

The last of the powder sifted down into the golden liquid just as Jonathon hopped around the runner. "Is that Inca Kola—" Jonathon froze, horrified, as he saw the powder settling in the liquid, the packet still in Carlos's hand. "What are you doing?" he breathed.

A rapid exchange of glances passed between Carlos and the runner. The runner swore softly, shook his head, and stepped away.

Carlos studied the tainted bottle he held in his hand, watching the powder disappear into the golden liquid. Exhaling in sadness, Carlos shook his head. There was no other way. He lifted the bottle toward Jonathon. "This is for you," he said quietly.

Holding both hands up in refusal, Jonathon hobbled backward. "Uh-uh. I'm not drinking that. You just poisoned it—I saw you!"

Then his eyes narrowed in confusion. "What are you trying to do, kill me?" The question was demanding.

Carlos shook his head. "I am not trying to kill you. I would not bring you all the way to Lima just to kill you now."

"You would if you wanted the reward."

"Jonathon, a reward is not my concern."

"*Then what is?*"

Defeated, Carlos sighed. "I have told you. These tunnels are my concern."

"So you're going to kill me to protect them!"

"Jonathon, this will not kill you. It is not poison, it is an herb."

"Then you drink it."

Carlos shook his head. "I cannot. It is an herb that will fog your memory so you do not remember the tunnels clearly. I need to be alert to get you through Lima safely." His eyes pleaded with Jonathon. "I am sorry. I wish you could keep all you have discovered, but we cannot have you telling people where the tunnels are. These tunnels are sacred to us. We must keep them secret."

Jonathon's heart hammered in his chest, his mind racing with thoughts. His emotions burned. "I thought I had become a friend, not a threat."

The words pained Carlos. "You are my friend, Jonathon, but you must understand, this drink is not for you. It is for all the Inca descendents."

Lifting his eyes from the bottle, Jonathon met Carlos's gaze. "When we first entered these tunnels you asked me to trust you, and I did. I trusted you and every runner who showed up. I did everything you asked me to do and more." His words came with sincerity. "Now I'm asking you to trust me, Carlos, . . . please. *Ama qella, ama suwa, ama llulla, ama hap'a.*"

For a long time, Carlos stood still, studying Jonathon; their eyes reading each other's emotions. Finally Carlos nodded. "I do trust you, my friend. We will leave when it is safe." Setting the bottle in a crevice, he retreated across the chamber. The other runner followed.

Holding still, Jonathon studied the golden liquid as it fizzled in the dim light and the powder dissipated in the drink. Carlos said it was an herb to help him forget the tunnels—to help him protect a people who had befriended him.

The words Carlos spoke a lifetime ago in the mountain depths came back to Jonathon's memory. *"Be full of faith and stay loyal. Hold to the belief that life is good and everyone really does try to do their best. Honor your family and your friends. Even give honor to a stranger for you may discover he is your best friend, your closest family, or even your very salvation."*

His eyes never left the glass container nestled in the tunnel wall. "So, if I drink it, how long before I get amnesia?"

Stunned at the comment, Carlos looked up. "You don't have to drink it, Jonathon. I trust you."

"I know, and I also trust you." He turned to his friend and smiled. "So just in case I don't get a chance to say it again, I'm saying it now: *Gracias*. Thank you for saving my life. And, if you ever see Severino—if he lived after helping me escape—tell him that for me too, please. Tell him thank you for saving my life."

Jonathon moved toward the crevice and retrieved the bottle.

EIGHTEEN

THE AMERICAN CLINIC in Lima exploded into activity. Doctors and nurses rushed reports through police-lined hallways. Outside, more officers controlled the crowds of reporters and others waiting for word. The center of the chaos was an American teenager, missing in the mountainous jungles of southern Peru for over a month and found alive.

In the emergency room, medical personnel called for x-rays, others rapidly cut the clothes from Jonathon's body. He sensed IVs being started and cold antibiotics entering his body. Doctors asked him questions, the same ones over and over. Jonathon couldn't respond. The bright lights above hurt his eyes, and the noises pierced his hearing. He rolled his head in protest. The tunnels had been so dark and quiet. He just wanted to be left alone.

None of the people surrounding him seemed to notice.

Beneath the hot lamps, he kept his eyes closed to the light and trembled with cold and emotion. His body shook so hard at times that it hurt. Someone draped a heated blanket over him. He felt a new drug entering his veins, this one colder than the rest. A voice told him it would help him sleep, but he didn't need the drug to sleep. He only needed quiet and darkness—like the tunnels. He felt the medicine's chill spread up his arm. Soon his body felt warm and heavy.

Above him he sensed movement through the crowd, a new person, leaning close. "Jonathon, it is me, Juan."

Through the spreading drug, Jonathon recognized the voice. He lifted his good hand, searching for Juan with his eyes closed. Juan's grip claimed his, and their hands tightened.

"*Buenos*," Jonathon whispered in tired greeting.

"*Buenos*, Jonathon. You made it!"

Jonathon managed a weak smile as the medicine tried to claim him.

Seeing the struggle, Juan tightened his hold on Jonathon's hand to assure him. "Go ahead and sleep, Jonathon. I will call your parents and tell them you are fine."

Accepting Juan's word, Jonathon allowed the medicine to take over. He felt movement slow, noises dull, and lights fade as the drug eased him into sleep, back to the tunnels and away from the chaos around him.

Outside the American Clinic, a man turned and left the pressing crowd. A smile eased across his hardened face. He had a message to deliver and, with luck, a reward to collect.

Nurses entered the room to check Jonathon's vitals every half hour. Medical doctors came and checked his injuries and his progress, but Jonathon slept, his breathing deep and regular. Still sedated, Jonathon dreamed he slept in the tunnels, in a secluded and safe chamber.

But, as darkness claimed the earth, the chamber didn't stay safe. Through the tunnels, he heard a noise. Opening his eyes, Jonathon saw a rock wall begin to move. He stared at the movement, trying to focus through dizzy eyes. A form approached through the darkness, its face distorted. A mummy stared at him with evil eyes and gave a low, evil laugh.

As their gazes met, the mummy's lips curled back to expose decayed teeth, a hideous grin of triumph. Jonathon tried to move, but he was tied to the ground by a giant web. The hideous mummy shuffled its decrepit body closer. Caught in the webbed trap, Jonathon struggled to break free, to cry out and escape, but he could not.

Standing above him now, the creature gave a low laugh of evil. A gnarled hand took hold of Jonathon's arm trapped in the web. The mummy brought forth his other hand and in it, Jonathon saw a tremendous spider. Black and red, the tarantula looked at Jonathon with eight eyes, fangs dripping deadly poison.

Groaning in the hospital bed, Jonathon fought to wake from his nightmare, but the drugs held his body prisoner. He wanted to force his eyes open in the night, to tell himself it was a dream, but they felt glued shut.

Near his bed came movement and the low laugh of evil. This time Jonathon flung open his eyes, his heart pounding in his chest. It was the same laugh in his dream.

In the darkened room, a stranger stood by his bed, his face and form hidden in shadow. At Jonathon's waking the man gave a wicked smile. "So the American wants to watch himself die. *Que bien.*" In his hand the man held, not a spider, but a syringe.

Jonathon watched the man reach for the injection port on the IV. In that instant, Jonathon realized it wasn't a dream. Someone had come to kill him!

The man inserted the needle, and his thumb moved to the plastic plunger. With a surge of adrenalin, Jonathon knew he couldn't let that liquid reach his bloodstream. He grabbed for the narrow tubing that entered his arm and tried to pull it out before the man injected the solution, but the tape held the IV in place.

Seeing his victim react, the man depressed the plunger, sending poison into the line. Roaring a protest, Jonathon bent the tubing and yanked in fury. The IV ripped free from his inner arm, splattering liquid and blood across the man's face. Still moving, Jonathon rolled out of bed and staggered to his feet.

A curse and a fist assaulted Jonathon, the powerful blow smashing against his face. Jonathon stumbled against the bed. Too drugged and too weak to fight back, he felt hands grab for his neck, squeezing hard. Inside Jonathon the air and blood stop flowing, started pounding beneath the man's strangle hold. He struggled, trying to break the death hold, but the stranger was winning.

The desperation in his body changed to a tingling sensation, followed by a numbness. An odd thought filled Jonathon's mind. He survived the tunnels only to die now, in a hospital, so close to seeing his family. Sagging toward the floor, Jonathon wondered if they would be disappointed that he didn't wait for their arrival.

Just then a light pierced the darkened room and a movement came through the doorway. Jonathon heard a muffled shout, felt a shuddering of movement, and then the grip on his neck broke away.

Released from the deadly vice, Jonathon sank to the cold, tile floor, his body desperately trying to draw wheezing breaths of air through its damaged system. Shouts filled the corridor. They sounded distant and strange. Then Jonathon heard nothing more.

◆　　　◆　　　◆

Morning lit the Lima sky. He groaned at the intrusion of light, yet the effort brought immediate pain to Jonathon's throat. Recoiling in agony, he reached for his throat.

"Easy. Breathe slowly. Your throat will hurt for a few days," a voice directed.

Jonathon tried to follow the advice, taking short, shallow breaths through his throat. It worked. The pain subsided, and he felt his body relax. The intensity of the sunlight burned his eyes. Wincing, he turned away from the light and covered his eyes with a bandaged hand. He heard movement near his bed and then the sound of curtains closing. The room darkened, and Jonathon lay still, trying to reclaim his memory.

"You're awake," the voice noted.

Jonathon forced open his eyes and turned blurred vision toward the voice. Through his drug-induced haze clarity came slowly at first, but then a smile spread across Jonathon's battered face. "Juan, is that you?"

"Sí, mi amigo. How are you doing?"

He swallowed and closed his eyes. "I'm here."

"After last night I'd say that's quite a miracle."

At those words, Jonathon's memory began to sharpen. He touched his neck gently and winced at the pain. "I guess that wasn't a dream, huh?" It hurt to talk.

"No, it was not. It was very real."

"Did they catch him?" Jonathon lifted his hand from his throat and again rested it over his eyes, shielding them from the dim light of the room.

"No, but they now have police officers guarding your room and the outside of the hospital. Only a few people are approved to enter your room. That is quite a security force for one teenager." Juan watched the youth. "So, do you want to tell me why you need all this protection?"

"Because I'm good looking?"

Juan chuckled at the teen's battered face. "Right now that may be debatable."

Beneath the covering of his hand, Jonathon opened his eyes slightly, staring into nothingness. He wanted to change the conversation. "How long have you been here?"

"Since I pulled that man off you last night, and I'm not leaving until your parents get here."

Jonathon exhaled slowly. "That was you? I owe you big time. Thanks." He lay still a moment, finding more strength. "Does my dad know I'm here?" he whispered.

Juan studied the teenager, respecting Jonathon's need to change the subject. He nodded. "He does. In fact, he's flying to Peru right now. Your mom is coming, too."

Jonathon managed to lift a corner of his dried lips at the words. "Good."

Juan continued. "They were ecstatic when I told them you were alive. You should have heard them. Your dad was overwhelmed. He kept saying he'd knew you would make it. He never lost faith in you."

A tired smile accompanied Jonathon's nod. "*Ama hap'a*," he whispered. "Have faith."

Juan's eyes darted to the youth, wondering where he had learned Quechua. After a silent moment, he swallowed and decided to test a thought. "How are you feeling?"

"Tired."

"You should be. You've been through a lot." He moved toward the bed, reading Jonathon's face as he spoke. "The doctors say you are pretty dehydrated, but they are taking care of that. You broke your hand severely at one point and cracked some ribs. The ribs are healing fine, but your hand will need to be surgically reset when you get home. You lost quite a bit of weight too. I can see that. And you are covered with cuts and bites." He nodded. "The cut on your cheek will probably leave a scar."

"Yeah."

Speaking deliberately, Juan carefully watched for signs of reaction from the youth. "The doctors are saying it's a miracle you survived the jungle."

Jonathon didn't respond.

"The *selva* can be pretty tough."

At Juan's words, Jonathon's hand dropped from his eyes, and he turned away. Slowly Juan nodded at the teen's reaction. "I see you are getting used to the light."

"I guess." The words made his throat hurt. Jonathon licked his lips and tried to swallow but could not produce enough saliva.

Juan lifted a bottle of water from the nearby table. He opened it and dropped a straw down the narrow neck before offering a drink to Jonathon. Jonathon took a small sip and then laid his head back on the pillow. Watching Jonathon's expression, Juan spoke quietly. "And noises no longer seem to hurt your ears as much either."

Jonathon did not respond.

Tapping the bed rail, Juan pressed his lips together before venturing forward with his words. "Who are Carlos and Severino? You have mentioned them in your sleep."

A physical reaction crossed Jonathon's face, but he stayed silent.

Hesitant, Juan continued. "Ever since they brought you in, you have been talking about them and other things, strange things. The doctors say you are just reacting to the drugs, but I do not think so."

In the bed, Jonathon's face tightened more, but he offered no explanation.

Juan's grew somber. "So, who wants you dead, Jonathon?"

The question brought pain to Jonathon's expression. Juan leaned closer, his voice low. "Listen to me, Jonathon, last night someone injected poison into your IV and tried to strangle you. The only reason the police are not in here questioning you right now is because they do not know you are awake. As soon as they know, they will be asking who wants you dead and why."

A swallow moved down Jonathon's damaged throat; the muscles in his jaw worked rapidly. Within himself the teenager fought a silent battle.

Drawing a breath for courage, Juan voiced his candid conclusion. "Jonathon, I know you were not lost in the jungle for five weeks. The *selva* does not make you sensitive to light or sound." Now his voice quieted to a whisper of air. "You have been talking in your sleep about hidden tunnels and Inca mummies."

The words caused Jonathon to shut his eyes, agony lining his face.

Juan wasn't ready to give up. "Where were you, Jonathon?" At Jonathon's refuting head shake, he continued. "I may be able to help, but you have got to tell me the truth."

"I can't."

"If you are afraid—"

"No!" Jonathon's light brown eyes opened quickly. "I'm not afraid—not for me."

Juan studied Jonathon's expression, surprised at the conviction he saw in the teenager's eyes. His next words came slowly. "Jonathon, if you are trying to protect someone or *something*, you need to tell me. Unless I know what happened, I cannot stop the authorities. They will question you and, as intelligent as you are, I really do not think you can handle their inquiries alone."

From the bed, Jonathon's face twisted with agony and inner conflict. Moments passed. He swallowed and closed his eyes. Juan was right—he would need help to protect what he knew. With his defenses washing away, Jonathon gave in to that knowledge and nodded. "I wasn't lost in the jungles for five weeks."

Slowly, almost afraid to ask, "Then where were you?"

He swallowed, forcing his injured throat to reveal the truth. "In the secret tunnels."

Overwhelmed by the words, Juan swayed slightly against the bed rail.

Groggy against the pillow, Jonathon spoke, his words soft. "They exist. I fell into them and Severino found me there. He's an Inca descendent. His family has a sacred room inside the tunnels filled with mummies and gold. His sister cares for the mummies there."

The revelation matched the information Juan had studied. He slowly nodded. "The Incas assigned young, unmarried girls to care for the mummies in their family."

"They still do." Taking a breath to ease the pain in his throat as he spoke, Jonathon continued. "Severino took me to their house and took care of me, but I thought they were keeping me captive. I didn't realize they were protecting me from terrorists in the area. When I decided to be stupid and get home on my own, the terrorists took me hostage. Severino and his friend Carlos saved my life. They helped me escape from the terrorists and got me safely to Lima . . . through the tunnels." Suddenly the words lodged in his throat, and Jonathon closed his eyes, emotions hurting more than his throat.

"So the terrorists want you dead."

He managed a nod.

"Why?"

Forcing his voice to cut through his emotions, Jonathon tried to answer. "Because I interrupted their meeting, I've seen where they meet, but mostly because I've seen their faces. I can identify them to the police." He shook his head at the memory. "I'd be dead already if it wasn't for Severino and Carlos—and I don't know if Severino is still alive."

At the comment a smile began to lighten Juan's face and he lifted a small envelope off the bedside table. "You got a letter this morning. It was hand-delivered to the nurse's desk and has no return address, only an *S* written on the back. Maybe it's from Severino." He passed the packet to Jonathon.

With hands hampered by bandages and IVs, Jonathon took the envelope and tore open the end. A small, folded letter fell out. Picking it up, Jonathon began to read. As his gaze fell on the script, his hands started shaking.

> *Jonathon,*
>
> *Carlos told me what you did for him and for us. There are not enough words to express my gratitude. Thank you! Inka Kola . . . se pasa! That's great! Carlos also told me what you said. Thank you and you are welcome.*
>
> *In case you ever begin to doubt, here is a memento.*
>
> *Friends, Severino.*

Folded in the bottom of the letter lay a single Inca coin—gold and very real.

Tears burned in Jonathon's eyes as he lifted the coin from its paper bed. "He's alive! Severino made it!"

"I am glad. I am glad you both survived."

His emotions sobering, Jonathon lifted his gaze to Juan. "I'm not making this up, Juan."

Their eyes met and Juan slowly nodded. "I believe you."

Jonathon passed Juan the letter and coin. In awe, Juan read the letter. When he finished he fingered the treasured coin, turning it over in his hold, running his thumb across its surface. The markings, the size—everything about the coin testified of its authenticity. For a long time, Juan could not speak around the lump in his throat. Then Juan's eyes lifted, shining with tears. "This is at least six-hundred years old. Jonathon, this coin looks like real Inca gold."

"It is real, and so are the tunnels, Juan. They do exist. The Incas still guard them, and their sacred mummies are hidden inside." Now Jonathon smiled. "The lost Inca empire *survived*!"

Around his emotions, Juan managed a nod. "For years I have only hoped—"

"You don't have to hope any more. They exist! But Juan, if the world finds out they *will* lose everything and, for the second time in history, they *will* become the lost Inca empire. We can't let anyone know about this . . . not even the authorities. You've got to help me. I don't want to lie, but I can't say anything about the tunnels or mummies when they question me either."

With understanding, Juan nodded. "I will help. If the tunnels are revealed, it will be the Inca descendents who do it—not me and not you. We will guard their heritage."

His words brought a sense of peace to Jonathon. "Thank you."

Yet Juan held Jonathon's gaze as a look of seriousness locked onto his face. "But it will mean you will have to focus only on the terrorists. Are you ready for that?"

In the bed, Jonathon swallowed, his mind moving quickly through his thoughts, his decision already made. "Yes."

"You will have to identify the terrorists and tell the authorities everything you know."

"I know."

"The terrorists will not accept your testimony quietly. They will try to silence you again, like they did last night.

Jonathon gave a nod. "I know that, but I will do whatever it takes to protect the tunnels and my friends."

The quiet power of Jonathon's words brought a smile to Juan's lips. Slowly he nodded his own agreement. "Then, if this is something you want to do, I will stay with you through every question."

"Thank you."

"We will get through this together and protect what you know."

Juan passed the letter and coin back to Jonathon, but the teen shook his head. "I want you to keep the coin, Juan."

The words stunned the older man, and for a moment he hesitated. "No, you should keep it so you will always remember."

"I can never forget."

Juan's thumb brushed over the coin one final time before he pressed the treasure into Jonathon's hand. "This is yours. It is a sign from Severino that he considers you now, and forever, one of them. He gave you something you could use to betray him. You could sell that coin or show it to the world, and he knows that, but he gave it to you anyway because he trusts you. To the Inca people, that kind of trust and loyalty is priceless."

"*Ama llulla.*"

"*Ama hap'a.*"

Together they smiled as they shared a connection beyond words. Juan gave a nod. "By giving you that coin, Severino is telling you he considers you one of them, a member of their family—their *ayllu.*"

"Family, *ayllu.* I'm honored." Jonathon looked at the coin in his palm. "I won't betray him, Juan. I won't betray either one of my families ever again. Now I understand what you and Dad mean. Some things are worth more than glory and fame. Some things, like family, are priceless."

Smiling warmly, Juan nodded his approval.

Jonathon rubbed the coin gently. His eyes glistened. "I've been thinking," the young man shared. "I'm going to ask my dad if I can return next summer and work the season at Machu Picchu. Then, on my days off, maybe Severino and I can get together."

Juan's smile grew. "I am sure he would like that."

Behind them the door opened. A man, pale and American, pressed through the door, accompanied by a woman with dark hair. Jonathon looked up, surprised. "Dad? Mom?"

Tears burst down David's face as he saw his son. "Jonathon!" Without restraint he rushed across the room and gathered his son into his arms. Jonathon returned the embrace, his own tears starting. "Dad, I'm so sorry! I love you, Dad. I really do."

Without a word, Juan moved to the door. Stepping through the portal, he glanced back at the reunion and smiled with contentment. Jonathon had come to Peru a boy, but he was going home a man.

Leaving them to their privacy, Juan pulled the door shut and walked away. His heart felt full.

He would enjoy seeing Jonathon again next summer.

ABOUT THE AUTHOR

WRITING has been part of T. Lynn Adams's career since she was a teenager. At the age of fifteen, she walked into a newspaper business with a story idea and was challenged by the editor to write it for them. She did and has been writing for newspapers ever since. She has also been published in many national and international publications. Currently, she is the editor of a regional agriculture newspaper.

T. Lynn Adams lived in Peru for eighteen months and deeply treasures that experience, the people, and the culture. While there, she learned about the secret tunnels of the Incas. She also had many encounters with members of the Shining Path, but like all Peruvians she met, they treated her with courtesy and respect despite their reputation.

T. Lynn Adams and her husband are raising six children and she openly admits to enjoying their teenage years, their friends, and *most* of their music. Her teens love to tease her about not being able to fry an egg and about the time she burned a bag of potato chips inside the oven. With the bag hidden there to keep it from being devoured by her teenage sons, she didn't remember the chips until after she turned on the oven. Since that episode, she has discovered the best hiding place in the entire house is *(whisper)* the dishwasher. No teenager wants to get near one!

Her family is one of the most influential things in her life. They love to spend time together, and even though they are not perfect, the most common sound in their home is laughter.